DEATH OF A COUNTRY FRIED REDNECK

"Any idea who set the bus on fire?" Hayley asked.

Bruce rubbed his eyes. He looked tired and irritated from having to be up so late.

"Nope," Bruce sighed. "Might've been the body they found in the bus."

"What?" Hayley said, twisting her head away from the smoldering, twisted-metal bus to Bruce.

"You didn't hear? Cops don't know yet if this was an accident, a suicide or a murder. What they do know is somebody was inside the bus and he or she is now a smoking charred corpse."

"Do they know who it was? Do they know anything?"

"Like I said, Hayley, the body's burned up pretty good. There's no way of identifying it yet."

Hayley's mind raced.

A dead body inside the bus?

Who could it be?

And how did the bus get here?

"Oh, I have heard one interesting rumor," Bruce said. "I heard Officer Earl talking on his cell and I could've sworn he said they found something in the corpse's mouth and it looked like a chicken bone . . ."

Books by Lee Hollis

DEATH OF A KITCHEN DIVA

DEATH OF A COUNTRY FRIED REDNECK

Published by Kensington Publishing Corporation

A Hayley Powell
Food & Cocktails Mystery

DEATH of a
COUNTRY FRIED
REDNECK

LEE HOLLIS

KENSINGTON PUBLISHING CORP.
http://www.kensingtonbooks.com

KENSINGTON BOOKS are published by

Kensington Publishing Corp.
119 West 40th Street
New York, NY 10018

All Kensington Titles, Imprints, and Distributed Lines are
available at special quantity discounts for bulk purchases for
sales promotions, premiums, fund-raising, and educational or
institutional use. Special book excerpts or customized print-
ings can also be created to fit specific needs. For details, write
or phone the office of the Kensington special sales manager:
Kensington Publishing Corp., 119 West 40th Street, New York,
NY 10018, attn: Special Sales Department, Phone: 1-800-221-
2647.

Kensington and the K logo Reg. U.S. Pat & TM Off.

ISBN-13: 978-0-7582-6738-2
ISBN-10: 0-7582-6738-X

First Mass Market Printing: November 2012

10 9 8 7 6 5 4

Printed in the United States of America

Chapter 1

Hayley Powell didn't think she was screaming that loud. But when her boss Sal Moretti came barreling out of his office, strawberry yogurt dripping down the front of his light blue, short-sleeve dress shirt, angrily pointing a pudgy finger at her and blaming her for scaring him so badly he spilled his breakfast all over himself, she finally managed to shut her mouth and contain herself.

It was a natural reaction. This was huge news. Her all-time favorite singer—four-time Grammy winner and last year's Sexiest Man Alive according to *People* magazine—country music hottie Wade Springer was coming to town to perform two charity concerts. How could she not be screaming?

However, if she'd had the slightest clue at the time that Wade's imminent arrival in her little home town of Bar Harbor, Maine, would lead to murder, she definitely would not have been so excited.

But, right now, without the power of hindsight, Hayley was in a joyous and celebratory mood. She jumped up from her desk, which was situated in the front office at the *Island Times* newspaper, scurried into the small bathroom in the back, and quickly returned with a paper towel. She began frantically dabbing at the bits of strawberry that rested in the crease of Sal's shirt just above his ample belly.

"I'm sorry, Sal. I'll go to the store and get you another yogurt," Hayley said apologetically.

"Forget the yogurt. I want another shirt," Sal bellowed. "My wife spent almost twenty dollars on this at Walmart!"

Hayley suspected Sal would never be caught at New York's Fashion Week anytime soon.

"I don't get what's the big deal about some Nashville crooner coming to Bar Harbor," Sal grunted. "Big name celebrities come here every summer. We've had the president of the United States bring his family here. Martha Stewart owns a home on the other side of the island. I've never even heard of this guy!"

"You mean to tell me you've never listened to his number one hit, 'I'm Not a Wife Beater, I Just Wear One'?"

"I don't listen to music. I'm a newsman. That's why I prefer NPR," Sal said, snorting. He grabbed at a tiny piece of strawberry that Hayley missed and popped it in his mouth.

Sal snatched the paper towel out of Hayley's hand and continued to wipe the yogurt off his shirt himself.

Hayley smiled and dutifully scooted back behind her desk. She scrolled down the e-mail on her computer announcing Wade's upcoming Bar Harbor appearances.

"Wade has always been committed to the environment. He even wrote the theme song for that Oscar-winning documentary about the ice glaciers. Remember that? I loved that song. He talked about the planet being like a big cocktail left on the bar too long and how the ice cubes have all melted away," Hayley said to her half-listening boss, who was now pouring himself a cup of coffee. "Anyway, when the College of the Atlantic heard he was going on tour in the northeast, they wrote him a letter requesting he do a benefit concert to help raise funds for their ocean research department. My friend Jamie McGibbon—he's a professor there—well, he sent me an e-mail with the news that Wade's people just confirmed the dates. You know Jamie. His wife owns the ice cream shop that has the pumpkin spice flavor you love so much . . ."

"Is there a point to this story?"

"Well, no, Jamie just wanted me to be the first to know about Wade Springer performing at the Criterion Theatre."

Sal perked up. "Wait, so we have a scoop?"

"I could go get us each one. You know how much I love the salted caramel."

Sal sighed. "No, Hayley. A news scoop! We've got the story that this singer is coming to town—before the *Herald*?"

"Yes, Jamie wanted me to be the first to know because I'm such a huge fan."

"Have one of the reporters write something up so we can post it on our website before word gets out and the *Herald* beats us to the punch."

"All our reporters are out covering the city council meeting."

"Then you do it."

Hayley wasn't a reporter. She was just the office manager who wrote a regular cooking column called "Island Food & Spirits" where she shared anything on her mind along with a few tasty food and cocktail recipes.

Sal could read the doubt in her face.

"Just because you write about seafood casseroles and rhubarb pies doesn't make you any less of a journalist.

And a journalist drops everything he or she is doing to alert the public to any breaking news."

"Got it!" Hayley said, as she began typing furiously. She noticed Sal heading for the door. "Where are you going?"

"I'm starving. I'm going to get some blueberry pancakes at Jordan's."

Hayley raised an eyebrow, amused.

"Don't give me that look. I didn't say I was the one who has to drop everything. I'm the editor. I delegate. I pay *you* to drop everything!"

Sal marched out of the office.

Hayley quickly typed a few sentences quoting an unnamed source at the college—since she didn't want Jamie to get into trouble for talking out of school, literally—and then posted the item on the paper's website.

Within seconds, the office phone rang and Hayley picked it up. "Island Times, this is Hayley."

There was loud screaming on the other end of the receiver.

Even louder than her own high-pitched shrieking earlier.

Hayley knew exactly who it was.

"Hi, Liddy," she said, smiling.

"Is it true? Is he really coming?"

"Yes! Can you believe it?"

More screaming. From both of them. It was like when they were teenage girls and ran away from home together, taking a Greyhound bus to Boston to sneak into a Backstreet Boys concert. They had made it as far as Bangor just an hour outside of town before their parents had the bus pulled over and the cops dragged them home.

Liddy was one of Hayley's closest friends. They had

grown up together. Their lives diverged a bit when Hayley found herself divorced and struggling to raise two kids while Liddy made a big splash in the local real estate market during the boom and was now tooling around town in a Mercedes and flying off to Manhattan every month for retail therapy.

"We have to meet him!" Liddy squealed. "I'm on the board of directors of the Criterion Theatre so I'm sure I can arrange it."

"Liddy, are you serious? That would be like . . . a dream come true," Hayley said. She couldn't allow herself to believe that it was even possible.

"Of course. And now that he's divorced from that hillbilly, the one who can barely carry a tune, what's her name?"

"Stacy Jo Stanton," Hayley offered.

Actually, Stacy Jo was a successful country singer in her own right, but Liddy just couldn't bring herself to admit it.

"Right. Her. Well, now Wade's available again so he might be in the market for some female companionship while he's in town, and since you're dating Lex Bansfield and I'm one hundred percent single, that someone could be me!"

Liddy was right. Hayley was dating Lex Bansfield, the handsome caretaker of one of the multimillion dollar oceanfront estates, but she wasn't sure where that was going, or how serious it was, and she certainly didn't consider herself partnered at this point. But realistically, Hayley knew that neither she nor Liddy stood a chance of ever dating someone like Wade Springer. Liddy loved to get carried away sometimes.

"I had a dream the other night when I fell asleep listening to one of Wade's albums on my iPod," Liddy said, taking a long pause for dramatic effect. "I dreamed that someone was spooning me from behind and when I opened my eyes I was wearing one of Wade's signature ten-gallon white cowboy hats and he was snuggling against me, one strong arm pulling me into his buffed furry chest, and in this deep voice he said, 'Mornin' sunshine,' and I just . . . Oh God, it's so hot in my office! What's the weather like outside?"

"Forty-two degrees. It's not your office. It's you," Hayley said, laughing.

"Oh, before I forget, I read online that Wade just fired his personal chef who was cooking for him while he's on tour."

"What? Why?"

"The guy bought some bad shrimp and gave everybody food poisoning. Luckily Wade was doing a sound check and didn't eat any, but four crew members were hospitalized. Isn't that good news?"

"I don't see how that's good news," Hayley said.

"He fired his chef! Maybe the tour organizers are planning to hire someone local to fill in while they're here on the island."

"I know where this is going. Even if that's true, there's no way I'd ever get the job."

"Why not? You're an award-winning cooking columnist!"

"I got third place. And there were only five columns nominated."

"It's all about perception. You're still award winning! Now don't dismiss this opportunity like so many others."

Hayley chose not to press Liddy on what other opportunities Liddy believed she'd dismissed. That was another discussion. Right now was all about bringing Liddy back down to earth.

"Okay, let me think about it."

"There's no time to think. We both know Wade's favorite dish is country fried chicken. He's a Southerner, after all. You need to write about that in your next column. Show these guys you've got what it takes to satisfy Wade's palette."

Hayley thought about it for a second and realized Liddy had a good point. Why not write about Wade's local concert and include a recipe for his favorite dish? Chances are he would probably never see it, but what would be the harm? And if someone close to him did happen to read it, then maybe there was a slight possibility that she would be considered. It certainly was worth a shot.

"I'm hanging up now, go write," Liddy said, and then there was a click.

Hayley was jammed with phone calls and managerial duties at the office until quitting time, so she didn't have time to write her column. It would just have to wait until after she fed her kids dinner and took her dog, Leroy, for a walk.

When she arrived home, Leroy, her dirty white shih tzu with a pronounced underbite, was running around in circles, bursting with excitement over her arrival. Much like Hayley's own reaction to the news Wade Springer was coming to town.

Hayley's two kids, however—sixteen-year-old Gemma and fourteen-year-old Dustin—were nowhere to be seen. Neither had *ever* displayed even a fraction of the excitement over their mother coming home from work that Leroy could be counted on to do.

Ever.

She assumed they were both out with friends.

Suddenly, a screech came from upstairs.

Scratch that. Gemma was home.

Hayley grabbed her ears to cover them. Lord. Where did she get that loud earsplitting screaming from?

Gemma came pounding down the stairs, the phone pressed to her ear. Her face was beet red and Hayley noticed the hand holding the receiver was shaking.

"Honey, are you all right?" Hayley asked.

"Shhhh, Mom, please! This is important!"

She was all right.

Gemma turned her back to Hayley and whispered frantically into the phone, a few excited giggles escaping every few sentences.

After giving Leroy a doggie treat, Hayley filled a pot with water and placed it on the stove and turned the heat on the burner up to high. She had made some of her homemade spaghetti sauce, left over from the night before, so a quick pasta dinner would be easy to prepare and give her more time to get to work on her Wade Springer tribute column.

Gemma finally finished her call.

She screamed again.

Leroy, startled, dashed out of the room and hid behind the couch.

"Mom, Reid Jennings asked me out on a date! I can't believe it! Reid Jennings!"

"I'm so happy for you! Who's Reid Jennings?"

"He's a new kid. His parents just moved here this year. They bought that seafood restaurant on the pier after the last owner skipped town."

Hayley had heard of the family, but didn't know much about them.

"Anyway, Reid's an artist and a really, really talented one," Gemma gushed.

"He paints?"

"No. He's a singer-songwriter and he's playing at that new agey coffeehouse next to the organic food market on Cottage Street, and he asked me to come tonight and hear him perform one of his original songs!"

"So it's not really a date. He just wants to fill the seats."

Gemma gave her mother a withering look.

"Way to pop my balloon, Mom," Gemma said, sighing. "Is it so hard for you to allow me this one ounce of happiness?"

"I'm sorry," Hayley said. "I didn't realize your life was so full of disappointments and despair."

"Don't count me in for dinner. I couldn't possibly eat now. Oh, and Dustin's at Cameron's house so he won't be eating, either."

Hayley immediately shut off the burner and dumped the pot of water into the sink. She turned to see Gemma halfway back up the stairs to her room.

"So how old is he?"

"I don't know. A little older than me."

"How much older?"

"He's a senior."

"Seventeen?"

"Eighteen, okay? Come on, Mom, enough with the third degree."

"I'm not convinced it's wise for you to be dating an older boy."

"Stop being so overprotective. I'm old enough to make my own decisions," Gemma said, continuing up the stairs to her room.

"So what time do we have to be there?" Hayley asked.

Gemma stopped cold. "Be where?"

"The coffeehouse. We're not staying late because I have a column to write."

"Mom, you're not invited."

"It's a public event. And I'm sure Reid will appreciate an extra body there to help fill the house."

"Why are you doing this to me?"

"Because I don't like the idea of you dating someone I've never met, and since I know you and that you will never bring him around to meet me, this is a nice alternative to me actually crashing one of your real dates."

"Fine!" Gemma sighed. "But we have to be there by seven-thirty."

Hayley didn't like the fact that she would be out late. She just wanted to pour herself a glass of red wine and write her Wade Springer column. But her kids came first. She had to do this.

The coffeehouse was half full when they arrived on time at seven-thirty. Lots of teenagers sipped lattes and flavored teas and were slouched over wooden tables, talking. Hayley guessed she was the oldest one in the room.

Gemma had dressed to the nines and stood out from the others, who were in jeans and t-shirts. Hayley refused to sit alone at a table in the back, much to Gemma's chagrin, and joined her at a table up front directly in front of the microphone that had been set up.

The coffeehouse owner, a frizzy-haired redheaded woman in her late twenties wearing a bulky wool sweater and jeans skirt, stepped in front of the mic and gave a quick rundown of upcoming events before turning it over to Reid.

Hayley almost gasped out loud when Reid entered from the back, a guitar slung around his shoulder. No wonder Gemma was so googly-eyed and excited over the attention he had given her. The kid was incredibly handsome with the face and body of a male model. His brown hair was scraggly and mussed and he wore thick glasses that did little to hide his beautiful puppy-dog brown eyes. He seemed perfect.

Hayley glanced over at Gemma, who was the only one wildly clapping at his introduction. It took a moment for everyone else to catch up. After most people stopped applauding, Hayley had to physically restrain her daughter from clapping anymore so Reid could start his song.

Reid launched into his number, and Hayley was surprised by what a soothing, melodic voice he possessed. He also played the guitar well, and Hayley noticed he quickly had the crowd in the palm of his hand.

When it was over, Gemma jumped to her feet, forcing everyone else to haul their butts up out of their chairs and give Reid a standing ovation.

Reid looked over at Gemma and gave her a wink.

Yeah, the kid was cute. Probably a heartbreaker, too. But Gemma was right. Hayley had to let her make her own decisions and her own mistakes.

Hayley and Gemma hung around long enough for the crowd to thin out and Reid to finish accepting accolades from his friends for his performance.

Finally, when the coffeehouse was nearly empty, Reid ambled over and gave Gemma a warm hug.

"Thanks for coming," Reid said with a smile that lit up the room.

Hayley had to gently grab Gemma by the elbow to stop her from swooning.

"This must be your sister," Reid said with a straight face, nodding to Hayley.

The easiest play in the book to impress a girl's

mother. But damned if it wasn't effective one hundred percent of the time.

"Oh God, no! That's my mother!" Gemma screamed.

"I had her very young," Hayley said, but then caught herself. "But I'm not condoning motherhood at an early age whatsoever."

Reid laughed.

"You were very good," Hayley said, and meant it.

"Thank you, Mrs. Powell," Reid said. "That means a lot to me."

The kid had obvious talent and a laid-back charm. He was hard to resist.

"Can I buy you two some coffee or tea?" Reid asked, slipping an arm around Gemma. Her body jerked slightly from the thrill of his touch.

"No, we need to get home. I have some work to do before tomorrow," Hayley said.

"Yes, Mom's a columnist for the *Island Times* and has left things to the last minute as usual. I, however, have already finished all my homework and would love to join you for some tea."

Checkmate.

Hayley decided not to drag Gemma home with her. The coffeehouse owner was stationed behind the counter and could serve as a makeshift chaperone. And Reid seemed like a nice enough kid. So she told Gemma to be home by ten, and turned to leave. As she was heading out the door, she heard Gemma say breathlessly, "Your singing gave me goose pimples. Look, I still have them."

Hayley walked the four blocks home and wondered why girls always fall so hard for a guy with a handsome face and a nice singing voice. She had thought Gemma would go more for someone with brains, a whip-smart college prep kid with plans to be a doctor or lawyer. But no, she was obsessed with the soft-spoken artist who had a way with a guitar.

Where did she get that from?

Oh, well. No time to ponder that question. Hayley had to get home and write all about her idol, Wade Springer.

ns... she was obsessed with the soft-spoken, action who had grown in the guitar.

Not could she just wait until the point...

Oh, well. No time to ponder this question. I have had to get home and tell us all about her idol, Mark Palmer.

Island Food & Spirits
by
Hayley Powell

In the immortalized words of every teenage girl in America, I would just like to say "OMG!" I can not tell you how beside myself I am with excitement about a truly amazing and fantastic upcoming event that is about to happen in our tiny little town! And best of all, it's showcasing an idol of mine who's so popular I can't believe he is also about to grace the stage of our very own historic landmark the Criterion Theatre.

I'm just so over the top deliriously happy that I almost can't even type his name without wanting to start screaming like I'm twelve and at the mall waiting for a Justin Bieber appearance! I actually believe—no, I *know*—I am going to have to grab my friend Liddy and go to the big city—No, Liddy, *not* New York! I'm talking about our big city of Bangor—to get myself some new blue jeans, a sassy shirt, and, dare I say, cowgirl boots with heels!

So if you haven't heard by now, hold on to your seats because the impossibly gorgeous and wildly successful Wade Springer (insert *screaming!*) is coming to Bar Harbor to do not one but *two* charity country music concerts for the College of the Atlantic's ocean research department.

I can say with certainty that this is probably one of the most exciting things that has happened here since the bar my brother Randy owns, Drinks Like A Fish, had a two for one special on their to-die-for Lemon Drop Martinis, and because they were so popular, the Hannaford grocery store *and* the Bayside liquor store both ran out of vodka over the weekend. We almost had a New England version of the Watts riots on our hands from all of the angry Lemon Drop lovers in town!

Anyway, what a great coup for the college to get Wade to perform. I, for one, will be first in line for tickets since I have been Wade's number one fan ever since he first arrived on the Nashville scene. I adore country music, much to the chagrin of my kids, who find it quite embarrassing when their friends come over and I'm in the kitchen singing into a hairbrush microphone at the top of my lungs "Man! I Feel Like a Woman" along with Shania Twain. Honestly, though, sometimes it's worth the eye rolling and screaming, "Oh, Mom, for the love of God, stop!"

I pride myself on knowing almost everything there is to know about Wade, and I probably shouldn't admit this since

I might start sounding like a groupie, but he is by far the best country music star around. I'm sorry, Brad Paisley! Sorry, Toby Keith! And sorry, close second, you hunk of beef, Tim McGraw! But Wade wins!

I can't help it if I just happen to know that his favorite color is blue just like mine and that when he was ten years old, his best friend was his black-and-white border collie, Rip. And that when he was thirteen, he had his first kiss. At sixteen, he started his own band with four friends and two of those friends are still in the band with him now. At eighteen, he turned down a baseball scholarship to a prestigious college to continue writing and playing his first love, country music!

I could go on and on, but I'll stop now because I don't want to start sounding like Kathy Bates in that movie *Misery* or anything. But for me, anyone whose favorite food of all time is country fried chicken is definitely number one in my book!

So for this week's column, in honor of my beloved Wade Springer's upcoming local concerts, I'm going to dish up (and I don't mean to brag) my first-place, award-winning country fried chicken that won at last summer's Memorial Day BBQ cook off at the town ball field.

Let's get started! The best way to start a delicious country fried chicken dinner is with a cold frothy beverage, so everyone grab your favorite chilled beer or two or . . . okay, six-pack, and enjoy them with my blue ribbon country fried chicken recipe.

Hayley's Blue Ribbon Country Fried Chicken

3 eggs
½ cup water
1 cup of your favorite hot sauce (I'm
     keeping mine a secret)
2 cups of self-rising flour
1 teaspoon pepper
Salt and pepper to taste
Garlic powder
One 1½ to 2½ pound chicken, cut up
Peanut oil for frying

In a medium-size bowl, beat eggs and water, then add the hot sauce and stir. In another bowl, mix the flour and pepper. Season chicken pieces with salt, pepper, and garlic powder. Dip seasoned chicken in egg, then coat with flour and set aside.

In a Dutch oven or deep frying pan, pour enough peanut oil to fill halfway to the top and heat to 350 degrees.

Fry your chicken until golden brown and crispy, white meat around 8 to 10 minutes and dark meat 12 to 14 minutes, flipping the meat halfway along. Remove from oil and place on paper towel–lined plate and let sit for five minutes. Enjoy!

Chapter 2

"Hayley, I can't stop thinking about you and your country fried chicken," the man said.

Hayley spun around and spied a man leaning against the side brick wall of the store.

He was tall, north of six feet, with broad shoulders and a relaxed gait as he stepped toward her. Hayley could see that he was wearing a cowboy hat but his face was still hidden in the shadows.

She had just stopped at the Big Apple convenience store on her way home, to pick up a Snickers bar, because she was having a sugar craving, and he was waiting for her when she came outside. It was already dark and the light from the street lamp was blinding her enough so she couldn't make out who it was.

But that voice.

Low and with a distinct southern drawl.

It had to be him.

It was Wade Springer.

She could only guess that he had read her column when it hit the stands earlier today and searched the town high and low to find her. This was possibly the most romantic moment of her entire life. It was like in that movie, *Field of Dreams*. If she baked it, he would come. Okay, so not exactly like that movie. But close enough. And here he was. Not twenty feet from her. She resisted the urge to run into his arms and profess her undying love to him forever and ever.

Hayley squinted to get a clearer look at her favorite country music legend.

Wait a minute.

It wasn't a cowboy hat he was wearing. It was more like a Boston Red Sox baseball cap. And he really wasn't that much over six feet. Maybe five ten, ten and a half at most. Were her eyes playing tricks on her? Did she just *want* this to be Wade?

The man stepped into the light from the street lamp. She was right. It wasn't Wade Springer at all. It was Lex Bansfield.

He walked over and gave Hayley a sweet kiss on the lips.

"My mouth's been watering ever since I picked up the paper today and read your column. When are you going to make me some of that fried chicken?"

Hayley smiled and kissed him back, not wanting Lex to see the clear disappointment òn her face.

"Maybe you can come over sometime this week and I'll make a batch for you and the kids," she said, unwrapping her candy bar and taking a generous bite. She offered some of it to Lex, but he shook his head.

That's when the strong smell of fish wafted up into her nose and she scrunched up her face. "Lex, where have you been?"

"Cleaning out my fishing boat. I'm lending it to Ned Weston while I'm out of town."

"Out of town? Where are you going?"

"Didn't you get my e-mail?"

"No, I've been a little busy today."

Waiting for Wade Springer to call.

"I'm leaving tomorrow," Lex said.

"Where?"

"Boss is flying me to the family estate outside of Phillie. He wants some trees on the property cut down and he only trusts me to do it right. I'll be back in a couple of weeks."

"I hope he's flying you first class. He can certainly afford it."

Lex's boss, Edgar Hollingsworth, was heir to a frozen seafood dinner empire and, despite his demanding nature, very generous to his summer estate caretaker.

"Nope," Lex said, winking. "Boss doesn't fly commercial. We're taking his private jet."

"You poor thing," Hayley said, stroking his cheek. "What will you do while I'm gone?"

"Oh, I'll try to carry on," Hayley said, laughing. There was no way she was ever going to admit to Lex that she would probably spend the entire time tracking down another man, even though it would just be so she could get her picture taken with him.

"Well, behave yourself and try to stay out of trouble," he said.

"I always do."

Lex gave her a skeptical look.

Even Hayley didn't believe it. Trouble just seemed to find her. And, at the time, she had no idea just how much trouble was brewing.

Lex pulled Hayley into him and squeezed her tight. Lex made Hayley feel safe. But she wasn't quite sure of her feelings for him. She was happy he wanted to take things slow. The fact was they hadn't known each other that long. And as perfect as he seemed on paper, there were still lingering doubts. He wasn't the most emotionally available man. Whenever she wanted to talk seriously about their relationship, he'd make a joke or a glib comment, like he was uncomfortable discussing his feelings.

In other words, he was your typical man.

But he was kind and sweet and drop-dead gorgeous and worth getting to know more, and perhaps one day they would wind up together. But for now, though, Hayley was content with the way things were.

Dating. But no strings attached.

Okay, maybe a string or two.

But they were a long way from being exclusive.

Only time would tell.

Lex kissed Hayley one more time.

The fishy smell was overwhelming.

"Do me a favor and go take a bath," Hayley said, plugging her nose with her fingers.

Lex tipped his baseball cap and then got in his Jeep and drove away, leaving Hayley standing in the parking lot of the Big Apple, clutching her half-eaten Snickers bar.

Hayley didn't get much sleep that night. She spent hours tossing and turning in bed, fantasizing about Wade Springer showing up at her house—no, wait, her office was better because that way there would be lots of people there to witness him barging in and picking her up in his strong arms. Just like at the end of one of her favorite movies, *An Officer and a Gentleman,* when Richard Gere showed up in his spiffy white navy officer's uniform and swept Debra Winger off her feet in front of all her factory coworkers as they enthusiastically applauded while he carried her off into the sunset.

She really needed to stop eating sweets before bed.

Hayley finally gave up trying to sleep and went downstairs at 4 A.M. to put a pot of coffee on and watch reruns of *The Dog Whisperer* with Leroy, who was also wide awake from the sound of a raccoon foraging through a neighbor's nearby garbage bin.

At one point, they were interrupted by the police scanner Hayley kept plugged in and sitting atop her refrigerator. (Sal wanted all the employees to keep scanners in their homes in case a major news story broke.) The dispatcher ordered a squad car to a local residence. The owner had been out of town on vacation and returned home to find the place ransacked.

This was disturbing. Bar Harbor was such a safe town, but lately it had been plagued by a series of break-ins. The police were going crazy trying to find the culprit and just when things would calm down, the thief would strike again.

A house.

A car.

Even a candy store.

He was nondiscriminating in his targets. Hayley hoped they would catch him soon. What would Wade Springer think about performing in a town with such a high crime rate?

Hayley tried not to think about Wade Springer anymore. The column had only come out yesterday. What were the odds someone from the tour would even read the paper, let alone her small inconsequential article buried in the back. She was being ridiculous.

Maybe there was some other way to get to Wade Springer. It's not like she thought they were going to be lifelong friends. She just wanted to meet him and tell him how much his music meant to her.

Maybe she really *was* turning into Kathy Bates in *Misery*. Would she eventually lure him to her house and keep him hidden away in the guest room and stop him from escaping by hobbling his ankles with a sledgehammer?

Was she that crazy?

Okay, now she *really* needed to stop thinking about Wade Springer. She was scaring herself.

Mercifully, the sun finally crested over Cadillac Mountain in Acadia National Park, the first point the sun hits in the United States every morning, and Hayley went into the kitchen to make breakfast for the kids.

She was at the office early, and she checked her e-mail. Sure enough, there was Lex's e-mail alerting her to his plans to travel to Philadelphia. She scrolled down further. Nothing from Wade Springer or his people.

Fine. No big deal.

It was a pie in the sky thought anyway.

Bruce Linney was the next to arrive. He and Hayley had a somewhat love–hate relationship.

He loved her. She hated him.

No, that was unfair. Bruce just liked to push Hayley's buttons and it drove her crazy, but she understood that he had a crush on her, and was especially jealous of her budding relationship with Lex.

Bruce was the paper's crime reporter, which meant he was a part-time employee, because there really wasn't that much crime in Bar Harbor.

Until recently, of course.

Bruce wasn't bad looking. In fact, he could be considered by most to be rather handsome. It was just that his irritating personality oftentimes overshadowed his positive physical attributes.

Bruce was on a tear. "Did you hear he struck again?"

"Yes," Hayley said. "I'm sure the cops will catch him soon."

"I'm not waiting for those clowns to get off their asses and solve this," Bruce yelled before catching himself. "No offense to Sergio."

"None taken," Hayley said absentmindedly as she continued scrolling through her e-mail. Sergio was the chief of police and the boyfriend of Hayley's younger brother, Randy.

"I'm going to collar this guy myself. I recently invested in some spy equipment I ordered online and I've narrowed down the area where he's most likely to hit next. . . ."

Hayley was no longer listening to Bruce. She had just received a text from Liddy. Her mouth dropped open in shock.

Liddy wrote, **Caravan of tour buses just rolled into town. Word has it Wade Springer is at a booth in Jordan's ordering breakfast as I'm writing this. Meet you there.**

This was it. Code red. Her chance to meet Wade.

Bruce was still talking. "It's scientific, really, how I was able to pinpoint the area he might strike next. I used this computer program. . . ."

Hayley sprung to her feet. "We need petty cash!"

"So go to the bank at lunch," Bruce said, a bit put out that she was interrupting his analysis of the recent crime spree and how he was going to expertly crack the case.

"Sal might want a poppyseed bagel when he gets in and I won't have any money to go get him one! I'll be right back!"

Hayley moved so fast she blew some papers off her desk. She was out the door before they even had a chance to float to the floor.

By the time Hayley reached Jordan's restaurant on Cottage Street, the line to get a table was out the door.

Liddy was the last one in line and did not look happy about it.

"Can you believe this?" she spat out. "Word spreads fast in this town. There's no way we're ever going to get inside, let alone get a glimpse of Wade."

"It's all right. I should've known this was hopeless."

"Well, I'm still on the board of directors at the Criterion, so we have that to use to get a meeting. But by then, I'm sure his people will have already hired a personal chef for Wade."

"Look, I took a shot and wrote the column. There's only so much we can do. Even if they read it, there's no guarantee they'll ever allow me to cook for Wade."

Liddy's mind raced and then something hit her.

"There could be another way."

"What?"

Liddy pulled Hayley closer. "The only other way into the restaurant is from the back."

"You mean through the kitchen?"

"Exactly!"

"And then what?"

"You're in the kitchen! You make Wade Springer's breakfast."

"What about Kelton, the cook? He's not going to let me take over for him."

"Oh, please. He owes you. You let him cheat off your physics pop quiz sophomore year. He'll let you make one omelette."

Liddy had a point. Kelton had always had a soft spot for Hayley.

Maybe this wasn't such a wild idea after all.

Hayley dashed around the side of the restaurant.

"You go, girl!" Liddy screamed, pumping her fist. She stopped when she noticed everyone in line staring at her.

Hayley entered the kitchen. Smoke from the bacon

frying nearly gagged her and she waved it away as she approached Kelton, who was pouring blueberry pancake batter on the grill.

"Hi, Kelton," Hayley said with a little trepidation.

Kelton turned around, surprised. "Hayley, what are you doing here?"

Kelton was what you would call a gentle giant: close to three hundred pounds that pushed against his hopelessly stained white t-shirt, with a scruffy beard, but the kindest eyes and the sweetest smile. Kelton had been friends with Hayley since kindergarten.

"Wait. Let me guess. Wade Springer."

Busted.

"I can't get you a table, Hayley. I'm sorry. I turned down my own mother."

"I understand, Kelton. I'm not here to eat. I'm here to cook."

Kelton raised an eyebrow. "You after my job?"

"Yes. But just for one order."

Kelton smiled. "I get it. You want to prepare his breakfast order. I read your column. Pretty shameless ploy, Hayley."

"I'll owe you big-time," Hayley said.

Kelton looked at her for a moment. Hayley wasn't sure he was going to go for it. He might get in trouble with Dave, the owner. But, then again, Kelton and Dave were best friends, so how much trouble would he really get in?

Kelton reached up and grabbed a piece of green paper that was clipped to a clothespin above the pickup station and handed it to Hayley.

"Southwest omelette, side of sausage, hash browns. Don't screw it up."

Hayley gave Kelton a hug. "Thank you, Kelton!"

"Consider us even for that physics quiz in high school."

She couldn't believe he still remembered.

Hayley grabbed an apron with a giant red lobster on the front and tied it around her waist and quickly got to work. An omelette was pretty standard stuff and there was not going to be much opportunity to make one that really stood out, but a few spices sprinkled here and there and a couple of added ingredients to give it a little kick just might do the trick. She also added some cheese to the hash browns and cooked the sausages to perfection, working so hard at her presentation, it was as if she were competing on *Top Chef*.

Hayley took a deep breath as she set the plate out on the pickup station and rang the bell.

Kelton came up behind her and put a comforting hand on her shoulder.

"Good luck."

"Thanks," Hayley said, patting his hand.

The waitress buzzed past, picking up the plate and taking it over to the corner booth where Wade sat with his manager. Wade's back was to Hayley so she never got a good look at his face. But she saw him cut off a piece of the omelette with his fork and raise it to his mouth to take a bite.

She noticed him talking to his manager. Was he talking about the omelette or were they just going over the song list for the upcoming performances?

She stood there in the kitchen, peeking out through the pickup station, watching Wade eat the entire breakfast. When he was finished, he reached out and touched the waitress on the arm and said something. The waitress, a world-weary hardened local who was not easily impressed by anyone, broke

into a wide smile and nodded and then made a beeline for the kitchen.

She entered through the swinging door and said
with a thick Maine accent, "Wade Springer wants to
personally give his compliments to the chef."

Hayley froze.

This was it.

She couldn't believe this hare-brained scheme of
Liddy's actually worked.

Kelton was beaming. "Well, don't just stand there,
Hayley, go take a bow."

Hayley took a step forward as if she were in a dream.

That's when someone grabbed her by the arm.

"What are you doing back here, Hayley?"

It was Dave, the owner of Jordan's. Dave Jordan.

Damn.

"Kelton, I told you not to let anyone back here."

"Oh, come on, Dave, it's Hayley."

"I'm sorry. Springer's security people will be all
over me if they find out I'm letting locals overrun the
place. I'm going to have to ask you to leave now,
Hayley."

"But she cooked his breakfast and now he wants to
say thanks," Kelton protested.

"You let her do your job?"

Hayley was feeling bad now. This was exactly what
she didn't want, Kelton getting into trouble.

"You know she's a good cook. Don't you read her
column?"

Hayley could tell Dave was sympathetic. But she
also knew he had a business to run, and what would it
look like if Wade's people found out he let just
anyone off the street prepare a meal in his kitchen for
a famous customer? And she also knew that the tour
being in town meant a boom in business for Dave and

he couldn't risk upsetting anyone enough to boycott his restaurant.

"Kelton, thank you. But Dave's right. I'm going to go now."

Hayley was red faced and felt foolish as she retreated out the back door, knowing her best chance to meet Wade Springer had just slipped through her fingers.

Chapter 3

When Hayley arrived home from work, her loyal dog, Leroy, was at the back door to the kitchen to greet her as always. She heard a pair of high-pitched voices chattering away in the living room. Probably Gemma and a friend. No effort was made by the girls to even acknowledge her arrival after a hard day at the office.

Thank God for the unconditional love of a dog.

Leroy was running around in circles and looked like he was about to pass out from the excitement. Gemma and her friend were too engaged dissecting the details of Gemma's "date" at the coffeehouse with high school heartthrob Reid Jennings.

"Omigod, you should have heard his voice. So deep and smooth, and, Carrie, he was singing right to me. We locked eyes. It was so romantic. It would have been perfect if my mother hadn't been there!"

"I'm home, so I can hear you!" Hayley said as she shed her jacket and checked the cupboards to inspect what food was in the house for dinner. It was slim pickings and Hayley dreaded having to go to the grocery store, which would be packed with nine to fivers just off work.

"Hi, Mrs. Powell!" Gemma's friend said.

"Hi, Carrie," Hayley answered.

Carrie Weston. A friend of Gemma's since first grade. Carrie was a sweet girl, rather shy, and not as popular as Gemma. She didn't like sports and was too insecure to try out for cheerleading or for any plays or for the student council. She was a bit of a wallflower with flat brown hair and a little thick around the middle. She had a pretty face, with a large mole which she hated, and she rarely smiled except when she was with Gemma. Hayley always feared that when Gemma rose in popularity once she hit high school, she would drop Carrie as a friend to hang with more of an "in" crowd, but to Gemma's credit, she stayed loyal. Especially since Carrie was always available to listen to all of Gemma's breathless stories of her love life.

Hayley knew one reason Carrie was so quiet and introspective.

She had a lousy home life.

Her mother died of cancer when she was three, and her father was left to raise her. Ned Weston, Carrie's father, was a big drinker with a foul temper, and he was very strict with Carrie, never trusting her and always suspecting she was up to no good. Hayley disliked Ned but tried to be civil, given the fact that their daughters were besties.

Hayley walked into the living room and gave Carrie a smile. "Don't let her talk your ear off, Carrie. I'm sure you'd like to discuss other topics besides the incomparable Reid Jennings."

"Oh, I don't mind, Mrs. Powell," Carrie said. "I'm just glad Gemma's found someone she likes."

"I'm very picky," Gemma added.

"Yes, we know. And not just about boys," Hayley said. "Are you dating anyone, Carrie?"

Carrie looked surprised by the question. "Um, no. Not at the moment."

"I'm making it my personal mission to find her a boyfriend before school's out next summer so we can double date at the beach," Gemma said.

"Anyone you have an eye on?" Hayley asked.

"Well, there's one person that drives me crazy every time I see him, but the only problem is he doesn't know I'm alive," Carrie said.

"I can't tell you how many times I've gone through the same thing," Hayley said.

"Plus, after reading your column in yesterday's paper, I'd have to fight you for him," Carrie said, laughing.

"Oh, I see," Hayley said. "You're a Wade Springer fan, too?"

"Oh . . . My . . . God! So hot!" Carrie said, swooning.

Funny how the mere mention of his name made girls of all ages melt.

"I know, right? Whenever I'm feeling depressed, I play one of his songs in my car and it never fails to brighten my spirits," Hayley said, immediately realizing she was regressing in age with every word she spoke.

"What's for dinner?" Gemma said, already bored by the subject of Wade Springer, who she clearly did not find remotely as interesting as Reid Jennings.

"I just went shopping two days ago and the cupboards are already bare," Hayley said.

"What can I say? Growing kids, healthy appetites, you know the drill," Gemma said.

"How about we go out for pizza? My treat. Carrie, would you like to join us?"

Hayley could see that Carrie wanted to come along, but she hesitated. "Well, my dad's working late tonight, and I'm not supposed to call him unless it's an emergency, but as long as I'm home by nine I should be fine."

"Great. We can drop you off after we eat. What about Dustin?"

"Already ate," Gemma said. "He's out with some friends making a horror movie with his iPhone. They took all the ketchup we had in the house to use as blood."

"Who knew I gave birth to the next J.J. Abrams," Hayley said as she scooped some dog food into a bowl for Leroy, refilled his water bowl and followed the girls outside where they piled into the car and headed toward Geddy's restaurant on Main Street just up from the town pier.

As Hayley looped around town and took a right on West Street past the old mansions that lined the coastal side of the street toward the pier, she drove past the Harborside Hotel, a very well-appointed four-star hotel, one of the best in town. Suddenly a scream from the back seat startled her.

"Omigod! There he is!" Carrie was out of control, yanking the door open, about to jump out of the car.

"Carrie, wait!" Hayley yelled as she jerked the car to the side of the road and hit the brake. "Who are you talking about?"

"Wade Springer!" Carrie was already out of the car and running across the street to the hotel parking lot where two tour buses were parked.

Hayley looked at Gemma, who rolled her eyes and folded her arms and let out a deep sigh. "Go on. Make it quick. I'm starving."

"We'll only be a minute," Hayley said, making sure no cars were coming before swinging open the driver's side door and racing across the street to catch up with Carrie.

Hayley found Carrie in the stately lobby of the

hotel. Her whole body appeared to be shaking and she was on the verge of tears.

Hayley put an arm around her. "Honey, are you all right?"

"I saw him. He was right there. I got so close I could almost touch him."

"Did you say anything to him?"

"I tried. But I just froze up. And then he went into the bar with some people and I haven't been able to move since."

The bar was part of the hotel's Italian restaurant, La Bella Vita. Hayley loved their meatballs and was forever trying to duplicate their secret recipe.

"So he's in the bar right now?"

Carrie nodded.

Hayley took Carrie's hand. "Come on. Let's go meet him."

She pulled Carrie by the hand, but Carrie still didn't move.

The shock of seeing her idol in the flesh.

Hayley completely understood.

"Come on, honey. One step at a time."

Carrie put one foot forward, then another, and finally started walking. Hayley decided it was up to her to make Carrie's night.

Hell, meeting Wade Springer would make Carrie's year.

And Hayley's, too.

Also, if she just happened to mention that she was the one who prepared that mouth-watering breakfast he enjoyed at Jordan's earlier in the day, then so be it.

As they rounded the corner, Hayley in the lead, she slammed into something. The impact nearly knocked Hayley off her feet.

Carrie gasped.

It wasn't a wall Hayley hit.

It was a man.

Over six feet tall and probably close to three hundred pounds. An African-American guy with huge biceps and a stern face.

"Excuse me," Hayley said apologetically before trying to walk around him. "We're trying to get to the bar."

The towering side of beef didn't move.

"I know she's underage but we're not ordering anything," Hayley said. "We'll just be a minute. There's someone we want to meet."

Still no budging.

Finally the giant spoke. "Sorry. Private party."

"Can't we just pop in for a second? We want to meet Wade."

"You and everybody else. No one gets in there. I have my orders."

"I see," Hayley said. "But this girl . . ."

Hayley grabbed Carrie and pulled her out from behind her and shoved her in front of Wade's bodyguard. "This girl's lifelong dream has been to meet Wade Springer and I promised her I would do everything I could to make that happen. And you're the only one standing in the way of her dream finally becoming a reality."

"Sounds to me like you shouldn't make promises you can't keep."

Carrie finally found her voice. "What if we told you I was dying and we're here as part of Make-A-Wish."

"I'd say I don't believe you for a second," the guard growled.

Hayley tried one more time. "Could you at least . . . what's your name?"

"Curtis," the guard said, not cracking a smile.

Hayley put out her hand to shake. Curtis kept his massive arms folded.

"Curtis, could you at least go in there and tell Wade two of his biggest fans are out here and would love the opportunity to just say hello?"

"Never going to happen," Curtis said.

Carrie stepped back, defeated. "Come on, Mrs. Powell, let's go."

Hayley gave Curtis a scowl to match his own. "You are not a very happy person, Curtis. Haven't you heard an occasional smile and a positive attitude help you live longer? Think about it."

And with that, Hayley spun around and followed Carrie out of the hotel, trying to hold on to her last shred of dignity after behaving like a star-struck groupie.

After taking the girls out for pizza at Geddy's, Hayley drove Carrie to her house on Ledgelawn Avenue. When she pulled up, Hayley felt a knot in her stomach. Ned Weston's car was in the driveway and all the lights were on in the house. He had beaten them home. Through the rearview mirror, even though it was already dark outside, Hayley could make out the look of fear on Carrie's face in the back seat.

"Thanks for dinner, Mrs. Powell. See you at school tomorrow, Gemma," Carrie said quickly as she bolted out of the car and scurried across the lawn toward the front door of the house.

Before she had a chance to reach it, the door swung open and the angry face of Ned Weston peered out. He was a bear of a man, though no match for Curtis, Wade Springer's unhappy watchdog.

Ned could have been considered a handsome man, with a sexy shaved head that reminded Hayley of that hot British Starfleet commander from Star Trek, Patrick Stewart. But Ned's dark and unfriendly personality ruined any chance that a woman might be attracted to him.

In fact, he struck Hayley as downright menacing.

Hayley watched Ned's face turn beet red as Carrie tried to explain why she hadn't been there when he got home from work. Carrie pointed toward the car and Ned whipped his head around, glaring at Hayley.

Hayley offered a weak smile and a quick wave, but Ned didn't acknowledge her. He just grabbed Carrie by the arm and dragged her into the house, slamming the door shut behind him.

"What a jerk," Gemma spit out from the back seat.

"You think she's going to be all right?" Hayley asked.

"Oh, yeah. He'll yell at her for a while until he gets tired and then he'll just go watch ESPN or Fox News. It's not like he ever hits her or anything. She'd tell me if he did."

"Well, that's good to know."

Hayley slowly pulled the car away from the curb, keeping one eye on the house, wishing there was something she could do to help poor Carrie, but knowing she was powerless to do anything, and it was an awful feeling.

Chapter 4

The following morning Hayley had finally given up hope that Wade would ever read her column or have any idea that she could cook.

Any chance of getting hired to be his personal chef was a mere pipe dream.

So after making the kids' lunches and downing two cups of coffee, she fired up her Subaru wagon and drove to work, satisfied that at least she could get a good seat at one of the concerts thanks to Liddy's position on the board of directors at the Criterion Theatre.

When she arrived at work, Sal was standing near her desk in the front office chatting to Bruce, while chowing down on a bagel with cream cheese. Bruce was running down a list of suspects he had made up the night before regarding the recent rash of break-ins.

Bruce was determined to solve the case and become the town hero.

Solving a crime. Meeting Wade Springer. Hayley chuckled to herself. We all have our goals in life.

Maybe it was time for her to find a more serious

one. She made the decision to forget all this silliness and just focus on her next column.

That's right about the time the phone rang.

"Island Times, Hayley speaking," she said as she slid behind her desk and picked it up.

"Okay, you know how when you go to bed every night and get down on your knees and thank the good Lord he brought me into your life?"

It was Liddy.

"Um, no, Liddy, I really don't do that," Hayley said, laughing.

"Well, honey, you better start because I'm your guardian angel and I am about to bring loving light and happiness into your otherwise dreary life!"

"What have you gone and done now?"

"I just came from a board of directors meeting at the Criterion."

"Please tell me you got us front row seats."

"Oh, sweetie, this is much bigger than that. Are you wearing something nice? Because, in twenty minutes, you're going to meet Wade Springer in his hotel room!"

"What?" Hayley screamed.

Sal was so startled by her shriek he spilled coffee down the front of his shirt. Another Walmart shirt bit the dust.

He glared at Hayley, but she was too excited to notice. Sal pushed past Bruce and stalked off to the bathroom to scrub the stain.

"What are you talking about?" Hayley asked breathlessly, lowering her voice in a vain attempt to restore a little office etiquette.

"Well, the reason Wade has come to town early is because he's a big outdoorsman and wants to do some biking, hike some trails, maybe climb to the top of Door Mountain. He's going to play tourist."

"And he needs a local guide and you recommended me?" Hayley said, trying not to scream again.

"Honey, when was the last time you climbed a man, let alone a mountain?"

Liddy had a point.

"And do you even own a bike?"

She had had a moped once. But then it broke down and she couldn't afford to fix it so it was now sitting in her garage, rusted from being parked under a leak in her roof after a heavy rainstorm.

"So anyway," Liddy said, almost as breathlessly as Hayley, "I suggested at the meeting today that since we have some time before the concert, it might not be a bad idea to do some publicity, meet with a couple of papers for interviews, do a local radio show, really talk up why Wade is here and his passion for ocean research, and since you work for the *Island Times.* . . ."

"Liddy, I write a cooking column."

"Well, they don't have to know that. I told his manager you were the town's premier entertainment reporter!"

"You lied?"

"Of course I lied. Haven't you ever heard the phrase 'desperate situations require desperate measures'? Now find a mirror and make sure your hair isn't too frizzy."

"I can't go now. I just got into the office. And Sal's here."

"This is a once in a lifetime opportunity, Hayley. It's now or never. Are you going to let something as insignificant as a job get in your way of meeting Wade Springer?"

"Says the woman who just got a commission from a two-point-three million dollar house sale last month."

"Hayley, this is your chance. And if you don't do it,

then I am going to go and say I'm the *Island Times'* answer to Nancy O'Dell and meet him in your place."

"I don't know. . . ."

"You're a smart woman. You can think of some way to get out of there. Now get off the phone. You're wasting valuable time."

Hayley hung up and sprung to her feet. "We need petty cash!"

Bruce gave her a curious look. "Didn't you *just* go to the bank yesterday?"

"Sal's birthday is coming up and I want to plan a little party. Some wine, a block of cheese, and some crackers."

Sal ambled out into the front office, the remnants of his coffee stain still visible on his lime green short-sleeved shirt. "My birthday isn't for another three weeks."

"You always tell me I leave things to the last minute. Well, this is my effort to improve before my next job evaluation."

Sal really couldn't argue with that.

And it was a good thing, too, because Hayley was already out the door.

There were still enough tourists in town to make parking nearly impossible near the Harborside Hotel so Hayley ran all the way to the town pier, veering right on West Street. She was out of breath and sweating when she burst into the lobby. She paused to catch her breath before casually approaching the desk clerk, a young bearded man in his midtwenties whose massive frame was squeezed into a black vest which was obviously too small for his size.

"I'm here to see Wade Springer," Hayley said, practically choking from her run across town.

"And you are?"

"Hayley Powell," she said, wheezing. "Entertainment reporter for the *Island Times*."

The clerk cocked an eyebrow. "Really? I didn't even know they had one."

He picked up a phone and punched in some numbers.

Hayley pulled a compact out of her bag and checked herself. *Disaster* was an understatement. The sweat from her sprint to the hotel had caused her mascara to run and her hair looked as if she had just stuck her finger into an electric socket.

The clerk hung up and stared at Hayley.

Uh oh.

Looked like the jig was up.

"Go on up. Room two-thirty-three," he said, and returned to his computer.

As Hayley turned to go, she thought she heard the clerk mutter *lucky bitch* under his breath.

Hayley stopped off in the ladies' room and tried to repair her frazzled appearance. But she knew Wade's time was limited so it wasn't as if she could do a complete makeover. She wiped off the runaway mascara, pulled her wild hair into a ponytail, sprayed a little perfume from her bag into the air and stepped into the mist, and then hoped for the best.

When she arrived in front of the door to room 233, the butterflies were definitely free in her stomach.

And her hand was shaking as she reached up to knock on the door.

She patted down her blouse, groaning to herself that this was the shirt that made her look fat, but she wanted something roomy to wear this morning because she wanted fried clams for lunch.

The door swung open and a man was there.

But it wasn't Wade.

This guy was short and stout with dyed yellow hair.

And wearing sunglasses.

Indoors.

"Hayley? I'm Billy Ray Cyrus."

"No you're not." Hayley couldn't help herself. He didn't look anything like Miley's dad.

"There are two of us. And it's been a pain in my ass ever since he became famous for 'Achy Breaky Heart.'"

"I see. I'm sorry, Mr. Cyrus."

"But then he only had one hit and kind of disappeared and I was just reclaiming my life and identity again and then—boom!—his spawn becomes this huge child star and so his name is right back in the public eye all over again and once more my life is ruined. But you're not here to talk about me and my issues. Please, come in."

He grabbed her by the arm and yanked her inside, shutting the door behind him. "We've been hiding from screaming fans and nosy paparazzi all day. I don't know how Wade thinks he's going to go jogging in the park later without getting mobbed."

The room was a suite. With a large living room and plush furnishings. Fresh flowers and bowls of fruit.

Hayley had no idea there was anything so glamorous in Bar Harbor.

Or maybe they just dressed it up for Wade.

"You have five minutes. We have the *Bangor Daily News* and the *Herald* coming in a little while. I tried to read your column in the *Times* but couldn't find it."

"I've been on vacation."

Billy Ray led Hayley to the couch and she sat down. "Can I get you anything to drink?"

"No, thank you."

At that moment, Wade bounded out of the bedroom wearing a black dress shirt and jeans and his signature white cowboy hat.

It was like a dream.

Billy Ray began to leave but Hayley reached out and snagged his shirt. "Maybe some water. I'm having trouble breathing."

Billy Ray nodded as he pulled free from her grip and disappeared out the door, leaving Hayley alone with Wade.

Wade stuck out a strong, big, masculine hand. "Wade Springer, nice to meet you."

Hayley was speechless.

Probably for the first time in her life.

She nodded.

Just staring at his hand.

Not taking it.

To the point where it got really uncomfortable.

Finally, Wade gave up trying to shake her hand and took a seat on the love seat opposite her. "So, fire away. What do you want to know?"

"Nothing."

"Well, that's just about the shortest interview I've ever sat through."

"No, I mean I'm not sure there's anything you can tell me that I don't already know about you. How's Rip?"

Wade gave her a funny look. "My dog?"

Hayley nodded.

"Dead."

"Omigod. I'm so sorry."

"Died about ten years ago."

"See, I knew that. I'm just really nervous."

"Well, take a deep breath and relax, Hayley."

Hayley nodded.

Not taking a deep breath.

And not relaxing.

"Why don't I start with a question to break the ice?"

Hayley nodded again.

"How long have you been an entertainment reporter?"

Suddenly Hayley felt a pang of guilt. She was sitting just a few feet away from her all-time favorite country music singer, but she was there under false pretenses. She didn't feel right lying to Wade of all people.

"About five years."

Five years? Where did that even come from?

The door opened and Billy Ray came in and handed Hayley a bottled water.

"You have three minutes left, Hayley. Make it count."

Hayley just stared at Wade, unable to speak, her mind a blank.

This was a disaster. She felt like jumping to her feet and bolting out of the room and forgetting this whole thing.

"Is that you?" Billy Ray said, scooping up a newspaper that was lying on the coffee table that separated her from Wade.

Hayley's heart sank.

It was a copy of the *Island Times*.

And it was open to her cooking column.

Billy Ray scrunched up his face as he looked at it.

"Something wrong, Billy Ray?" Wade asked.

Billy Ray read a few paragraphs and hurled the paper down on the table. "She's a fraud. She's not an entertainment reporter. She writes a column about food and drinks."

"My two favorite subjects," Wade said with a smile.

Billy Ray hovered over Hayley threateningly. "I think you should go now."

"Yes, of course," Hayley said, casting her eyes downward as she stood up, her face flushed with embarrassment.

Billy Ray escorted her to the door.

A deep southern voice boomed from behind them.

"Wait, Billy Ray. This is the woman I was telling you about."

Stop the presses. Wade Springer? Talking about *her*?

Hayley casually pinched herself to make sure she hadn't fallen asleep at her desk and was dreaming.

"Do you know she snuck into the kitchen of that little cafe we ate at yesterday and cooked me my breakfast?" Wade said.

He turned to Hayley and winked. "Best omelette I ever had. I went to give my compliments to the chef, I forget his name. . . ."

"Kelton, he's a friend," Hayley managed to get out.

"Kelton, that's right. Anyway, he came clean and told me about Hayley."

"I could have that restaurant shut down for something like that," Billy Ray said.

"Oh, don't be squawking like a flustered hen, Billy Ray. I think it's about the sweetest thing I ever heard," Wade said, charmed.

"I have some phone calls to make," Billy Ray sniffed, knowing he wasn't getting anywhere with his boss, so he may as well retreat to another room.

"I'm sorry. I've been entirely inappropriate misrepresenting myself," Hayley said.

"You're not misrepresenting yourself now. I know exactly who you are."

"Thank you for understanding. I better go."

"You're not going anywhere."

Hayley couldn't think of anything more exciting than being held against her will by Wade Springer.

But she knew *that* was definitely a dream.

"Not until I get a taste of that famous fried chicken I read about."

"So you read my column?"

"Every word. And it just so happens I need someone to cook for me while I'm in town. Nothing fancy.

Some grits for breakfast, maybe a packed lunch for when I go sightseeing, a light supper. Think you can handle that?"

Hayley knew it would be impossible again for her to speak so she just nodded.

"Great. You can start tomorrow."

"What about your dinner tonight? I can whip something up when I get off work."

"No, I already have plans."

"Oh. Okay."

"You and I are going to go out to celebrate your coming to work for me."

Hayley's jaw nearly hit the floor.

Did Wade Springer just ask her out on a date?

No, of course he didn't.

On the other hand, it did sound a lot like he just asked her out.

On a date.

With him.

Sometimes dreams really do come true.

Chapter 5

Mass hysteria.

That's the best way to describe what was happening in Hayley's house as she prepared for her dinner with Wade Springer.

What to wear.

How to flatten her hair.

And why did she have to eat a tub of ice cream after work? Her stomach was now actually protruding over her belt. Would Wade mind her wearing stretch pants to dinner? Jenny Craig would be so disappointed in her. This was all too much.

Deep breaths, Hayley. Deep breaths. She had to focus.

Makeup. She needed to put on her makeup. And not too much mascara because she sometimes looked like a hungover raccoon.

She hadn't been this excited about a date since the first night she had gone out with Lex.

Of course, that night she wound up arrested before she even left the driveway. But that was another story.

Wait.

Hayley stopped herself.

Date.

She was thinking about this dinner as a date. What on earth was she doing? This wasn't a date. Wade was her employer as of today. She was letting her imagination run wild.

She needed to calm down.

Hayley fumbled through her bedroom closet for a sweater that didn't have too much noticeable dog hair on it. She yanked out a sleek black one. Black was slimming, right?

A pair of white pants.

Some slip-on shoes.

Nothing too dressy.

But smart.

And professional. Yes, that was key. She had to be professional.

She applied some CoverGirl and Olay Simply Ageless Foundation.

Yeah, right. *Simply Ageless.* Who comes up with that stuff?

She frowned at a small zit on her face as she stared at herself in the dresser mirror, and then rubbed more foundation on her face.

This was such a complicated process.

Gemma burst into the room. Hayley noticed that she was wearing a too tight t-shirt and way too short cut-off jeans for a girl her age, but she didn't have time to argue with her daughter. She would deal with it later.

"Mom, did you check the voice mail? We have a code red situation. Lex called and wants you to call him back when you get a chance."

"Now why would Lex calling be a code red situation?"

"Because you're going on a date with another man, and not just any man. A huge country-singing superstar and maybe he knows about it and is calling to test you."

"First of all, Gemma, this is *not* a date."

Maybe if she said it enough times she'd actually believe it.

"I'm working for Wade," Hayley said. "We're just meeting to discuss menus. Even if he did know, Lex couldn't possibly object."

"Then why are you so dressed up?"

Hayley brushed some dog hair off the front of her sweater. "This is not dressed up."

"For you it is."

Hayley flashed her an annoyed look.

"Now listen to me, Gemma. I don't want you breathing a word about this dinner to anyone, do you hear me? I don't want it spreading all over town. There's enough gossip around here as it is."

Gemma gave her one of those panicked looks that said, *I'm going to reassure you, but I am totally lying.* "Okay."

"What did you do?"

"Nothing." Another panicked look.

"Gemma . . ."

"Okay, I may have posted something on Facebook."

"What? What did you post?"

"I might have said something along the lines of . . . *OMG! My mother is going out on a date with Wade Springer tonight.*"

"Gemma, you didn't!"

"Well, you are!"

"It's not a date."

"Don't worry. No one will read it."

"You have seven thousand Facebook friends and there are only five thousand year-round residents in Bar Harbor!"

"Don't hate me because I'm popular."

"Did you mention where we were having dinner?"

"Of course not."

"Good."

"But you might want to go talk to Dustin. Soon."

"Why?"

"He's downstairs tweeting and you know what a big mouth he's got."

Hayley flew out of the bedroom and down the stairs. Too late.

Dustin had already sent out seventeen tweets about his mother's big date with Wade Springer, even discussing the specials at Town Hill Bistro where they were planning to dine.

Hayley immediately called Wade and suggested they not go to dinner since she didn't want gawkers interrupting them. Instead, she suggested a drink at the Balance Rock Inn, a very high-end bed and breakfast set back from the rocky shores of the Atlantic Ocean, where guests could enjoy a cockail outside and watch the cruise ships in the harbor set out for their next destinations.

There was also an outdoor gazebo with cushioned chairs and love seats in which to enjoy a glass of wine with your significant other, but that was way too romantic, so there was no way Hayley was going to suggest they sit there.

Too late.

When Hayley arrived at the Balance Rock Inn, Wade was waiting for her in the gazebo. She hoped and prayed he wasn't thinking she was trying to make more out of this than it was.

A simple business meeting.

Wade looked gorgeous in his red print open shirt and white cowboy hat and tight jeans and cowboy boots. He had a simple gold neck chain that sparkled in the moonlight.

"I took the liberty of ordering us some wine," Wade said as he took Hayley's hand and led her over to one of the love seats. "I'm more of a beer kind of guy, but I knew I was meeting a lady, so I went for the Pinot Noir."

"Thank you," Hayley said nervously.

Wade poured them each a glass and handed her one. They clinked glasses. "Here's to your fried chicken. May I not gain too much weight while I'm here in Bar Harbor."

Hayley sat there sipping her wine, feeling completely out of her element. But Wade was perfectly at ease, talking about how he hiked the Precipice Trail today, which climbs a thousand feet up the east face of Champlain Mountain in the park. He said how strenuous it was, but how much he loved it and couldn't wait to conquer more trails while he was in town. He couldn't believe how beautiful Acadia National Park was, a little jewel so far removed from the hustle and bustle of the major cities. He was an outdoorsman, happiest when pushing his physical limits.

God, Wade was sexy.

Hayley took another sip of wine. "Did you get the menus I e-mailed you? I want to know about any allergies you might have, or if there is something you really don't like, although I'm pretty familiar with your eating habits, having read about you all these years."

"I'm sure I'm going to love everything you cook for me, Hayley," Wade said with a wink.

Was that wink a flirtatious gesture?

Hayley took another sip of her wine.

Great. She was calming her nerves with lots of alcohol.

Always a sound plan of attack.

Suddenly, her eye caught something.

There was a figure crouched down behind some bushes a few feet away, watching them. He was small and wiry, the size of a kid, maybe eleven or twelve years old.

Hayley squinted to get a better look, and then there was a blinding flash that surprised both her and Wade, followed by a rustling in the bushes as the kid ran off in the dark.

Hayley shrugged. "I guess a fan wanted a photo for his scrapbook."

"Happens all the time," Wade said, smiling, and then he refilled their glasses with more wine.

Hayley wasn't exactly tipsy when she and Wade left the Balance Rock Inn, but she was feeling warm and fuzzy inside, and fought every urge to rest her head on Wade's broad shoulders.

If she could reach one.

Wade was tall.

Maybe on her tippy toes.

Wade insisted on walking Hayley home, but Hayley laughed and assured him the town was very safe and her house was just a few blocks away, and it was such a beautiful night.

He gave her a sweet peck on the cheek that nearly caused her to lose her balance.

Before he could press the matter of escorting her home any further, she left.

As she walked home, Hayley felt confident she could prepare at least three meals a day that would make Wade happy and she was getting more excited about the idea of being Wade Springer's personal chef.

When Hayley got home, she noticed Liddy's Mercedes parked in the driveway.

The house was lit up like a Christmas tree, unlike

most of the other homes on quiet residential Glen Mary Road.

Hayley shook her head, smiling to herself. Liddy and the kids were probably on pins and needles waiting to hear every detail of her night with Wade. She was tired, but would give them a few highlights before she turned in for the night.

But when Hayley walked in the back door and through the kitchen there was no welcoming party to greet her. She heard the sound of rummaging down the hall and followed it to the living room, where she stopped and gasped.

The room had been turned upside down. The shelves were emptied, books and framed photos piled high on the floor. The couch and chairs were moved, the dining room table upended.

"What is going on here?" Hayley said as she spotted Liddy on her hands and knees going through a basket of magazines.

Liddy's face was pale and gaunt. Like she hadn't slept in days. She wasn't even wearing one of her signature Donna Karan ensembles. She was in a sweatshirt and jeans and flip-flops.

Liddy in flip-flops?

This had to be something bad.

Real bad.

"Where are the kids?" Hayley asked.

"Upstairs," Liddy said. "They're searching the bathroom. I think I went up there to use it the last time I was here, but I'm not sure."

Liddy looked lost and broken.

"My God, Liddy, what's happened?"

"My diamond earrings? The pair I bought at Tiffany's on my last trip to New York and spent a fortune on when I knew I shouldn't? But then I said to myself,

'Liddy, you deserve this!' and I called you from the counter so you could talk me out of it, but I really wanted you to tell me to go for it and you didn't disappoint . . ."

"Yes, Liddy, I remember. What about them? Did you lose one?"

Liddy nodded and then burst into tears.

Hayley rushed forward and embraced her.

Not the end of the world. At least, in Hayley's mind. She was raising two kids as a single mother and just wanted to pay her heating bill for the winter. But Liddy was an entirely different creature altogether. And, to her, this *was* the end of the world. So as her closest friend, Hayley needed to be there for her.

"Don't worry, honey, we'll find it."

She started to pull out of the hug, but Liddy clutched the sleeve of her sweater tightly.

"I've searched everywhere. The kids are still looking upstairs. This is the last place I could've lost it. And we've turned this whole house upside down and . . . nothing."

"You guys find anything up there?" Hayley called, finally freeing herself from Liddy's grasp and walking over to the foot of the stairs.

"Nope," Dustin said before she heard him walk back into his room and turn his attention to his PlayStation.

"Sorry," Gemma said before her cell phone chirped and she, too, abandoned the search.

"I know I'm making too big a deal out of this, especially with all the starving children in the world, but I loved those earrings, Hayley, and if I wear just one, I'll look like a really well-off gypsy."

"Don't worry. We'll find it."

"I'm sorry. I didn't even ask you about your big date. How was it?"

"Fine. Nothing special," Hayley said before adding, "And it wasn't a date."

Hayley decided not to go on and on about the deliciously charming and gorgeous Wade Springer, and how the night could not have gone more perfectly. There was no reason to rub salt in the wound. Her friend was hurting.

So, instead, she pushed her ratty stained couch to the other side of the room and joined in on the search for her best friend's missing diamond earring without missing a beat.

That's what friends are for.

Chapter 6

Hayley couldn't breathe as she stood in front of the magazine and newspaper rack at the Big Apple convenience store where she picked up her coffee before work every morning.

She wasn't near a mirror, but she knew her face was beet red.

Her heart was pounding.

She stared at the photo on the front page of the *Bar Harbor Herald*, the *Island Times'* rival paper. It was a picture of Hayley and Wade Springer canoodling in the gazebo at the Balance Rock Inn, along with a caption, "The Way to a Man's Heart Is Through His Stomach."

The article went on to say that Hayley was being hired to be the official chef for Wade while he was staying in Bar Harbor, and that the big question now was, *Is it really business, or pleasure?*

The figure in the bushes.

The flash.

It was a photographer.

And the *Herald* probably bought the picture so they could trump up some silly story about a romance brewing between a world famous singer and a simple-minded local girl. She always knew the *Herald* was just a shameless tabloid dressed up like a quirky small-town paper.

At least her own paper, the *Times,* wouldn't stoop this low.

Right in the next rack was the *Island Times.*

The same photo was on the front page.

Their caption said, "What's Really Cooking Between Wade Springer and Our Very Own Food and Cocktails Columnist?"

No.

Sal would never print something like this without warning her first.

But, then again, she had left work early the previous day, before the paper was put to bed and she had turned her cell off because she didn't want any calls interrupting her meeting with Wade.

She forgot to turn it back on.

Hayley fished her phone out of her coat pocket and fired it up.

Sure enough, there were four messages.

All from Sal.

Message #1:

"Hey, Hayley, I'm at the office late. We're about to go to press and I got this kid Darrell Rodick here in the office with a photo of you and Wade and I just wanted to get your side of the story to see if there's something here. Call me back."

Darrell Rodick was a ruthlessly ambitious fifth-grader and amateur photographer who fancied himself the town's paparazzi. The only trouble was, very rarely did celebrities frequent Bar Harbor, and, when they did, it was in the summer. He once ambushed a pretty girl who had appeared once on *The Vampire Diaries* while she was biking around Eagle Lake.

The kid was a big pain.

And Hayley was about to call his parents and tell them so.

Message #2:

"Uh, Hayley, please call me back. I'm not sure what to do here. We're nearing deadline. My wife just saw the Rodick kid heading over to the *Herald* offices, and you know how I don't like to be scooped."

Hayley knew what was coming next.

Message #3:

"Hayley, I need to decide what to do soon and you're off the grid for some reason so I'm going to make an executive decision and print the photo. I know you're not going to like this, but we just interviewed the bartender at the Balance Rock Inn and he confirmed you two looked like you were on a date."

The bartender?

Seriously?

Message #4:

"Okay, Hayley, it's done. Sorry about this, but I had to go with my gut. I didn't want the *Herald* getting the jump on us. Maybe you can do an exclusive interview with us. Just to clarify things in case we got something wrong."

Hayley was fuming. Her face got hotter.

Yes, she was ticked off at that bratty shutterbug Darrell Rodick for spying on her. Yes, she was furious with Sal for turning the *Times* into a small-town version of *Star* magazine. But, most of all, she was really pissed at the unflattering photo of herself.

Wade, of course, looked stunning and natural as always, like he was accepting a Country Music Award.

But she just wasn't photogenic. Her head was thrown back and her mouth was open, laughing, and it looked like she had some kind of weird underbite. She looked just like her dog, Leroy. They do say dogs tend to resemble their owners.

Hayley rushed out of the Big Apple, hopped in her car, and drove straight to the office. When she blew through the front door, Sal was nowhere to be seen. She stormed into the back bullpen, but his office door was closed and locked.

"So is it true?" a man's voice said from behind, startling her.

Hayley spun around.

It was Bruce.

He dangled a copy of the *Times* in front of him.

"Of course it's not true. I should sue for libel. Where the hell is Sal?"

"Don't know. My guess is he's hiding from you," Bruce said, studying the photo on the front page. "Sure looks to me like something's going on between you two."

"We're not going to go through this again, Bruce," Hayley said, remembering how Bruce reacted when she first began dating Lex. She knew he had the hots for her and they had known each other a long time, but there was no way she would ever go there. Especially with a coworker.

"Have you talked to Wade? Has he seen the papers?"

Hayley's heart nearly stopped.

She hadn't thought of Wade. What must he be thinking? Would he suspect that Hayley had ulterior motives for going to work for him? Wade knew she was a columnist at the paper. Would he think she had pursued the job as his personal chef so she could pump him for intimate details about his personal life? Or maybe he would suspect she was some kind of pathetic fame-whore trying to make herself part of the story.

Hayley couldn't bear the thought of her beloved Wade making those judgments about her.

Bruce folded the paper in his hand. "So?"

"No, I haven't talked to Wade. Why waste his time with this garbage?"

"I couldn't agree more," Bruce said, following Hayley back out to the front office, where she sat down at her desk and turned on her computer, ready to begin the day's work.

"It makes me sick to my stomach that this is our front-page story when there is a serious crime spree going on in this town," Bruce said.

Hayley clicked on her e-mail and was relieved she hadn't yet received one from Wade's people, terminating her.

Maybe they hadn't seen the papers yet.

"Did you know this mysterious robber broke into another home yesterday when the residents were at work? In broad daylight. He's getting more brazen every day," Bruce said.

Hayley tried ignoring him.

"I do have a suspect, though," Bruce said, trying to stir Hayley's interest.

Hayley clicked on her file of recipes and searched for the perfect one for her next column, but curiosity got the best of her and she swiveled around in her office chair to face Bruce.

"Who?" Hayley asked.

"That punk ass, Jesse DeSoto," Bruce spit out.

Jesse DeSoto was an obvious choice. A nineteen-year-old high school dropout hellion who got a perverse joy out of picking on younger kids. Hayley despised him because when Dustin was in fifth grade, he became a target. Hayley had noticed Dustin's mood changing at home, but her son refused to admit he was getting chased home from school and pushed around by Jesse.

Until Gemma witnessed one particularly nasty

episode where Jesse had Dustin flat on his stomach and was shoving his face into a snowbank. Gemma had raced to his rescue, and, luckily, Jesse had always thought Gemma was cute, so when she ordered him to stop bothering her brother, Jesse immediately let Dustin go with the promise of never touching him again.

And he had kept his word. Hayley was going to call Jesse's mother to complain, but Dustin begged her not to and she finally let the whole matter go. Still, she was no fan of Jesse's, and Bruce was probably right.

"What evidence do you have?" Hayley asked.

"Nothing concrete yet. But it's only a matter of time. I'm going to tail him and catch him in the act and blow this whole story wide open."

"Good for you," Hayley said, humoring him.

"And then maybe we can shove all this ridiculous coverage of some subpar singing cowboy off the front page."

For once, Hayley agreed with Bruce.

Well, except for the part about Wade being subpar.

Bruce wasn't a country fan. He was more of a heavy metal enthusiast. He had looked like Steven Tyler in high school.

Maybe that's why she once had a thing for him.

Too bad he cleaned himself up.

Chapter 7

By the end of the morning, Hayley's budding romance with Wade Springer was the talk of the town. She waited for the phone call from Billy Ray Cyrus, relieving her from her chef duties, but it didn't come.

So on her lunch hour, Hayley drove over to the grocery store and picked up the items from a list of ingredients for Wade's breakfast, the first meal she would be officially preparing for him.

He and a few of his bandmates had gone whale watching today, so they had just picked up a few sandwiches at a local deli, and were planning to grab dinner at the hotel when they got back. So Hayley didn't really have to worry about starting her new cooking gig until the next morning.

She dropped the food off at her house and returned to work. There was still no sign of Sal. He managed to keep himself scarce all day with an occasional e-mail claiming he was chasing a story in Bangor.

Interesting, Hayley thought.

Sal rarely wrote articles anymore, being editor in chief. It was pretty obvious he was avoiding her. She knew Sal like her own brother. And she knew he would probably show up with her favorite fresh bagels from

Morning Glory bakery hoping she would be so excited she would forget he printed that photo.

And he was probably right.

Hayley could never carry a grudge for too long.

When Hayley turned off her computer at the end of the day, she was confident she still had her moonlighting gig as Wade's chef.

So she wasn't that mad anymore.

In fact, when she had driven over to the grocery store during lunch, she'd felt like a regular celebrity because all the stock boys and cashiers kept pointing and whispering as if Rihanna was in the seafood department buying fresh shrimp.

Hayley decided to cap off the day by going for a drink at Randy's bar, Drinks Like A Fish.

It was Happy Hour.

Randy had killer drink specials.

What could be better?

And she needed to see some friendly faces.

Randy was tending bar. He was two and a half years younger than her. At least that was the case if you compared birth certificates. Hayley now claimed Randy was older by three years and counting. She always believes if you say something over and over again, eventually it becomes accepted as the truth.

So she was never going to back down from shaving a few years off her age.

Liddy was sitting at the bar sipping an espresso martini. She looked distraught and was talking Randy's ear off, undoubtedly bemoaning the missing earring tragedy. Next to Liddy was Hayley's other BFF, Mona.

Mona was married with six or seven kids. Who could keep count? She had just popped out another one a few months ago.

Mona was wearing a bulky sweatshirt advertising her seafood business. Mona was a successful fisherman selling lobsters and scallops at high-end prices to locals and tourists alike during the summer. She was so successful, she pretty much took the other three seasons off.

Hayley approached the bar and Randy broke out into a wide smile.

"Hey, sis," he said as he poured a Jack and Coke and slid it over to Hayley, who was standing behind Liddy and Mona, hugging them from behind.

"I've looked everywhere and nothing. Zip. Zilch. Oh God, do you know how much I spent on those earrings?" Liddy moaned.

Hayley knew this would be the number one topic of discussion for weeks to come.

Randy reached for Mona's glass. "Another Diet Coke, Mona?"

"Yeah, why not? I'm in no rush to go home to all that screaming and whining."

"Oh, come on," Randy said as he refilled Mona's glass from the soda fountain. "Your kids are very well behaved."

"I'm not talking about my kids. I'm talking about my deadbeat husband. And if he doesn't stop getting me pregnant, I'm going to kick his ass."

"Are you . . . ?" Hayley asked.

Mona nodded, patting her stomach with a frown.

"You've got to be kidding! Again?" Hayley said.

"Why the hell do you think I'm drinking Diet Coke? I hate this crappy stuff. It's all chemicals!"

Randy put the refill on a coaster in front of her. "Don't you two believe in using contraceptives?"

"I'm not an idiot, Randy," Mona moaned. "We've tried everything. I'm this freaking medical miracle. I defy the odds. I'm like immune or something. The Pill? I'd get better results from aspirin when it comes to my ovaries."

Hayley slid on to a stool next to Mona. "Well, I think it's great news. I can't think of anything better for a child than to have you as a mother."

"Tell my rugrats that, will you? I swear they have secret meetings at night discussing plans on how to drive me bat-shit crazy," Mona said, downing her glass of soda.

Mona reached out and took Hayley's hand. "So how are you doing? I saw the paper."

"I was hoping Bruce would do a story," Liddy said, gulping down the last of her espresso martini. "I wasn't sure he was going to take a missing earring seriously when I called him."

"I was talking to Hayley." Mona sighed. "About the photo of her and Wade Springer on the front page of both papers today."

"Oh. That. I forgot," Liddy said. She reached over and squeezed Hayley's hand. "All publicity is good publicity, I always say."

"But what if you don't want *any* publicity?" Hayley asked.

"I don't understand the premise of your question. Who doesn't want publicity?" Liddy said, dropping her head down on the bar. "Where could I have lost my earring?"

"Maybe this guy or girl who has been breaking into houses and stealing property lately is behind it," Randy said, trying to be helpful.

Liddy sprang up from the bar. "Yes! Of course! How could I have not made the connection?"

"Why would anyone steal just one earring?" Mona asked.

Liddy ignored her. "Randy, have you talked to Sergio? Does he have any leads?"

"I'm afraid not," Randy said, wiping down the bar

with a towel. "The culprit has been really smart so far and made very few mistakes."

"Then that clears Jesse DeSoto," Hayley said. "If that boy had a penny for every IQ point, he wouldn't even be able to buy a forever stamp at the post office."

"Jesse DeSoto?" Liddy asked.

"Bruce suspects Jesse may have something to do with the crime spree," Hayley said.

Liddy grabbed her bag off the bar. "Of course! That kid's bad news. And always causing trouble. It has to be him!"

"Now don't go jumping to conclusions," Randy warned. "This isn't the Salem witch trials."

"Those bitches were guilty! And so is Jesse DeSoto. I'm going over to the police station to talk to Sergio right now and bring him up to speed on my investigation."

Liddy raced out the door.

"What investigation?" Hayley asked. "I just said Bruce suspected him. He has zero proof."

"Let her go," Mona said, shaking her head. "I'd rather she be out there stalking some lame-ass troublemaker kid than in here wailing to us about her missing piece of junk jewelry."

"Actually, those earrings were really expensive," Randy whispered as he leaned in to Hayley and Mona. "She paid five grand for them."

"Five thousand dollars?" Mona yelped. "I bought my truck for less than that. Granted, it was used and needed new brakes, but holy crap!"

Suddenly the door to the bar was flung open, and a man stumbled in, fighting to keep his balance as he made his way to the bar.

He was young, early twenties, with longish brown hair, tall with a bean-pole build. He was wearing a black cowboy hat. He pushed it back as he steadied himself with one hand on the bar. His face was pale and gaunt.

Hayley noticed his eyes were almost coal black. Maybe it was the lighting. But he looked like he had a dark soul.

He punched the bar with his fist.

"Bartender, whiskey straight up," he said, slurring every word.

Randy took a deep breath and then said gently, "I'm sorry, sir, but I think you may have had enough for tonight. Let me pour you a cup of coffee. On the house."

"I don't want coffee," the man said, his head swaying. He pounded the bar again with his fist. "I said I want whiskey."

Randy stood his ground.

"Don't make me climb over this bar and get it myself," the man warned.

"I'm not serving you, sir. Now, I offered you some coffee. If you don't want it, then I suggest you turn around and walk out of my bar."

The man reached over the bar and grabbed Randy by the shirt. "Do you have any idea who I am?"

"Yes. You've been in here the last couple nights. Drunk. Which was fine, but now you're being belligerent and I want you out of my bar," Randy said evenly.

Hayley reached into her pocket for her cell phone. She was getting ready to dial the police if the situation escalated.

The man with the coal black eyes stared at Randy, his nostrils flaring. Randy glared back.

Neither was budging.

Finally, the man let Randy go and it looked as if he was going to leave peacefully. But, then, without warning, he lunged across the bar and took a right-hook swing at Randy.

Randy jumped back, but not fast enough. The man's fist connected with his jaw and Randy fell back against a shelf.

A couple bottles of Smirnoff flavored vodka crashed to the floor, sending glass flying everywhere.

Hayley punched 911 immediately into her cell phone and waited for the dispatcher to pick up. Thankfully, it was a small town and the officers would be there in a matter of minutes, if not seconds.

Randy regained his senses, and bounded around the bar to drag the guy out. But before he reached him, the drunk cowboy grabbed an empty Budweiser bottle and smashed it against the bar and then waved the jagged shards at Randy's face threateningly.

Hayley gasped, still waiting for someone at the station to answer.

Mona was off her stool and jumped on the guy's back. She wrapped her arm around his throat and squeezed as hard as she could.

Hayley and Randy stared in disbelief. This pregnant lobster woman was fighting like a mixed martial arts champion.

The man struggled, trying to shake her off, but Mona held him tight. He desperately clawed at her arm, but Mona was strong. She hauled lobster traps for a living.

There was no way she was letting go.

Saliva came spitting out of the guy's mouth as he tried to breathe. He dropped to his knees. Mona went right down with him, not releasing her grip in the slightest.

She had this guy.

And she was going to finish it.

Finally, the dispatcher at the station picked up and Hayley screamed for her to get some officers over to the Drinks Like A Fish bar.

But there was no rush at this point. The drunk was passed out.

Probably a combination of Mona's headlock and too much alcohol.

He started to snore.

Randy was already sweeping up the broken glass with a broom behind the bar.

Hayley just stared at Mona in disbelief. "Where did you learn that?"

"I like watching the Military Channel. They have the most kick-ass shows about self-defense training and that kind of shit."

Hayley looked down at the sleeping cowboy on the floor. He had to be part of Wade Springer's entourage.

Perfect.

She was already involved in a bar brawl with one of his people and she hadn't even cooked Wade his first meal yet.

Chapter 8

Hayley was up at five in the morning to cook Wade's first meal of the day. She decided to prepare a full farmer's breakfast as well as her homemade Maine blueberry muffins and some freshly squeezed orange juice.

After cooling the muffins, she scrambled the eggs, fried the bacon, whipped up the grits, and squeezed the oranges. She carefully arranged the covered plates on a wooden tray and slipped the whole thing into a pizza warmer, carefully balancing it as she clicked the leash onto Leroy's collar and led him out the back door to her car in the garage.

The kids weren't even up yet. It was still dark outside. But she knew Wade had an early sound check at the Criterion Theatre and had requested his breakfast be delivered at 6:30 A.M.

After Hayley dropped off the food to Wade, her plan was to drive Leroy to the vet because he was due for a few shots.

Leroy excitedly scampered toward the car because he thought they might be going for a hike in the park. Only when they pulled up to the veterinarian's office would the cold hard truth hit him head on. Panic would then set in. So she had some time to enjoy his rare good behavior.

Hayley pulled into the nearly full parking lot of the Harborside Hotel and found an empty spot. She got out and walked around behind the Subaru wagon and popped open the hatchback where she had carefully placed Wade's breakfast.

"Stay here, Leroy, I'll be right back."

Leroy started yapping.

"I'm serious," Hayley sighed. "This will only take a moment."

Leroy continued yapping.

"Leroy, shut up!" Hayley yelled as she lifted the pizza warmer with Wade's breakfast. But she knew it was hopeless. Once Leroy got going, there was no stopping him. She knew what had to be driving him wild. It had to be another dog.

Sure enough, when Hayley turned around, she saw Wade walking out of the hotel with a giant St. Bernard on a long, studded, black leather leash.

Wade spotted her and waved.

Hayley set the pizza warmer back down. "Hush, Leroy!"

Wade ambled over to them. "Morning, Hayley."

Hayley checked her watch. "It's almost six-thirty. You ready for your breakfast?"

"Sure thing. But I have to take Delilah out for some fresh air first," Wade said, rubbing the top of the St. Bernard's head.

"Now? I don't want your food to get cold."

"Understandable. But I don't want Delilah peeing on the carpet in the hotel. This tour is expensive enough as it is without having to reimburse for property damage."

Of course Wade wanted to walk his own dog instead of handing her over to a roadie to exercise her for him.

God, what a man.

Leroy stopped barking and was staring at Delilah curiously.

Maybe it was because Delilah was staring at Leroy with a dopey grin.

If this were an animated movie, there would probably be little red hearts shown thumping in her eyes.

Some drool from Delilah's slobbering mouth landed on Hayley's shoe.

"What's your little spitfire's name?" Wade asked, his deep baritone drawl sending shivers up Hayley's spine.

"Leroy, and he's a pain in my butt. He's always barking at other dogs."

"He doesn't seem to be barking now."

Wade was right.

For once, Leroy was being quiet.

Hayley turned to see if he was okay.

Leroy was staring back at the obviously love-struck St. Bernard.

Leroy then jumped over the seat into the back of the car where Hayley had just set down the pizza warmer. He ran right over it to get to Delilah.

"Leroy, no!" Hayley wailed as she threw open the flap to the pizza warmer and peered inside. "I think he just crushed your blueberry muffin."

"No worries. I'm not hungry right now anyway."

Hayley glanced at him, concerned. "You're not?"

"I can eat later. Why don't we take the dogs for a walk along the shore path? We may have found a love connection."

"But you hardly know me and, well, I am technically working for you and . . ." Hayley noticed Wade grinning. "You were talking about the dogs, weren't you?"

Wade nodded before bursting out laughing.

Hayley wanted to die on the spot.

Leroy craned his neck to sniff at Delilah. Delilah stepped back, acting coy and feminine, despite the fact that she was five times the size of her suitor.

"I have to get Leroy to the vet and then I have a ton of errands to run and—"

"What time does the vet open?"

"Eight."

"It's not even seven. Come on, let the dogs get to know each other. And who knows? Maybe we'll get to know each other a little, too."

Hayley nodded. "Okay."

After all, he was the boss. If he would rather take a walk than eat the delicious meal Hayley had slaved over the stove to prepare for him, that was his decision. She tried not to be offended. But then it occurred to her that she was being asked on a morning walk by Wade Springer.

Screw the eggs.

Hayley and Wade strolled along the narrow dirt path that followed the shoreline from the harbor to the stately mansions on the other side of town owned by some of the richest families in the country.

The sun had just started coming up.

The waves crashed violently against the rocks, and Hayley and Wade let Leroy and Delilah off their leashes to go explore the seaweed and snails and starfish that had come in with the last tide.

Delilah was so exited to be off her leash, she nearly knocked Hayley off her feet as she broke into a run.

Hayley lost her balance and nearly fell flat on her face before Wade caught her around the waist to keep her steady.

Another shiver shot up her spine.

And then she noticed a flash.

Just like the one at the Balance Rock Inn.

There he was.

Darrell Rodick. That obnoxious pint-size paparazzi.

"Darrell Rodick, stop taking pictures!"

He was about thirty feet away.

She could see him checking his digital camera.

"Awesome!" he cried. "It looks like you're hugging! I'll get at least fifty dollars for this one!"

And off he went.

Hayley was not going to let the little runt get away with this again.

She started chasing him.

Wade called after her, "Hayley, relax! It's no big deal!"

But there was no way she was going to let herself be plastered all over the front page of both papers again.

She huffed and puffed and ran as hard as she could.

Hayley had maybe run for about thirty seconds before she began sweating and heaving, and her feet ached.

Darrell was already out of view, having ducked into a wooded area, and it was painfully clear that he was a wiry little kid with boundless energy and she was a woman in her thirties who hadn't been out for a healthy run in months. Ever since someone took a potshot at her in the park. But that's another story.

She slowed down and was about to turn back toward the shore when a man jumped out of the bushes and grabbed her.

Hayley spun around in his arms and slammed the palm of her hand into the bridge of his nose, a trick she had learned in a self-defense class she had taken with Mona.

The man threw his hands in front of his face and yelped. "Jesus Mary!"

She recognized him immediately.

"Bruce, what the hell are you doing?"

"I think my nose is broken."

"Serves you right for scaring me like that."

"I was staking out Jesse DeSoto but he spotted me and took off running. I thought you were him. I wanted to question him."

"By leaping out of the bushes?"

"He's a slippery little bugger and I figured it was the only way to get him to talk to me," Bruce said, fumbling for some Kleenex in his jeans pocket. "My nose is bleeding. Thanks, Hayley."

"I'm sorry, Bruce."

"What are you doing out here so early?"

"Walking Leroy."

Bruce pressed the tissue to his nostrils and moaned and then said, "I see you've got company."

Hayley turned to see Wade walking toward them, both Leroy and Delilah back on their leashes.

The two dogs were brushing against each other flirtatiously.

"You never cease to amaze me, Hayley," Bruce said.

"What do you mean?"

"I never thought you to be the type to get all girly-girl giggly over the first overrated singing cowboy that looks at you twice."

"And I never thought you to be the type to be jealous of anyone who pays me a little attention because you're too much of a coward to admit you like me."

There.

She said it.

And she'd been waiting a long time.

Without another word, Bruce turned on his heel

and stalked off, the wad of blood-soaked tissue pressed to his nose.

"And when did you ever hear me giggle once?" Hayley yelled at him.

But he was already out of earshot.

Why didn't she have this many men interested in her in high school?

She would have had a much better experience.

Island Food & Spirits
by
Hayley Powell

Just the other day as I was leaving the office, I decided to pick up a few items at the grocery store because, as most of you have probably heard by now, I am currently Wade Springer's on-tour personal chef (insert *squealing!*). But enough of that right now. Back to my point.

As I was walking toward the front doors of the store, which are made of glass, I happened to see a reflection of a person I knew. I couldn't quite place the name, but she looked so familiar. I spun around to get a better look and say hello. But, strangely, no one was there. Which is a miracle since it was 5 P.M. and we all know how crowded the store gets when people get off work. I looked up and down the parking lot. No sign of her. So I turned back around and, wouldn't you know, there she was again!

That's when it hit me. The slightly chubby, out-of-shape person who looked vaguely familiar to me in the reflection of the glass was me!

I let out a horrified *scream* at the exact moment poor Mrs. Crowley chose to exit the store. I shocked her so badly with my screaming, she threw her grocery bag straight up in the air! It turned upside down, and the next thing I knew, it was raining cans of cat food from the sky! They all began hitting the ground around us and rolling wildly all over the parking lot. I felt so awful for scaring this poor woman half to death that I started running around gathering the runaway cans. I was huffing and puffing and waving my arms like a madwoman so no one would hit me with their car while I was bending over collecting all the cans.

I had to stop because I was completely out of breath. That was the moment I decided to take matters into my own hands and get rid of some of my unwanted pounds. First thing in the morning I was going to call the local gym and make an appointment with a personal trainer for some exercise tips that would help me get into better shape. But, first, I had to get into the store for my groceries and pick up one of those delectable black forest cheesecakes at the bakery. I know what you're thinking, but in the immortal words of my personal heroine Scarlett O'Hara, "Tomorrow is another day."

I called Abbey at the local gym, and made an appointment to drop by during my lunch hour. Maybe start with a little running on the treadmill. Nothing too taxing. As I breezed through the doors with newfound determination and a very high energy level, I felt my jaw drop to my chest as I stood there surveying the room in my ratty sweats and baggy, stained sweatshirt. Apparently this was where all of the beautiful people in Bar Harbor hung out. Where did they all come from? And what the hell happened to their body fat? Had any of them ever touched a plate of biscuits and gravy in their lives? Standing there slack-jawed, looking at their perfectly toned bodies, I suddenly felt every biscuit and gravy plate I had eaten in my entire lifetime just clinging to my whole body!

Seriously, some of them were actually wearing spandex! I hadn't seen spandex since those old MTV videos of Olivia Newton-John singing "Physical."

So much for the gym. I turned around and hightailed it out of there.

No, tomorrow I will just start walking to work. And I'll need everyone's help. No matter how many of you I try to flag down, yell for you to stop, or try jumping in front of your car begging for a ride, *please* just smile and wave to me as you drive right past me, and be happy in the knowledge that you are, in the end, helping me. And just ignore any curse words I may scream out as you drive away. I'm sure I will get used to the seven-minute walk to the office in no time!

But now for today's recipes. Of

course, I haven't been able to get biscuits and gravy off my mind since my ill-fated trip to the gym. But I told myself that it is totally fine for me to make them because how else will I know if they will be the perfect accompaniment to Wade's country fried chicken if I didn't whip up a test batch to try ahead of time?

But, first, a nice cocktail should set the right tone, allowing you to relax before you begin your baking. So mix, shake, pour, and enjoy!

Cranberry Martini

1 ounce vodka
½ ounce Cointreau
3 ounces cranberry juice
Ice
Lemon slice for garnish

Combine all of your ingredients in a cocktail shaker and shake for 20 seconds. Strain into a chilled martini glass and squeeze a little lemon juice in, then garnish and forget your troubles.

Homemade Country Biscuits

2 cups of all purpose flour
4 teaspoons baking powder
¼ teaspoon baking soda
Pinch of salt
3 ounces cold butter, diced
8 ounces buttermilk
In a bowl, combine the dry ingredients

and knead in the butter with your fingers. Add buttermilk and gently knead on a floured surface only until the dough is mixed together.

With a floured rolling pin flatten out to about an inch thick and use a 3-inch round biscuit cutter or a glass right from your cupboard to cut out the circles. Place on a greased baking sheet.

Place in a preheated 400 degree oven for 15 to 20 minutes or until golden brown. Remove and brush melted butter on them if you like.

Country Gravy

1 pound ground pork sausage
2 tablespoons butter
¼ cup all purpose flour
Salt and pepper to taste
3 cups milk

Brown the pork sausage in a large skillet over medium high heat. Remove cooked sausage to a paper towel–lined plate, leaving drippings in pan.

Melt butter into the sausage drippings.

Reduce heat to medium. Add flour, stirring constantly until mixture turns a golden brown.

Gradually whisk the milk into the skillet. Once the milk mixture is thickened and begins to bubble, return the sausage to the skillet.

Season with salt and pepper and reduce heat and simmer for 15 minutes. Spoon over warm buttered split biscuits and let the feasting begin!

Chapter 9

After spending most of the day running errands, Hayley raced home so she could prepare Wade's dinner. There really wasn't any question what he wanted for his first meal.

Hayley's blue ribbon country fried chicken.

She hauled a picnic basket out of the downstairs hall closet and found a red-checkered tablecloth to line the bottom. Then she carefully placed the still piping hot chicken fresh from the fryer onto a plate and put it inside the basket before covering it up with the cloth.

She had already prepared some macaroni and cheese, and sautéed carrots for a vegetable, and some fresh biscuits during her lunch hour, which were already in the trunk of her car. She also prepared a separate plate of chicken for the crew and placed that in the backseat.

She would have just enough time to drive the meal over to Wade at the hotel and get back home in time to make dinner for the kids.

When Hayley pulled into the parking lot, Billy Ray Cyrus, Wade's publicist, was pacing back and forth in front of the entrance.

She smiled and waved at him as she got out of the car and retrieved the picnic basket from the back seat.

Billy Ray rushed over to her.

"Hayley, do you have a moment?" he asked breathlessly.

"Sure, if you help me carry Wade's dinner inside."

"Absolutely."

Hayley popped open the trunk, put the picnic basket down on the ground, and started handing Billy Ray plastic cartons of food. She was planning on arranging the food personally on Wade's plate.

Presentation was important to her.

"Wade posted Mickey Pritchett's bail," Billy Ray said. "We're expecting him back here anytime."

"Mickey who?" Hayley had no idea who he was talking about.

"One of our roadies. I believe you met him last night at one of your local bars," Billy Ray said, sniffing. "Smells delicious."

"Thank you. Oh, right. Him," Hayley said, scowling. "That guy's a jerk."

"I know. He can be a handful when he's been drinking. Wade's given him so many chances."

"Why does he keep a guy like that around?"

"Wade was very close with Mickey's father, Buddy. They grew up together in the Louisiana bayou. When Buddy died, Wade became a father figure to Buddy's sons Mickey and Clarence. Clarence worked through his grief and got a scholarship to college but Mickey became lost and started rebelling. Caused all sorts of trouble. Whoring, thieving, vandalizing. His mother finally couldn't take it anymore and, with a heavy heart, kicked him out. Poor Mickey had nowhere to go. So Wade took him in, and tried to teach him the value of hard work. He was hoping that by hiring him for this tour, well, it might straighten

Mickey out. But obviously that hasn't happened," Billy Ray said, shaking his head.

"Why are you telling me all this?"

"Well," Billy Ray said, taking Hayley gently by the arm, "I heard the man he assaulted was your brother, and I was wondering if you would consider talking to your brother and asking him to drop the charges. So long as Mickey makes restitution and pays for any damage he caused to the bar. We'll deduct it from his paycheck every week until he's all paid up."

Hayley wasn't inclined to help a foul-mouthed drunken idiot like Mickey.

"Wade sure would appreciate it," Billy Ray quickly added.

The magic word.

Wade.

"Sure. I can talk to Randy. I'm sure he doesn't want to make a big deal out of this anyway."

"Oh, thank you, Hayley, thank you," Billy Ray said, relieved. "Mickey's not such a bad kid. He just doesn't know how to hold his liquor."

"No problem," Hayley said, filling Billy Ray's arms with a tray of biscuits.

"Why don't I run this inside and come back and help you with the rest," Billy Ray said, turning on his heel and running into the hotel, balancing the Tupperware and trays piled high in his arms.

Hayley decided to get the basket of chicken inside quickly before it got cold. Leaving the car's hatch open, she picked up the picnic basket off the ground and turned around, slamming into someone.

"Oh, I'm so sorry. I didn't see you . . . ," Hayley said, her words trailing off as she looked up into the man's face.

It was Mickey Pritchett.

"Howdy, ma'am," Mickey said with a drawl.

"Hello," Hayley said coldly, liking him even less now that he called her ma'am.

"I just wanted to apologize for my behavior at the bar the other night," Mickey said, taking off his hat in an effort to be more sincere.

"That's all right, Mickey," Hayley said, just wanting to get past him.

She made a move, but Mickey stepped in front of her, blocking her escape.

"There's just no excuse for acting that way. I don't know what got into me," Mickey said.

"I'm sure it was at least eighty-proof," Hayley said.

Mickey laughed. "Well, yes, ma'am, I reckon you're right. I do love my whiskey."

"Now, if you'll excuse me . . . ," Hayley said, making another attempt to get around him.

Mickey stepped in front of her again.

He stared down at her with those coal black eyes.

His smile was forced and unconvincing.

"Something sure smells good."

"It's Wade's dinner. Fried chicken."

"I'm not talking about the chicken, ma'am."

Hayley shuddered.

She glanced around.

There was no one around in the parking lot that she could see.

He pushed in a little closer.

"Get away from me," Hayley spat out under her breath.

"Now what happened to that small-town Yankee hospitality I've heard so much about?" Mickey asked, and then laughed.

He gripped her shoulders with his big hands. "Tour bus is parked right over there. Got a nice bed for two. Why don't you and I go lie down and get acquainted over some of your fried chicken?"

Hayley pushed him back with all her might. But he was so much bigger than her, he barely budged.

He grabbed her wrist and she dropped the basket of chicken. He wrapped his free arm around her and pulled her into him so hard he nearly crushed her face against his chest.

She could barely breathe.

She tried nailing the heel of her shoe into his foot, but he anticipated the move and she missed and smashed her ankle against the pavement of the parking lot. Hayley struggled as Mickey started dragging her toward the bus. His giant, long thin fingers pressed over her mouth before she could scream. She started pounding him with her fists to no avail.

She was like a rag doll in his arms because he was so damned tall and strong.

And then, suddenly, he let her go.

Hayley stumbled back, nearly falling to the ground. That's when she saw Wade.

He spun Mickey around and delivered a roundhouse punch across his face. The sudden impact took Mickey by surprise.

His nose spurted blood.

He just stood there, in a state of shock.

Wade looked like he was going to explode, his face was so red. "That's it, Mickey. Strike three! You are fired! You hear me? Fired! Pack up your stuff and get the hell out of here!"

"But, Wade, let me explain," Mickey pleaded.

Wade charged him. "Don't make me hit you again, Mickey. I said get out of here! Now!"

Wade turned to Hayley and said softly, "Are you all right?"

Hayley nodded.

"I don't know what to say," Wade said to Hayley. "I knew Mickey could be a dumb ass, but I never thought . . . I never imagined he would ever try anything like this."

"I'm fine. Nothing happened," Hayley said, still a little shaken over the whole situation—and at the thought of not being able to fight Mickey off if Wade hadn't showed up.

"I'm not leaving until you give me some traveling money," Mickey said, his tone now more threatening.

Wade spun around. "I'm not telling you again, boy. You got five minutes to clear your stuff out of the hotel and leave."

"Or what?" Mickey said, chuckling. "You're getting up there, Wade. I'm younger. And stronger. You don't think I can take you?"

Wade stood his ground.

He stared Mickey down.

Mickey shook his head. "I'm tired of you ordering me around, anyway. *Get me a water, Mickey. I need this shirt pressed, Mickey.* Just because you can carry a tune, you think you own the world. Well, the world doesn't revolve around you, Wade Springer, and maybe it's time someone brought you down to size."

"You threatening me, Mickey?"

"I'm going to do more than that," Mickey said, striding toward Wade.

Wade stepped in front of Hayley, protecting her.

"I'll kill you before you get the chance," Wade said.

His voice was low and even.

Hayley knew he meant it.

"You okay, boss?"

It was Curtis King. Wade's bodyguard. Built like a Mack truck.

And at this moment, a gift from God.

Mickey stopped advancing on Wade.

He glanced at Curtis.

He might have been able to take down Wade.

But Curtis?

Not in a million years.

"We're fine, Curtis," Wade said, never taking his eyes off Mickey.

"Yeah, no problem here, Curtis," Mickey said. "Just going to pack up my stuff, since my services are no longer needed."

And then he reached down and picked up Hayley's picnic basket. He reached in and grabbed a chicken breast and took a big bite.

"Now that's good chicken. You can consider this my severance pay" he said, before stalking off into the night carrying Hayley's basket of country fried chicken.

Chapter 10

"Should we call your brother's fella and have Mickey arrested again?" Wade asked Hayley.

Hayley shook her head. "No. Let's just forget the whole thing. Thank God you showed up when you did."

Hayley was shaking.

She was fighting back tears.

Wade stepped forward and wrapped her in his strong arms and hugged her.

"I'm so sorry, Hayley," Wade said. "This is all my fault. I brought Mickey here with me. I had no idea he was so out of control."

Hayley rested her head on Wade's broad chest.

She was feeling better already.

"You're not to blame, Wade. You were just being nice. Trying to give him a break."

As hard as it was to do, Hayley pulled away and smiled at Wade. "Now, I'm going to get out of your hair so you can enjoy your dinner."

"You're not going to join me?"

"No. I need to get home. Kids to feed. Column to write."

"But you have enough food here to feed the state of Mississippi."

"You should see what Billy Ray already took inside. I thought you might want to share it with your band and crew."

"They're out scarfing down mussels and beer at some seaside hangout. I'm here all alone," Wade said, offering a pathetic, fake sad face.

Hayley wanted to stay.

Deperately.

But she was still shaken up by Mickey and feeling a little vulnerable and didn't want to burst into tears and sob like a little girl in front of Wade.

No. It was best she go home.

There were still a couple more days left before Wade performed his two concerts and left town for good. Maybe she would have another opportunity to spend some more quality time with her country idol.

Hayley hugged Wade. "I'm going to go. Luckily I made some extra fried chicken just in case your crew wanted some."

Hayley reached into the backseat of her Subaru and handed Wade a plate with tin foil wrapped around it. Then she handed him a plastic container. "And here's some southern mac and cheese to go with it. I tried a new recipe so I'm curious to see if you like it."

"I'll be sure to report back," Wade said.

She looked up at him and he was smiling down at her.

Wade leaned down and kissed her on the lips.

Not hard.

Very soft.

Their lips brushing against each other very gently.

Hayley was shaking again.

But this time, it wasn't out of fear.

It was a good thing Wade was still holding her, because otherwise she would just have fainted dead away and probably chipped a tooth when her face hit the pavement.

There was an interminable silence before Wade finally spoke. "I sure hope that wasn't out of line."

"No, of course not."

"You going to sue me for sexual harassment?"

Hayley laughed. "No, you're safe."

Wade looked out at the fishing boats rolling with the waves in the harbor as they stood in the parking lot of the Harborside Hotel. He suddenly seemed very shy and awkward. "I'm very attracted to you, Hayley. From the moment you crashed my hotel room pretending to be an entertainment reporter."

"Don't remind me," Hayley said, cringing. "But Wade . . ."

"My least favorite word. *But.*"

"It's just that I've been seeing someone else."

She couldn't believe she was saying this to Wade Springer.

"And his name is Lex and he's a good man," she continued. "Actually, I'm not sure how serious it is or where we stand, but I need to figure that out before I start anything else."

"That's very admirable. In show business, we're not as respectful of others when we see something we want," Wade said, grinning. "I promise to behave."

"Thank you," Hayley said, resisting the urge to grab him and thrust her tongue in his mouth.

"At least, until you figure things out," Wade said, giving her a wink. "Good night, Hayley."

"'Night, Wade," Hayley said, watching him turn around and amble inside the hotel.

God, look at that butt.

Definitely one of the seven wonders of the world.

Hayley reached into her pocket, fumbled for her car keys, and opened the door. She sensed someone watching her and turned back around.

It was getting dark outside and there was a light on in one of the rooms on the second floor.

A man stood at the window staring down at her.

It was Mickey Pritchett.

He was wearing a white wifebeater and a pair of blue jeans. He pointed at her with a chicken leg, which at this point was nothing but bone. He seemed to be sending her the message that they had unfinished business and that he was watching her.

He had a sick, evil grin on his face.

Hayley jumped in her car and drove straight home. She wondered if she had been mistaken not calling Sergio and having Mickey arrested for attempted sexual assault. If Wade hadn't shown up when he did, she feared that's exactly where it was heading.

When Hayley walked inside the house, Dustin was in the living room sitting in the recliner with the TV remote, channel surfing.

Hayley plopped down on the couch. "I have some extra chicken left in the fridge. I could make that chicken and stuffing casserole you like so much for dinner."

"I already ate. I was starving when I got home. And Gemma made a salad because she's dieting again. At least until ten o'clock, when she gets hungry and raids the fridge for cold leftover pizza."

Hayley felt incredibly tired.

She stretched out on the couch.

Leroy scampered in and hopped up, snuggling in next to her.

Mark Harmon was on TV throwing out orders to

his crack crime-busting team on a repeat episode of NCIS on USA.

Hayley's eyes were heavy.

She couldn't even focus on Mark's chiseled, handsome face.

That had to be a first.

She always snapped to attention when Mark Harmon was on TV.

Wade Springer was definitely having a serious effect on her.

She ran her fingers through Leroy's white curly coat of hair and then closed her eyes and fell into a deep sleep.

Hayley heard a loud crackling sound.

And then voices.

Then another crackle.

More voices.

She slowly opened her eyes. It was pitch dark. Leroy snored softly, his head buried in her shirt. Dustin must have turned off the TV and gone to bed long ago.

She focused on the cable box clock.

It was 12:02 A.M.

The crackling sound started again.

She slowly sat up, a little disoriented, gently lowering Leroy's drooping head, which rested on her, to the couch.

She heard voices again. It was the police scanner she kept on top of the refrigerator in the kitchen. That's what she was hearing.

Something was going on.

There wasn't usually this much activity so late at night.

Hayley stood up and went into the kitchen, raising the volume on the scanner.

The dispatcher was talking to some officers. "We got a report of a vehicle on fire at Albert Meadow. Fire department is on the way."

"Roger," replied the officer. "We're about two minutes away."

"Make of the vehicle is a 2011 CJ Starbus. Looks like it's one from the Wade Springer tour."

Hayley grabbed her car keys off the counter and dashed out the door.

When Hayley arrived at Albert Meadow, a wide-open lawn and picnic area just off the town's iconic shore path, the fire department had already doused the flames.

The tour bus was just a shell of itself, black and charred and smoking.

There were only a handful of gawkers since it was so late at night. Hayley assumed they all owned scanners like she did. The rest of the town was sleeping.

She saw Sergio conferring with the fire captain and a few officers poking around the bus, checking out the scene.

Hayley was stumped as to how the bus got to Albert Meadow and just how it caught fire.

Buses just don't spontaneously burst into flames.

Did Wade know what was happening?

One of Sergio's officers began cordoning off the area with yellow police tape.

So it was a crime scene. Sergio and the fire chief probably suspected arson.

"Didn't expect to see you down here," a familiar voice said.

It was Bruce.

Obviously there to cover the story for the paper.

"Any idea who set the bus on fire?" Hayley asked.

Bruce rubbed his eyes. He looked tired and irritated from having to be up so late.

"Nope." Bruce sighed. "Might've been the body they found in the bus."

"What?" Hayley said, twisting her head away from the smoldering, twisted-metal bus to look at Bruce.

"You didn't hear? Cops don't know yet if this was an accident, a suicide, or a murder. What they do know is somebody was inside the bus and he or she is now a smoking charred corpse. Forensics is on their way down here from Bangor."

"Do they know who it was? Do they know anything?"

"Like I said, Hayley, the body's burned up pretty good. There's no way of identifying it yet."

Hayley's mind raced.

A dead body inside the bus?

Who could it be?

And how did the bus get here?

"Oh, I have heard one interesting rumor," Bruce said, yawning. "I was eavesdropping and heard Officer Earl talking on his cell, and I could've sworn he said they found something in the corpse's mouth and it looked like a chicken bone."

Hayley's heart nearly stopped.

She knew of two people directly connected to the tour who were eating chicken last night.

Her chicken.

Mickey Pritchett.

And Wade Springer.

Chapter 11

Even though it was an early Sunday morning, Hayley knew a news story of this magnitude would require the *Times*' staff to immediately report to work. When she reached the office, word of a charred body found inside the burned-out tour bus of Wade Springer in Albert Meadow had hit the town like a tsunami. Within an hour, all the TV reporters from the network affiliates in Bangor were in their cars, racing over the Trenton bridge onto Mount Desert Island to ask questions and get to the bottom of just whose body was inside the bus.

Rumors flew fast and furious all morning.

It was Wade!

No, wait, it was his publicist, Billy Ray Cyrus.

No, wait, it was the famous Billy Ray Cyrus, who came to make a surprise appearance at Wade's charity concert.

No, wait, it was Trace Adkins!

No, Jimmy Buffett!

No, Johnny Cash! No, he's already dead!

The names flying about just got more and more ludicrous.

Hayley received a call from Liddy, who was driving

by the Harborside Hotel on West Street on her way to an open house and swore she saw Wade Springer alive and well being escorted out of the hotel toward a waiting limo. But she wasn't absolutely one hundred percent positive it was him.

Hayley held her breath.

Please don't let Wade be the body on the bus.

Please.

By noon, the body had been transported to the county coroner's lab, and was finally identified from dental records that had been e-mailed from Nashville.

It was Mickey Pritchett.

Hayley felt a sudden jolt of elation knowing the body wasn't Wade.

Then she felt a twinge of guilt.

She despised Mickey. But nobody deserved to die like that.

Wade issued a statement just a few minutes later expressing his deepest condolescences to Mickey's family, not mentioning that Mickey and his mother were estranged. He also announced that the charity concerts would be postponed for a few days but would still go on because Wade had made a promise to the college and he intended to keep it.

Hayley couldn't imagine what had happened to Mickey. Wade had fired him. She had seen Mickey still hanging around the hotel eating the fried chicken he snatched from her when she left just a short while later.

Did he steal the bus?

If so, why did he drive to Albert Meadow?

And how did it catch fire?

Was Mickey a smoker?

Had he been drinking too much and then passed out with a lit cigarette in his hand?

She was dying of curiosity.

She picked up the phone and called Randy.

He picked up on the first ring.

"Randy, it's me. I was just wondering . . ."

"Sergio won't tell me anything."

"Damn. Well, I guess he's busy interviewing people on the tour."

"I'm sure you're going to hear from him before I do. He'll probably want to bring you in for questioning."

"Me? Why?"

"Hayley, I heard you were one of the last people to see Mickey Pritchett alive. Last night at the hotel. When you took your fried chicken over to Wade."

"Oh God, you're right."

Here we go again.

This wasn't the first time Hayley found herself smack dab in the middle of a police investigation.

"I just wish we knew more about what happened," Hayley said. "There are just so many unanswered questions."

"Everything will come out eventually," Randy said. "It always does. But if you want a heads-up, you know who you can call."

Hayley knew exactly who Randy was talking about.

Sabrina Merryweather.

The county coroner.

And Hayley's arch-nemesis in high school.

They loathed each other back then, but now Sabrina apparently had amnesia about her mean-girl tactics from yesteryear and considered Hayley a close friend. Hayley, on the other hand, had never forgotten even one single nasty slight or vicious comment.

But Sabrina was an invaluable source of information when it came to the cause of death and other interesting tidbits about a corpse.

It was just the idea of calling her that made Hayley

sick to her stomach. Sabrina could be so catty and annoying.

Still, she had to know.

"I'll call you back, Randy," Hayley said.

"You go, girl!" Randy said before she hung up on him.

Hayley called the coroner's office. Normally the office would be closed on Sunday but Hayley was betting someone would be there because of the Mickey Pritchett murder. And she was right. Hayley asked the woman who answered if Sabrina was there. The woman said rather haughtily that Dr. Merryweather was in the middle of something and would most certainly have to return her call. Hayley begged the woman to tell Sabrina she was on the phone. Hayley could hear the woman scoffing, but finally she agreed to check with Sabrina just to make sure.

Hayley didn't have high hopes. She presumed Sabrina was busy examining Mickey Pritchett's corpse and would probably have to call back later.

"Hayley! I'm so happy to hear from you! You never call me anymore!" Sabrina came on the line and said.

Hayley only remembered having called her once since high school. And that was to find out information on another dead body, last year.

"I know. Look, I'm sure you're super busy and I hate bothering you . . ."

"Oh, hell, that barbecued boy in the other room isn't going anywhere. You wouldn't believe how gross he looks. I often wonder why I got into this business. I just figured if I became a doctor, I might meet one. A really cute one. Talk about irony. Instead, I met a banker who decides to quit and become a so-called artist who likes to paint landscapes that nobody wants to buy, and now I'm the one supporting *him!* I really miss the days when our moms stayed home and our dads went to work."

Hayley couldn't remember a day when her mother didn't go to work. Unlike Sabrina, she didn't come from a wealthy family.

"So, Sabrina, this guy you're examining, Mickey Pritchett. I was wondering if you could tell me . . . ?"

"He works for Wade Springer. You know him, don't you, Hayley? Of course you do. I saw you two canoodling on the front page of *both* papers. Really, Hayley. Have you no shame?" Sabrina said, bursting out in a fit of giggles. "What I wouldn't do to be you! Is he really as cute in person as he looks in the papers?"

"Well, he certainly is handsome, but I'm just working for him . . ."

"I guess I'll see for myself in a few days. I got front row seats at both concerts."

"Oh, that's wonderful, Sabrina. So, about Mickey . . ."

"It's like you're psychic, Hayley, calling me today, because I was going to call you. After I saw your picture in the paper, I got all sad and frowny, and you want to know why? We never see each other! Ever! We are so overdue for a night out. So what I was thinking is, why not go on a double date?"

"Lex is out of town for a couple weeks."

"Who's talking about Lex? The guy is a hunk and nice to look at, but about as boring as a downed oak tree! I mean, seriously, what's he going to talk about? How many leaves he raked in one day? Yawn!"

"Then who . . . ?"

"You and Wade!"

"But we're not . . ."

"I saw the pictures! Don't tell me there isn't a spark between you two! And I am just dying to meet him. So let me make a reservation somewhere nice, even though now that summer's over, all the good restaurants are shut down. But I'll find something that works, and then the four of us—you, me, Wade, and my idiot husband, who I promise won't drone on about art or politics, because, well, let's face it, he's one of those bleeding hearts, and I assume since Wade is a country singer from a red state, he's probably conservative like my beloved Lee Greenwood who sang that classic 'Proud To Be an American' song—"

Hayley couldn't believe Sabrina had said all that without taking a breath.

"What do you say, Hayley?"

"Um, sure, that sounds like a plan," Hayley said, already panicking about committing Wade to a dinner with Sabrina and her husband.

But Hayley still needed information.

She could always call and cancel later.

Sabrina squealed. "I'm so excited! Omigod, did I just quote the Pointer Sisters? I loved listening to them as a kid!"

Hayley held the phone away from her ear to keep from going deaf.

"Well, I better get back to work," Sabrina sighed. "Duty calls. I hate when someone dies under suspicious circumstances on a Sunday. It ruins my entire weekend!"

"Wait. Before you go, I know your professional ethics are uncompromised and you would never talk to me about anything before you complete your autopsy and consult with the police . . ."

"What do you want to know?"

Sabrina obviously didn't care about ethics right now.

She thought Hayley was her ticket to an intimate dining experience with country superstar Wade Springer.

"Mickey Pritchett."

"Burned to a crisp."

"So the bus caught fire somehow and Mickey got trapped inside and burned to death?"

"The bus caught fire and Mickey certainly was in it. But that's not how he died," Sabrina said matter-of-factly.

"Then how?"

"There's a big hole in his chest. Somebody shot him."

Hayley nearly stopped breathing. "What?"

"He was murdered."

Chapter 12

After Hayley hung up with Sabrina, she resisted the urge to march into Sal's office and give him the scoop of the year. She knew he was in there, happy to be in the office on a Sunday because his wife hadn't yet come home from her mother's. Mickey Pritchett's death was about to be officially ruled a homicide. Sal would be able to get the jump on the *Herald*.

But she just sat there at her desk, staring at the wall.

She knew Darrell Rodick wouldn't be the only shutterbug with a digital camera running around town now. Bar Harbor was about to be deluged with tabloid journalists, all out in search of the most sensational aspects of this story.

A roadie on the Wade Springer tour shot dead and burned up inside a raging tour bus fire?

This was a huge scandal.

The reporters would eventually discover the bad blood between Wade and Mickey, and how Wade dumped Mickey from the tour on the night of his murder.

And then they would ask why.

Would it come out that Hayley had two run-ins with Mickey before he got shot?

Had someone seen Wade defend Hayley from Mickey's unwanted advances? Would she wind up a murder suspect again like she had been last year?

She couldn't possibly take the pressure of being in that kind of situation again.

She just couldn't.

The office was quiet. Everyone was probably at Albert Meadow pushing and shoving each other out of the way to get a one-on-one interview with Sergio, who was undoubtedly spearheading the case.

Hayley just started to type her next column.

But it was difficult focusing on recipes when she expected the phone to ring at any moment, with someone asking her to report to the police station for a sit-down interview with the chief.

And brother's partner or not, Sergio wouldn't hold back any punches when it came to interrogating her.

The afternoon crawled by and the phone rang just once. It was an elderly woman worried about her missing cat and wanting to place an ad. Hayley jotted down the information and promised to have it in to-morrow's paper.

Finally, just before quitting time, Bruce arrived. His sleeves were rolled up, there were ash smudges on his face, probably from getting too close to the burned bus, and his hands were grimy with soot. He barely acknowledged Hayley as he plowed through the front office to his cubicle in the back.

Hayley sat there for a few minutes. She heard him typing furiously on his computer. She couldn't take the suspense.

He was obviously writing a story.

He had just come from the crime scene.

It had to be related to Mickey Pritchett.

She stood up and strolled into the back bullpen, pretending to be searching for a file, but casually stepping behind Bruce and trying to read what he was typing.

Bruce sensed her presence immediately and spun around in his chair. "Can I help you?"

"Just getting a file. What are you working on?"

"Oh, nothing special, Hayley. Kind of a quiet day in town. Not much going on. What do you *think* I'm working on? Why else would I be working on a Sunday?"

"You don't have to be rude."

"I have a tight deadline."

"So you found out something?"

Bruce turned back around to his computer and continued typing.

Hayley craned her neck to see Bruce's screen. He was typing the words, *Wade Springer is without a doubt a person of interest.*

"Really? Sergio said that?"

Bruce stopped typing and sighed. "No, Hayley, those are my words. Sergio's not talking, but he's scheduled a press conference for tomorrow."

"So what makes you think Wade is a person of interest?"

"I got to Donnie."

Donnie was a local kid in his midtwenties, a hellion when he was younger, always in trouble with the law. But in a surprise turn of events, he grew up to become a cop. Hayley assumed all that time he spent in the local jail had made him fond of the police station, so it was a natural evolution for him to want to spend more time there as he got older. It was like a second home.

Donnie was also a major gossip.

And Bruce knew that.

Which is why he became his drinking buddy.

And drinking buddies talk about everything.

"What did Donnie tell you?" Hayley asked, treading carefully.

"Donnie said Wade's alibi is pretty shaky. According to his interview with the chief, Wade claims he took his dog out for a walk last night and was gone from the hotel for about an hour."

"Delilah."

"What?"

"Delilah's the name of his dog."

"Not really pertinent to the story, Hayley."

"Sorry."

"The problem is, nobody saw him. He could've been anywhere. He could've been at Albert Meadow shooting a hole in Mickey Pritchett's chest and setting fire to his own tour bus to try and cover up the crime," Bruce said, a big grin on his face.

"That's the most preposterous thing I've ever heard, even from you, Bruce," Hayley scoffed.

"Most of the crew from the tour were at your brother's bar in plain view doing shots and playing darts in front of a bunch of locals until closing time at one A.M.," Bruce said. "Wade's the only one who was unaccounted for."

"So you're going to write that in your article?" Hayley asked, her stomach churning. "You're going to suggest Wade left the hotel to go kill Mickey?"

"I'm not suggesting anything," Bruce said. "I just report the facts. And the fact is at this point Wade Springer is the only suspect."

Chapter 13

When Hayley delivered Wade's dinner that night, he was nowhere in sight. Billy Ray let her in the room.

She went to work setting out a Cajun shrimp pasta dish with a field greens salad and fresh garlic roll. She popped open a bottle of merlot and poured a glass to let it breathe.

Billy Ray explained that Wade was still at the police station talking to the chief, but he would be back shortly if she wanted to hang around.

Hayley declined.

It was getting late. And Gemma had texted her asking if she would mind picking her and Reid up at Reel Pizza Cinema where they were watching a movie and no doubt snuggling in the dark. Hayley was happy Gemma was so excited about this boy, but she was rather surprised they had progressed to a movie date so quickly.

It was less than a week ago when she had accompanied her daughter to Reid's coffeehouse concert and at that point they barely knew each other.

Gemma and Reid were waiting for her when Hayley pulled her Subaru wagon into the cinema parking lot.

She immediately noticed the two of them holding hands.

Reid circled around the car and got in the back seat.

Instead of sitting up front with her mother, Gemma jumped in the back with Reid. Hayley suddenly felt like a chauffeur, but bit her tongue.

"How was the movie?" Hayley asked.

"Boring." Gemma shrugged, not anxious to offer a critique.

"What'd you see?"

"I don't even remember the name of it," Gemma said. "We stopped paying attention after the first ten minutes."

"Well, what were you doing?" Hayley asked, cringing as the words came out of her mouth.

Of course, they were making out.

Gemma burst forth in a fit of giggles. "Nothing!"

Yes, definite confirmation they were making out.

Hayley adjusted the rearview mirror in time to see Gemma resting her head on Reid's shoulder.

He was gently stroking her hair.

When he noticed Hayley looking at them through the mirror, he quickly stopped.

Hayley wasn't sure what to think of this. They seemed to be getting much closer and were obviously very affectionate with one another.

She felt guilty because she had been working so hard writing her columns and cooking for Wade that she had completely missed the signs that her daughter was getting quite serious with this boy.

Or man.

He was eighteen.

God, eighteen.

And Hayley knew very little about him.

"Where am I dropping you off, Reid?" Hayley asked. "Where do you live?"

"Actually, if you wouldn't mind, could you let me off at Carrie Weston's house?"

Hayley raised an eyebrow.

"We were over there hanging out with Carrie before the movie," Gemma said. "But her father came home so we had to beat it and Reid left his guitar behind."

"I can walk home from there. I live close by," Reid said.

"Sure. No problem," Hayley said, glancing in the rearview mirror.

Reid saw her looking again and flashed Hayley a wide smile.

Perfect teeth.

The kid sure was a looker.

No wonder Gemma was all over him.

Like mother, like daughter.

The lights were all off at the Weston house when Hayley pulled up to the curb.

"It doesn't look like anyone's home," Hayley said.

"Not a problem," Reid said. "Carrie told me where they hide the key. I'll be in and out in under a minute. Thanks for the ride, Mrs. Powell."

"Good night, Reid."

Reid reached over and gently pulled Gemma closer to him before planting a very deep kiss on her mouth.

Gemma was noticeably swooning.

Hayley watched them through the mirror and her mouth dropped open.

This was not just a friendly kiss.

This was a full-on face assault.

She swore she saw tongues flying.

And it made her supremely uncomfortable.

Finally, Hayley cleared her throat and Reid got the message and released Gemma and pushed open the car door.

"'Night," he said, waving, and then slammed the door shut and ran across the lawn.

She waited until Reid was at the front door reaching into a planter for the house key before she pulled away.

Gemma all but flung herself against the back-seat window to stare at him longingly as they drove off down the street.

"Gemma, Reid seems like a really nice boy, but I'm not sure you two should be spending so much time together . . ."

"Mother, please, let's not do this now, okay?"

"Do what?"

"Have this talk. Let me enjoy this one tiny island of happiness in a sea of depression," Gemma said.

"Since when are you depressed?"

"I'm not. But I will be if you start limiting the time I'm allowed to spend with Reid. He's the best thing that's ever happened to me."

"I've said those very same words, believe me, many times! But you're very young and you need to be focused on your studies, because college isn't that far off . . ."

"I already know the speech, Mom. I've heard it all before."

"Then consider this a refresher course. I'm not saying I don't want you to see him, I'm just saying it doesn't have to be so intense. I don't want your grades slipping because you're spending all your free time with him."

"My grades are fine. You would be the first to know if I started slipping because my teachers would be e-mailing you constantly. And what's so intense about going to a movie?"

"Nothing. What was intense was that good-night kiss."

Gemma sunk down in her seat and giggled.

She was still flying high from it.

"So why do you hate him?" Gemma challenged.

"I certainly do not hate him. I like him. He seems like a decent enough kid. From what I know. I just don't want things moving too fast . . ."

"We're not having sex, if that's what you're getting at," Gemma announced abruptly. "I'm not ready for that."

Hayley almost lost control of the car, she was so taken by surprise, but managed to keep on the right side of the road.

"And the next sound you hear is your mother's sigh of relief," Hayley said, laughing.

"Mom, look," Gemma said, pointing to a house at the end of the street.

It was dark.

Nobody appeared to be home.

But there was a Chrysler parked out front and the driver-side door was open.

Hayley slowed down, and as the Subaru's headlight washed over the vehicle, she spotted somebody crouched down, fiddling with something underneath the dashboard.

"Mom, he's hot-wiring the car!" Gemma shouted just as the car's engine kicked on and the thief, who was wearing jeans and a orange sweat jacket with a hoodie that was hiding his face, hopped in the driver's seat.

He jerked his head around and saw the Subaru bearing down on him.

It was too quick for Hayley to get a good look at his face.

The thief hit the pedal to the metal and the Chrysler sped away into the night.

Hayley found herself slamming her foot down on the Subaru's accelerator and chasing after him.

Gemma's body jerked against the back seat, held down by the seat-belt strap.

"Omigod! I can't believe we're chasing a car thief!" Gemma screamed. "Mom, slow down!"

"I can't! We'll lose him!" Hayley yelled, jerking the wheel to the right and following the Chrysler on a back road toward the Kebo Valley Golf Course.

Hayley felt for her cell phone in the cup holder of the Subaru and tossed it back to Gemma. "Call nine-one-one! Tell them we're in a high-speed pursuit heading toward Eagle Lake Road and we need backup!"

"But, Mom, we're not cops!"

The car thief was well ahead of Hayley's Subaru and it looked like he was going to easily outrun them, when suddenly Hayley saw the brake lights flash on and heard the sound of squealing tires.

The car took a sharp turn off the road onto the golf course and smashed into a tree.

Hayley didn't have a moment to realize what had happened to the Chrysler before her own headlights lit up a deer standing frozen in the middle of the road.

Yes. Literally, a deer in the headlights.

She slammed on the brakes and the tires locked and Gemma was screaming as Hayley kept her hands gripped on the wheel, keeping it steady as the Subaru screeched to a stop just inches from the deer. The deer just stared at them for a moment, and once it realized it wasn't going to be roadkill, went prancing off into the woods.

Hayley turned to Gemma. "Stay here."

Gemma nodded.

There was no way she was going anywhere.

Hayley got out of the Subaru and ran over to the Chrysler, which was smoking from the impact of hitting the tree. The front end was crunched up like an accordian.

She saw someone moving in the driver's seat and heard him moaning.

"Are you okay?" Hayley asked.

"I think I broke my arm," the kid said.

Hayley reached inside the window and snapped on the overhead light to get a better look at the car thief.

Bruce had been right.

The thief was Jesse DeSoto.

Island Food & Spirits
by
Hayley Powell

I don't know why I'm in the mood for barbecue. I just can't seem to get it off my mind this week! So I think I'll be firing up the grill later, and making some delicious barbecue ribs! The best part of dining on ribs, of course, is the great side dish that goes with it—a good old homemade southern mac and cheese casserole! I have such a craving for it! It also goes great with my fried chicken recipe or even just as a meal all by itself.

But before we get to the recipe, I have to tell you about my little adventure with Leroy.

The other night I needed to clear my head after a long day of work and coming up with recipes for Wade Springer. I may have mentioned I'm his personal chef while he is staying in our town before his two sold-out concerts. But I'm never one to drop names or brag.

Anyway, I decided to walk Leroy on the Jesup trail, a scenic path that cuts through the woods around the golf course near my house. We were about a mile into our stroll when we came around the bend and walked smack dab into a small herd of deer! Not surprising, really, since the island is overrun with them. They eat *everything* in our yards and gardens! Just this past year, they ate every one of my beloved hosta plants in the front yard!

Well, it wasn't the deer that startled us, as they really didn't seem to be disturbed by our intrusion at all. What made me gasp, and unfortunately made Leroy start barking furiously with that high-pitched annoying bark of his, was the most enormous, gigantic eight-point buck I have ever seen in my life! I was pretty sure it was the same one the locals call "Bucky." I've been told the legend of Bucky the eight-point buck many times over the years. He's been a fixture in Acadia National Park and is probably the daddy to half of the island's deer population.

Of course, Leroy failed to notice the huge size difference between himself and Bucky and continued barking wildly and frantically pulling at his leash. As the other deer began to calmly walk away, obviously annoyed that their dinner was interrupted by some annoying yapping tiny little creature, I noticed Bucky was staring intently at us, and was starting to paw at the ground and snorting at us like a bull.

I decided this moment might be a good time to turn around and hightail it out of there, so I gave Leroy's leash a big tug, which choked him enough to stop his barking for a brief moment. We took off running so fast back in the direction from which we had come, you would have thought Mona and Liddy had just called me from my brother's bar Drinks Like A Fish and told me there was a 2 for 1 Happy Hour special!

Leroy was not happy about his walk being cut short, but as soon as the giant angry beast started charging us, he seemed to have a change of heart, and ran just as fast as he could right past me, dragging me along by the leash.

All I could hear was loud crashing and stomping through the underbrush behind us. I didn't dare turn around because I didn't want to know just how much Bucky was gaining on us. Suddenly, there was a loud crash, some grunting, and then silence. Curiosity was killing me, so I glanced over my shoulder and stopped dead in my tracks. Leroy tumbled over backward since he was running forward full tilt.

In his attempt to chase us down, poor Bucky had tried running between two trees that weren't quite wide enough for his gigantic antlers to fit through. Bucky's antlers got caught on both sides. He was completely dazed and the wind had been knocked right out of him! He just stood there, slowly shaking his head. He seemed to be no worse for wear.

Except for the fact he was no longer an eight-point buck. He was a six-point buck.

That was our cue to quietly slip away before this one sore buck came to his senses, freed himself, and finally finished us off!

As Leroy and I jogged home, I wondered if, instead of ribs, the venison steaks in my freezer might be a better accompaniment with our mac and cheese for the barbecue!

But, first, before heating up the oven, I'm going to have a nice Southern Screw and relax.

Cocktail, that is.

Southern Screw (driver)

2 ounces vodka
2 ounces Southern Comfort peach
   liquor
6 ounces orange juice

Pour all ingredients over ice in a glass and enjoy!

Southern Mac and Cheese

1 pound cavatappi pasta
2 tablespoons butter
3 tablespoons flour
1 cup milk
1 12-ounce can evaporated milk
2 cups shredded smoked Gouda cheese
1 3-ounce package softened cream
   cheese

¾ teaspoon salt
½ teaspoon red pepper flakes, divided
1 8-ounce chopped cooked smoked
    ham (if you have leftover ham
    from the night before, dice it up
    and use that)
2 cups corn flakes cereal, crushed
2 melted tablespoons of butter

Preheat your oven to 350 degrees.
Prepare cavatappi pasta according to
the directions on the box.

Melt 2 tablespoons butter over medium
heat in large saucepan or skillet big
enough to hold the pasta. Gradually
whisk in flour until smooth; cook while
constantly whisking for one minute or
until thickened. Slowly whisk milk and
evaporated milk into the saucepan and
cook until thickened. Whisk Gouda,
cream cheese, salt and a ¼ teaspoon of
the red pepper flakes until smooth.
Remove from heat and stir in ham.

Pour pasta into the cheese sauce and mix.
Pour into a lightly grease 13 x 9–inch
baking dish. Stir 2 tablespoons melted
butter and remaining ¼ teaspoon red
pepper flakes into the crushed corn
flakes and sprinkle over the mac and
cheese.

Bake at 350 for 45 minutes or until
golden brown and bubbly. Let stand for
5 minutes and then dig in!

Chapter 14

Hayley couldn't believe what she was reading as she sat behind her desk at the *Island Times* office perusing Monday's edition of the paper.

After she and Gemma caught Jesse DeSoto hot-wiring a car, after leading him on a high-speed chase, after Officers Donnie and Earl arrived on the scene and cuffed him and booked him, Bruce's local crime-beat article was all about the suspicious behavior of Wade Springer and how there were lingering questions about his role in the murder of Mickey Pritchett.

Bruce had been obsessed with Jesse, the bad-news delinquent. He had been tracking him, watching his every move, making it his personal mission to link him to the recent crime spree in town.

And, now, faced with undisputable proof thanks to Hayley and her daughter, Bruce couldn't be bothered.

When Bruce sauntered into the office later that morning, a smug look on his face, Hayley told him so to his face.

"Look, Hayley, I admit I've been interested in Jesse, trying to connect him to the rash of thefts and break-ins," Bruce explained. "But we're here to sell papers.

And frankly, Wade Springer is the bigger story. I had to write about him. There are dozens of punk-ass Jesse DeSotos in this town, but only one singer with a slew of number one records who is connected to a brutal murder."

"But all you've got on Wade is speculation. Just because no one saw him walking his dog, doesn't mean he's the one who shot Mickey Pritchett!"

"Doesn't mean he didn't do it."

"You're no better than the tabloids," Hayley said, folding up the issue with Bruce's latest article and hurling it into a trash can to make a statement.

Her statement didn't have the desired effect.

Bruce ignored it.

"Talk to Sal," Bruce said, still with the irritating smug look on his face. "I called him up and got his approval before we printed the story. It was his call."

"I don't care if Sal approved it. Your article had the breathless gossipy tone of a teenage girl's Facebook page, making things up about who's dating whom just to make herself look like she's in the know and more important than she really is."

"You're calling me a teenage girl?"

"I'm calling this article a load of crap. There isn't one solid fact in it that suggests Wade is guilty. And you come off as if you desperately want him to be."

"I don't even know the guy. And I'm not the one who goes on and on about him like he's the Second Coming. Let's face it. You're the one who's been seen traipsing over to his hotel room at night with feasts of food like some sex-starved Paula Deen."

"Traipsing? I don't traipse. And sex starved? Where do you get off? I've walked my dog past your house on many Friday nights, and it was hard not to see the glow of your television from the front window and the erotic images of some twentysomething sexpot getting off on a late-night Skinemax show!"

"Excuse me, you two, but this is a professional office!" Sal bellowed as he charged out from the back to shush them both. "Keep it down or take it outside!"

"Sal, I'm taking my break early," Hayley said, grabbing her bag, anxious to get out of the office before she said something to Bruce she would regret. "I need to cool off."

"Go. Take a walk. Go to your brother's bar and have a drink."

"It's ten in the morning," Hayley said.

"Since when has that stopped you?" Bruce asked, sneering.

Hayley took a deep breath.

Be the bigger person. Be the bigger person.

She turned and headed for the door.

She reached for the door handle, and was seconds from making a dignified exit, but she stopped.

She just couldn't resist.

She turned back around and stared at Bruce.

"I know you're just mad because it wasn't you, the big-time crime reporter, it was *me* who finally collared Jesse DeSoto," Hayley said quietly. "I robbed you of your one chance to be the big hero in town."

Bruce looked like he was ready to blow.

Sal grabbed his arm. "Easy, Bruce. Hayley, go. Walk it off."

Walk it off?

What was she, back on her high school basketball team having just been fouled by a player from the other team and pissed about it?

However, Hayley knew the smart decision was to leave so she followed Sal's orders and walked out of the office.

Hayley walked up Main Street at a clip, reliving the

argument with Bruce, how arrogant he was acting and how irresponsible he was for treating Wade like he was public enemy number one.

By the time she reached the end of the street and was staring at all the fishing boats bobbing up and down in the harbor off the town pier, Hayley was calmer.

Maybe it was she who was being unreasonable.

Bruce wasn't completely at fault.

There was a lot of pressure on everybody at the *Times* to increase readership and Bruce was no exception.

Wade Springer was a huge star.

In a very serious situation.

What if Lady Gaga was the person of interest and not Wade?

Would Hayley be treading as lightly, not wanting to upset or alienate her?

Hardly.

Although she did like her music.

Hayley slowly began to realize Bruce was just doing his job.

She hated to admit it.

But the wise thing to do was probably go back to the office and apologize.

Hayley turned to head back around and was startled by the sight of a wiry kid with a camera snapping her picture.

It was that bratty would-be paparazzi Darrell Rodick!

He was ambushing her.

"Darrell, what are you doing?"

He kept snapping away. "Tell me, Mrs. Powell, are you carrying Wade Springer's love child?"

"No! Why? Does it look like I'm gaining weight?"

Hayley threw her hands up in front of her face. "Stop taking my picture!"

Darrell wasn't listening.

His camera kept clicking and clicking.

"If you don't stop taking pictures, I'm going to smash your damn camera," Hayley said, reaching out to snatch the camera away from him. "I said stop!"

She got a hold of the strap, but he wrenched it away from her. "Mrs. Powell, I'll sue you if you try to take my personal property or damage it in any way."

"Yeah? Well, I'll have Chief Alvares arrest you for stalking," Hayley said, turning her back to Darrell, who just scooted around her and kept taking more pictures.

"This is a public street," Darrell said, aiming and shooting. "We both have the right to be here. And, for the record, you gave up your privacy the day you became a public figure."

"Since when am I a public figure?"

"Since you started dating Wade Springer."

"I'm not dating Wade Springer! I work for him!"

"Yeah, and I'm the governor of New Jersey."

Hayley could not believe she was fighting with a middle school kid.

Younger than Dustin, no less.

This was humiliating.

"I'm sorry, Mrs. Powell, but you might as well get used to the fact that for at least the time being, you're the Angelina Jolie of Bar Harbor."

Hayley could think of worse things to be.

"You'll never be able to hide from me," Darrell said, checking a few digital shots before he resumed shooting. "I'll always be around to record your every movement. Wade Springer's, too."

Something dawned on Hayley. She kneeled down and looked straight into Darrell Rodick's camera lens. "So you've been following Wade every time he's left the hotel?"

"From the second he hit town," Darrell said proudly. "He's never had a moment's peace, because I'm that good."

"So you must have seen him the other night! The night of Mickey Pritchett's murder. When he left the hotel to walk his dog."

"Sure. I followed him for like an hour, hoping to get a shot of him not cleaning up after his dog, but he had some plastic bags on him," Darrell said, disappointed.

Hayley reached inside her bag and pulled out a ten dollar bill and waved it in front of Darrell's face. "Think I can see a few of those pictures you took?"

Darrell grabbed the money out of her hand. "Sure. I can e-mail them to you, too, if you want."

He clicked through an endless file of photos before settling on one and handing the camera to Hayley so she could take a look.

Sure enough.

It was Wade and Delilah.

And they were on Devon Road about a half a mile from the Harborside Hotel. In the completely opposite direction of Albert Meadow where Mickey's body was burned to a crisp in the bus.

And best of all, the photo was time stamped.

11:15 P.M.

Hayley was so excited she bent over and took hold of Darrell's cheeks and planted a big kiss on his forehead.

"Mrs. Powell, please, control yourself! I know I'm irresistible, but have some decorum. We're on a public street!"

Hayley was euphoric.

She had just cleared Wade Springer of the murder.

And she was certain Bruce was not going to be too happy about it.

Chapter 15

After examining the photos for well over an hour, Bruce, to his credit, immediately began typing a follow-up story that confirmed Wade was nowhere near the scene of the crime at the time the fire was set.

But he refused to completely exonerate Wade because, in his mind, Wade still had a motive, and could have easily hired someone to do his dirty work for him.

After Sal signed off on the article, Bruce posted it online and it was set to be printed in the next morning's paper.

Bruce didn't exactly apologize to Hayley. But he did mumble under his breath that he may have been a bit overzealous in trying to get Wade indicted for murder. Although he kept mum on why it was he despised the country singer so much. And Hayley didn't ask.

The question now was, who did murder Mickey?

Hayley had slipped out at lunch to make some Tex Mex chili in her crockpot and to whip up some buttermilk cornbread for Wade's dinner. So after shutting down her computer for the day, she raced out of the office to pack up the meal and head directly over to the Harborside Hotel.

Sal wasn't saying much about her moonlighting as Wade's chef. He grumbled a bit when she took an extra forty minutes at lunch because she couldn't find all the ingredients for tomorrow's chicken and dumplings, but he soon realized having Hayley on the inside of Wade's entourage could actually turn out to be a lucky break when it came to unearthing information on the murder case. So he stopped complaining.

Hayley thought Wade was still at the Criterion Theatre rehearsing when she arrived to set the table and put out his dinner in his hotel suite at the Harborside. At least, that's what Billy Ray told her when she called earlier to confirm his schedule.

So she was surprised to hear someone in the bathroom taking a shower when the bellhop helped carry her crockpot and bread, covered with aluminum foil, into the room.

"Wade must have finished rehearsing early," Hayley said, pointing to the counter in the small kitchen area. "Just set it down there, Danny."

"Yes, ma'am," the bellhop said. He was a lanky young kid, pimply and very nervous as he sniffed to keep his nose from running.

Then he sneezed and almost dropped the crockpot. Great.

The kid had a cold.

Thank God all the food was covered.

Hayley followed him to the kitchen and put down the tray of cornbread, then fished in her bag for a five dollar bill to tip him.

"Thanks, Danny," Hayley said. "Next time, there's a ten in it for you if you stop calling me, ma'am."

"Yes, ma—" Danny stopped himself. "Mrs. Powell."

"Hayley."

The bellhop nodded, and wiped his nose.

His eyes were watery.

Then he sneezed again.

"Yes, Hayley."

Hayley escorted him out. She didn't want the kid near her food any longer than he had to be.

She shut the door behind him.

Hayley picked up a ladle, removed the lid from the crockpot, and stirred the chili slowly. She was going to try and get everything on the table and scoot out the door before Wade finished showering, to honor his privacy.

She knew he liked her, but she certainly didn't want to be an intrusion. Especially after a long day of rehearsing.

She poured some chili into a bowl, sprinkling a little red onion and cheddar cheese on top, and set it down on the table with a hunk of the cornbread. She heard the shower turn off, so she picked up speed and retrieved an ice cold beer and frosted mug she had put in the freezer earlier that day when she'd served breakfast, and set it down on the table with the food.

She was just turning to go when suddenly the door to the bathroom was flung open.

"Something sure smells delicious."

It wasn't Wade.

It wasn't even a man.

A pretty blonde, tiny in frame, but with breasts so big they could possibly end hunger in the Third World, flounced out of the bathroom in Wade's white terrycloth robe. "I hear you're quite a cook," she said.

Hayley recognized the woman instantly.

Who wouldn't?

It was Stacy Jo Stanton, Wade Springer's ex-wife.

She leaned over the table and took a big whiff of the chili.

Her boobs nearly crushed the buttermilk cornbread.

"Tex Mex chili. My favorite."

Hayley could barely move.

She was so surprised to see Stacy Jo in person after years of reading about her. But she wasn't thrilled by any means.

She was angry.

And jealous.

And feeling all the things she knew she shouldn't be feeling.

"Darling, the table should be set for two," Stacy Jo purred.

"I'm sorry, I didn't know you were coming."

"It was a last minute decision. Wade's obviously going through a lot right now, and even though we're not married anymore, we're still very, very close and I wanted to be here for him. You know, show him my support."

"I'm sure he appreciates it," Hayley said, forcing a smile.

"I keep in touch with Billy Ray," Stacy Jo said, picking up a piece of cornbread and looking it over. "He keeps me in the loop about what's going on. I arrived last night at the Bar Harbor Airport from New York and took a taxi straight here."

Stacy Jo took a bite of the cornbread. She chewed on it a moment, tasting it, and then set it back down on the table and pushed it away.

"You don't like it?"

"Oh, it's fine, darling. Just a little bland for me. I like to put jalapeño in my cornbread. Spice it up a bit. Because I'm not sure if you know this or not, but Wade likes things spicy. Real spicy."

She thrust her giant breasts out for emphasis on this last point.

"I'll be sure to remember that," Hayley said, glancing at the door, wishing Wade would get back soon.

Hayley was still holding the ladle. She resisted the urge to bop Stacy Jo over the head with it.

Stacy Jo stared at her for a moment, a fake smile on her face, and then walked over and took the ladle from her. She scooped out some chili and took a small taste. Chewed and tasted again.

Crinkled her nose.

"You know what, darling," Stacy Jo said. "I'm going to give you my recipe for Tex Mex chili so you get it right next time. How long have you been cooking for Wade?"

"Just a few days."

"Interesting. I'm surprised he hasn't said anything to you about the way he likes his food prepared."

"He seemed to really love my fried chicken."

"Honestly, darling, a complete idiot couldn't screw up fried chicken!"

Stacy Jo laughed. Her cheeks jutted out and her eyes got big and her face became red and splotchy.

Hayley took some comfort in the fact that at least Stacy Jo was ugly when she laughed.

"I'm sure I can teach you a few things. Give you some pointers," Stacy Jo said. "Trust me, darling, I know what I'm talking about. I've been braising Wade's meat for a long, long time. I know just how he likes it."

Hayley wasn't sure they were talking about food anymore.

She just knew she didn't want to be near this awful woman much longer.

"I can see why Wade hired you. You're cute. Like a cream puff. And we all know Wade's got one hell of a sweet tooth. But don't start getting any big ideas about becoming the first lady of Nashville, you hear? Because Wade and I are in a good place, and we're on the path to reconciliation, and I will not have some small-town Martha Stewart wanna-be getting in my way."

"I'm just an employee," Hayley said.

"Good answer, darling," Stacy Jo said. "Because we southern girls are like lionesses protecting our cubs when it comes to other women moving in on what's ours."

She raised her hands to show off her perfectly manicured sharp lavender nails. "And with claws like these, we can sure mess up the face of a wily predator from up north."

Hayley nodded. Her eyes focused on Stacy Jo's killer nails.

"And if that doesn't work, darling," Stacy Jo said, pointing one of her nails at Hayley's face. "I'm always packing. So tread lightly. Northern girls sometimes make us southern gals do crazy things."

North versus South?

Stacy Jo was threatening to reenact the Civil War right here in Bar Harbor?

And Hayley could tell from Stacy Jo's wild, crazy eyes that she was dead serious.

Chapter 16

Hayley was still a bit shaken up by her run-in with Wade's ex, Stacy Jo, when she left the Harborside, so she made a beeline for her brother Randy's bar for a relaxing glass of red wine before heading home to check up on the kids.

When she arrived at Drinks Like A Fish, Randy was tending bar and Mona sat on her usual corner bar stool complaining about her husband and kids, sipping on a Diet Sprite and not too happy about it.

There were a couple of bank tellers from the First National at a corner table nursing Cosmos and gossiping about their evil branch managers.

And, in the back, there was no missing the giant African-American man, in a bright yellow windbreaker that made him look like Big Bird, playing darts.

It was Wade's bodyguard, Curtis King.

Hayley slid on top of a stool next to Mona and put her arm around her and gave her a tight squeeze. "Heard you had a sonogram today."

"Yeah," Mona groaned. "Kid's healthy. I'm grateful for that. And I'm more grateful I'm not having twins."

"Usual, Hayley?" Randy asked, reaching for the Jack Daniels.

"No, school night. I'm just having one glass of red wine and then I have to head straight home. I've just missed you all since I've been working these two jobs."

Randy poured a glass full of merlot and set it down in front of Hayley. "Missed you, too, sis. It's been crazy busy in here the last few nights. At least until the murder. Now business has ground to a halt. No more of Wade's crew coming in to blow off steam."

Mona chuckled and pointed to Curtis, who had just nailed a dart in the center of the board. "Except him."

"What's so funny?" Hayley asked.

"Wait. You'll see," Mona said, grinning.

Curtis downed the last of his beer and ambled over to the bar, slamming the mug down in front of Randy. "Fill 'er up, sunshine."

Randy took the mug and poured him a cold one from the tap and slid it back over to him.

Curtis scooped it up and took a generous sip, which left a foam mustache on his upper lip.

He winked at Randy and returned to the dart board.

"Sunshine?" Hayley said, her mouth opened in shock.

"He's got a huge, and I mean HUGE, crush on your brother," Mona laughed.

"Ladies, please, let's not, okay?" Randy said, wiping down the bar with a rag.

Hayley glanced over at Curtis, who nailed the center of the board again and then casually glanced over to see if Randy was noticing his prowess with darts.

"He's looking over here, Randy," Mona said.

"Don't encourage him," Randy said in a quiet but urgent voice.

"I didn't even know he was gay," Hayley said.

"He came here the first night with a few of Wade's musicians, and got pretty drunk, and started getting a little randy. I told him I was taken, but that hasn't exactly discouraged him. He's been back every night. Won't take no for an answer."

"Did you tell him your boyfriend is the chief of police?" Hayley asked.

"Yeah, that didn't really do the trick."

"And Mickey Pritchett's murder hasn't kept him from coming around like the rest of Wade's crew," Hayley said, eyeing Curtis, who was busy chugging down his mug of beer.

"Well, there was no love lost between those two, believe me," Randy said. "Curtis was here the other night, slurring his words a bit after more than a few, but making it very clear he hated Mickey's guts. Seemed Mickey was a homophobe and really gave Curtis a hard time after he found out macho Curtis was a girly pansy boy. Mickey's words, not mine."

"I heard the guy tell Wade's drummer he wanted to put Mickey down for good," Mona said, stirring her Diet Sprite with a straw before pushing the glass away from her. "God, I miss beer. I can't wait for this kid to pop out."

"Mona, why didn't you mention this to me before?"

"You didn't ask," Mona said matter-of-factly.

"So Curtis had a motive to kill Mickey. They hated each other," Hayley said, her mind racing. "Randy, think. Was Curtis in here with the boys from the tour the night Mickey was murdered?"

"Yes, I'm certain of it, because he kept asking me out to dinner and I kept saying no," Randy said.

"But he was the first one to leave, around nine-thirty, don't you remember? Because that was around the same time my babysitter called me threatening to sue my kids for emotional abuse and I had to get home," Mona said. "We walked out of the bar together."

"Nine-thirty," Hayley said. "That gave Curtis plenty of time to go back to the hotel and force Mickey into the tour bus, shoot him dead, then drive it to Albert Meadow and set it on fire to try and cover his tracks."

"Doesn't he watch *CSI?* That never works," Randy said. "They always find evidence in the wreckage."

"I wish there was some way for me to search his hotel room to see if there's some clue that places him at the scene," Hayley said, spinning around on her stool and staring at Curtis.

"He isn't staying in the hotel," Randy said. "He's staying in the other tour bus. It serves as his office and makeshift sleeping quarters. He likes to keep an eye on the hotel from outside to monitor all the comings and goings. Part of his security process, I guess."

"And how do you know that?"

"Believe me, he's invited me back there every night he's been here for a quote, unquote, drink," Randy said.

Curtis strolled back over, wiped some remaining foam from his mouth, and placed his mug down in front of Randy.

Randy refilled it again.

"Honestly, Randy, you work too hard," Hayley said suddenly, loud enough for Curtis to hear. "I'm worried you're going to make yourself sick. You need to take a break every once and a while. As your younger sister . . ."

"You're two years older and what are you talking about?"

"Don't interrupt me. Let me look after the bar. Go get something to eat. Relax. Enjoy life for once, instead of working your fingers to the bone. You're so cute and I don't want you aging prematurely. Isn't he cute, Curtis?"

Curtis perked up and smiled. "Oh, yes. Very."

"You know what? I just had the craziest idea," Hayley said, fishing for something in her bag. "I got this gift certificate from Havana that I'm never going to use."

Havana was a quiet little Cuban restaurant on the other side of town.

And very romantic.

Candles on the table.

Impressive wine list.

The whole shebang.

Randy opened his mouth to protest, but before he could, Hayley was shoving the gift certificate in his hand. "Why don't you call Sergio and have a nice quiet dinner. Oh, darn, I just remembered, he's working tonight, isn't he?"

"Yes, there's this very big murder case . . ."

"Curtis, have you eaten?" Hayley was not going to let Randy get a word in edgewise and Randy knew it and was already looking resigned to the situation.

"No, ma'am," Curtis said, beaming.

"Why don't you go with Curtis? As friends. I'm sure Curtis has been working like a dog, too, looking after Wade. He deserves a tasty meal at one of our local hotspots," Hayley said.

"As long as Randy doesn't mind," Curtis said, eyeing Randy curiously, not sure if he was going to go for this plan.

Hayley was eyeing Randy, too, her back to Curtis. She was silently pleading with him.

Randy sighed. "No, Curtis, dinner sounds nice. Why don't you wait for me outside?"

Curtis upended his mug and swallowed the beer in one gulp. He nodded to Hayley and Mona. "You ladies have a nice evening. I know I sure will."

And he was out the door.

Randy glared at Hayley. "I swear, if Sergio ever finds out about this little undercover assignment . . ."

"He's not going to. I promise. I only need an hour. You don't even have to stay for dessert."

"I can't just close the bar," Randy said.

"Mona can take care of the bank tellers and anyone else who comes in. Any reason to avoid going home to her husband and kids, right, Mona?"

"She's got a point," Mona shrugged. "Besides, they're all out at the movies."

"Then it's settled. Let's do this," Hayley said.

"Why are you so obsessed with getting involved in all this?" Randy asked. "Is it because of Wade?"

"No. Wade's already been cleared. He has an airtight alibi. You know me. I just can't help myself. I still have all my first edition Nancy Drew books. That's why I work at a newspaper."

"But you're not an investigative journalist. You write a cooking column," Randy said.

"Please don't turn into another Bruce Linney. I couldn't take two of him. Now go! Curtis is waiting."

Randy took a deep breath and sighed again. Then he came out from behind the bar and went over to the table with the bank tellers. "I have to go, ladies. But Mona will be here to take care of you."

The women nodded and went back to their gossiping.

Randy shot Hayley one last look of annoyance and walked out the door to where Curtis was waiting.

The two strolled off down the street.

"I'll be back soon," Hayley said to Mona, who was already behind the bar washing glasses, before she shot out the door and raced down the street in the other direction.

When she arrived at the Harborside Hotel, Hayley was amazed to find the tour bus unlocked, especially given recent events. But once she was inside, it quickly became apparent there was really nothing of value to steal.

Just a lot of empty food containers and beer bottles. There was the nauseating smell of unwashed sheets and dirty clothes. She found discarded candy wrappers and a crumpled issue of *Health and Fitness* magazine.

Which Curtis probably flipped through while chowing down on junk food.

Hayley moved to a steamer trunk in the back of the bus hidden under a pile of clothes. She snapped it open and looked inside.

Mostly personal items. Shaving kit. A Dallas Cowboys ball cap. An autographed photo of Curtis flanked by Wade and Tim McGraw. Curtis was beaming at being in the middle of the two strapping sexy singers.

Well, it looked like Curtis and Hayley had the same taste when it came to men.

Hayley smiled and was about to put the photo back in the trunk when something suddenly caught her eye.

Sticking out from a pile of DVDs—mostly Adam Sandler comedies—was a glinting piece of metal.

Hayley knew what it was immediately.

A gun.

Hayley grabbed one of Curtis's dirty stained socks from the floor and used it to pick up the Smith and Wesson .38.

Was this the murder weapon that killed Mickey Pritchett?

Chapter 17

When Hayley called Sergio to tell him about the Smith and Wesson she found on the tour bus that served as Curtis King's makeshift office/crash pad, she neglected to mention that she had essentially committed the crime of breaking and entering.

Well, not breaking.

Just entering.

The bus was unlocked.

That somehow made her feel better.

She just told Sergio that she had heard rumors among the crew that Curtis was packing, and even though it wasn't unusual for a bodyguard to be carrying a weapon, it might be worth checking out.

Sergio agreed, given Curtis's feelings toward the victim (which Hayley also told him about), and went about obtaining a warrant to search the bus.

When Hayley got to the office the following morning, she hadn't even put her bag down when the phone on her desk rang.

Hayley scooped up the receiver. "Island Times, this is Hayley."

"Sergio had the gun sent up to Bangor to see if it's the same one that killed Mickey Pritchett."

It was Randy.

"Did Sergio arrest Curtis?" Hayley asked, waving to Sal, who blew in through the front door with a coffee and bagel and a pained expression on his face.

Probably another fight with his wife.

"No," Randy said on the other end of the line. "Sergio hauled him in for questioning, but apparently Curtis was very calm and cooperative. Said he was happy to answer any questions and do whatever he could to assist in the investigation."

"Could be covering," Hayley said. "He really despised Mickey."

"Or it could've been someone else."

"But who? Who else on the tour had a problem with Mickey? Wade certainly did, but luckily that little pain in the butt Darrell Rodick provided him with an alibi. I need to talk to the entire crew. Mickey was a loud-mouthed, mean-spirited bastard. I'm sure he ticked off more than a few people he worked with."

"And I'm sure Sergio will question all of them," Randy said. "Let him do his job, Hayley. For both our sakes."

"You're right," Hayley said. "I've really got to reign in this curious nature I have."

"Like that's ever going to happen," Randy said, snickering.

The front door flew open again, and Liddy breathlessly swept into the office, her eyes wide and arms flapping. "Hayley! Hayley! Hang up! We have to talk!"

"I'll call you back, Randy," Hayley said, hanging up, and then turned to Liddy. "Someone's already had too much caffeine this morning."

Liddy sat down in a chair next to Hayley's desk, opened her bag, and fished for a compact. She flipped it open and studied herself as she adjusted her hair. "I just came from the salon. How do I look? Too matronly? They always make me look like someone's spinster aunt. I really need a trip to New York to see a serious stylist."

"You look fine."

"You have to say that. You're my best friend and you don't want to hurt my feelings with an honest opinion. Maybe I should ask Mona. She doesn't care about my feelings."

"Is there a reason you popped by, Liddy? Because it's kind of busy around here today."

"Oh, please, you were just on the phone gossiping with your brother. How busy can it be? I came because I have some news I thought you would like to know about."

"You found your earring?"

"No. I can't even think about that. It'll just make me cry again."

"Then what's the big news? I have work to do."

"Well, it concerns the Mickey Pritchett murder. But if you're too busy . . ."

Liddy stood up to leave.

"Wait. What did you hear?"

"No. I don't want to disturb you while you are at work. It was thoughtless and rude of me to just drop by unannounced even though I am single-handedly keeping this paper alive with all my real estate advertising."

"Liddy!"

Liddy plopped back down in the chair. "Okay, listen to this. The salon doesn't actually open until ten, but sometimes they'll take VIP clients early in the morning so we don't have to engage in small talk with the usual riffraff."

"You mean, clients like me?"

"Oh, honey, you know what I mean."

"Yes, I'm afraid I do," Hayley said, shaking her head. "Go on."

"Well, I wasn't the only VIP getting my hair done this morning. Guess who was in the chair right next to me getting a blow-dry?"

"Kim Kardashian!"

Liddy gave Hayley a withering look.

"What? You told me to guess."

"Not literally. I was going to tell you."

"Sorry."

"Wade Springer's one mistake in life. That off-key harlot ex-wife of his."

"Stacy Jo Stanton."

"Yes, and I'll tell you something. That self-involved witch is so unfriendly. I tried chatting with her just to be friendly and she shut me down like I was . . ."

"The usual riffraff?"

"Don't test me, sweetie. You know I've got dirt on you all the way back to the days when we skipped school and smoked pot on top of Cadillac Mountain."

"So that's it? You just sat next to Stacy Jo at the salon?"

"Give me some credit, would you, please? I do have a life and career. I wouldn't be wasting my time running over here if I didn't have something juicy. Honestly, Hayley. No—after she dissed me she started texting on her BlackBerry like a wild woman. Texting and texting. It was on her lap so I had a clear view, if I craned my neck enough."

"I'm surprised Stacy Jo could see anything in her own lap given the size of her ginormous breasts."

"Meow."

"Just give me one," Hayley said. "I'm not a big fan of Stacy Jo. So could you tell who she was texting?"

"Based on what they were saying, I'm guessing it was a girlfriend back in Nashville. Someone she confides in, maybe a sister. It doesn't matter. It was what she wrote that stood out."

"What?"

"She was talking about Mickey Pritchett."

"Okay, that's not out of the ordinary. We're all talking about him."

"Yeah, but she was really trashing him. Said she was happy he was finally out of her life, he got what he deserved. Stuff like that."

"Why did Stacy Jo hate him so much?"

"From what I could tell, Stacy Jo and Mickey were involved in some kind of relationship that ended badly and I think Mickey was the one who broke it off."

Hayley's mind was reeling. "So what else did she text?"

"I don't know. It was about that time she caught me looking and moved to another chair farther away."

The front door crashed open again and Bruce stalked inside, carrying his Styrofoam coffee cup. He was in a seriously foul mood.

"Good morning, Bruce," Hayley chirped.

"There's nothing good about it," Bruce growled. "Judge just released Jesse DeSoto on bail. Some ridiculously small amount like five hundred bucks. His mother posted it. She probably stole it. They're all criminals. The whole damn family! I can't believe this. Now the little punk is free to just resume his stealing and vandalizing. What kind of town is this?"

Bruce took a sip of his coffee and spit it out. "Burnt again. I hate this town!" And then he stomped in the back toward Sal's office.

Liddy turned to Hayley and whispered in a sarcastic tone, "Why on earth isn't Bruce married already? He's such a catch."

Hayley couldn't help but smile. "If Mickey broke

Stacy Jo's heart, that's a clear motive. And she told me she's always packing, so she had the means."

"See? I solved the case," Liddy said. "I have to go. I have an open house in forty minutes."

"Not so fast. She had motive and means. But not opportunity. Stacy Jo didn't arrive in town on a flight from New York until Sunday night, a full day *after* the murder. She was taking a shower in Wade's hotel room yesterday when I brought over his dinner."

"What airport? Bar Harbor or Bangor?"

"She said Bar Harbor."

"Well, that doesn't make any sense. There is no flight from New York to the Bar Harbor Airport on Sunday night. They cancelled it because it was always empty."

"How do you know that?"

"Sweetie, with the number of shopping trips I take to New York a year, believe me, I've memorized all the flight schedules. And it's a small airport. When did you see her at the hotel?"

"Around five-thirty. After I got off work."

"There is only one flight into Bar Harbor from New York a day. And it arrives at six o'clock in the evening. It would've been impossible for her to arrive on Monday's flight and be here when you brought Wade's dinner. And we already know there is no Sunday flight. That means she had to have arrived on Saturday's flight. When Mickey was still alive."

Hayley jumped on the phone and called the airport. She knew they would never divulge Stacy Jo's flight information, but it was a twenty-minute ride to town from the airport. She would have either had to rent a car or take a taxi. Hayley knew that Larry Shaw from her brother Randy's class in high school drove that route in his cab. He met all the flights. Chances were if Stacy Jo took a taxi, he would remember seeing her. After all, she was famous.

Sure enough. When Hayley got Larry on the line, he confirmed dropping Stacy Jo Stanton off at the Harborside Hotel on Saturday night around 7:15.

Well before someone shot Mickey and set fire to the tour bus.

Motive.

Means.

Opportunity.

Chapter 18

"Have you been spying on me?" Stacy Jo said in a clipped tone, attempting to fold her arms across her chest, but unable to do so in a convincing manner due to her access cleavage.

"I just find it a bit curious that you lied to me about when you arrived in town," Hayley said, hands on her hips, bent over and trying to catch her breath.

She had literally been running all over town trying to track down Stacy Jo.

When Hayley had called the hotel asking to speak to Stacy Jo, she was put through to Wade's room where Billy Ray answered.

She was relieved when Billy Ray told her Wade had insisted Stacy Jo get her own room if she was going to spend time in Bar Harbor and stay for his concerts.

At least they weren't cohabitating.

Billy Ray last saw her going for a run when he returned from an early morning sound check at the Criterion.

So Hayley took an early lunch, dashed home and threw on some running shorts and a t-shirt, laced up her Reeboks, and took off in search of Stacy Jo.

She knew Stacy Jo was unfamiliar with the town

and wouldn't know much about the park trails, so chances were she was just doing a loop around the downtown area. Hayley was hoping to find her soon because she was dying from the run. She should have stuck to her plan to use that gym membership.

Hayley's instincts paid off. She was just about ready to give up after nearly an hour of jogging up and down the streets of Bar Harbor when she spotted Stacy Jo rounding the town pier just a block away from the Harborside Hotel. Stacy Jo was listening to her iPod, lost in her own thoughts, veering left toward the gift shops that would lead her back around to the hotel.

Hayley took a sharp turn and intercepted her. Stacy Jo pretended not to see Hayley, but Hayley ran straight at her until she was forced to stop.

Stacy Jo grimaced and yanked out her earbuds, staring at Hayley.

That's when Hayley hit her fast with her accusations.

How she had proof Stacy Jo lied about her arrival in town.

How taxi driver Larry Shaw backed up her claims.

When Hayley finally stopped talking, Stacy Jo took her sweet time responding. "When I got here is none of your damn business," Stacy Jo said. "Who are you to be stalking me? Don't you already have your hands full stalking Wade?"

"Please. I'm not exactly a fan of yours, Stacy Jo. I only own one of your songs, and it happens to be a duet with Wade, and, trust me, it would've done better on the country charts if he was singing with Shania."

"Oh, no, you didn't just say that," Stacy Jo said, flashing her incredibly long talons. "Watch your mouth, or I might just take an eye out."

"You don't scare me, Stacy Jo," Hayley said.

Stacy Jo glared at Hayley and then tried to push past her, but Hayley blocked her escape by stepping in front of her.

"I really think it's in your best interest to come clean," Hayley said. "If not to me, it's going to be to the cops, because they're going to find out anyway."

"Get out of my way," Stacy Jo barked as she gave Hayley a violent shove.

Hayley stumbled back and had to catch herself from falling to the ground. This sent a wave of fury surging through her, and she ran up behind Stacy Jo, who was running off, and grabbed her by her pink hoodie and spun her around.

"What are you doing? You're a crazy person!" Stacy Jo wailed before slashing her nails across Hayley's face and drawing a line of blood on her right cheek.

Then Stacy Jo reared back and swung her leg up in the air to deliver a swift kick to Hayley's stomach. But Hayley had enough time to step back and grab Stacy Jo's foot. She yanked it up, and Stacy Jo lost her balance and fell, landing hard on her butt.

She screamed bloody murder and sprang to her feet and charged Hayley, pummeling her with her fists.

Hayley felt like she was being attacked by a cougar. And given Stacy Jo was in her forties, that's exactly what she was.

Only, in another kind of jungle.

Stacy Jo was strong, a scrappy girl from a backwater town in the Deep South and she knew how to fight. That much was clear.

As they scratched and kicked and punched each other, Hayley saw out of the corner of one eye the harbor master calling 911 on his cell.

Hayley grabbed Stacy Jo by the wrists in an attempt

to calm the situation. "Stacy Jo, listen to me. We're causing a public disturbance and I think we should call a truce because otherwise . . ."

That's when Stacy Jo head-butted Hayley.

Hayley felt dizzy and saw those flashes of light like little stars in the sky. When she opened her eyes, she saw Stacy Jo running at her screaming some kind of indecipherable battle cry as if she were in that Mel Gibson movie *Braveheart* with blue paint on her face and wearing a kilt. Hayley loved that movie. She used to love Mel Gibson. Before all that bad publicity that exposed him as a drunk and a racist and a homophobe.

Well, at least she still had Mark Harmon.

Stacy Jo collided with Hayley.

More scratching.

More biting.

More kicking.

And then they were both falling. Locked in an embrace. Falling into an abyss. No, it wasn't an abyss.

It was shivering cold ocean water. Their vicious cat fight had led them right off the town pier.

Hayley screamed as she surfaced.

The water was freezing.

She grabbed at the seaweed tangled in her hair.

Stacy Jo screamed, too.

A desperate, frightened wail. "I can't swim!"

"Calm down, Stacy Jo," Hayley said, spitting out the salty water. "Your breasts are the perfect flotation device."

Stacy Jo splashed frantically in the water, coughing and sputtering to the point where Hayley felt bad for her and had to swim over and wrap an arm around her neck. She pulled her toward a rope ladder that would enable them to climb back up to the pier.

It was a good thing she remembered her training

from her days working as a lifeguard in the summer. Her official reason for doing it was her innate need to keep visitors to the island safe and happy, but she actually did it to spend the summer with bronzed and blond German exchange student Rolf Hoffman, who was heading up the lifeguard program.

"Grab the rope, Stacy Jo," Hayley sputtered, her lips blue and shivering as she guided Stacy Jo's hand to the thick rope.

Stacy Jo managed to hoist herself up, carefully navigating the ladder before finally reaching the surface of the pier. Hayley was right behind her, and when she reached the top, her face smashed into Stacy Jo's butt.

Could this day get any worse?

Yes, as it turned out, it could.

Stacy Jo had stopped suddenly, which was why Hayley was nearly smothered by her ample booty.

She was staring at the two uniformed police officers waiting for them.

It was Donnie and Earl.

"How are you doing today, Hayley?" Earl said, unhooking a pair of handcuffs from his belt.

"I'm great, Earl. Thanks. Donnie, how's your mother?"

"Fine, Hayley," Donnie said. "Just fine."

"Tell her I'm going to send her my pumpkin pie recipe. She's always asking for it and Thanksgiving is just a couple of short months away."

"No, ma'am," Donnie said. "I'm sure she'll appreciate it."

"If you don't mind, Hayley, could you please turn around? I'm sure you know the drill by now."

"Yes, Earl, I sure do," Hayley said as she turned around, facing a distraught Stacy Jo, as Earl snapped the cuffs on her.

This wasn't her first time arrested.

In fact, she was starting to get used to it.

Donnie went to put handcuffs on Stacy Jo, but she backed away, horrified. "You can't arrest me! Do you have any idea who I am?"

"Yes, ma'am, and I'm sorry, but I'm just doing my job," Donnie said, gently taking her by the arm and turning her around so he could get the cuffs on her. "Even if you were Carrie Underwood, I'd have to arrest you for causing a public disturbance. And I like her music so much better than yours."

It was a good thing Donnie had snapped those cuffs on Stacy Jo before he made that remark.

Otherwise, she would have mauled him like a Maine black bear.

Donnie and Earl drove the ladies to the station and, after booking them, put them in a cell together. Then they called Chief Alvarez, who at the moment was meeting with Sabrina Merryweather, the county coroner, to discuss her findings regarding Curtis King's Smith and Wesson.

Hayley and Stacy Jo were served a hot lunch including a piece of ham, mashed potatoes, buttered carrots, and a dry piece of chocolate cake.

Not bad for prison food.

Hayley had recently led a crusade to improve the quality of food served to anyone who might have the unfortunate experience of spending time in the local jail. Sergio had listened and implemented the changes, and Hayley was grateful they had been put into effect before her most recent incarceration.

Two times in jail in just over a year Not a good track record.

And this certainly was not going to insure her good standing in the P.T.A.

Stacy Jo refused to look at Hayley for the first hour they spent in jail together.

They ate in silence.

Stacy Jo asked to make a phone call, but was told by Earl she would have to wait until the chief got back. But, not to worry, she would have plenty of time to consult a lawyer before she was called before the judge.

Stacy Jo went to the opposite side of the cell to be as far away from Hayley as she possibly could. But as time wore on, and after Donnie refused to give her back her iPod so she could block Hayley out with music, she softened a bit.

"This is insane. We were just having a disagreement on the street. How is that a public disturbance?" Stacy Jo sighed.

"I think the harbor master called the police because it looked like we were going to kill each other."

Stacy Jo couldn't help but crack a smile. "Well, I have to admit, you were a much better fighter than I thought you'd be."

"Thank you," Hayley said. "I've never been accused of being a lady."

"What's that saying? You can put lipstick on a tiger, but she's still a tiger."

"Actually, it's lipstick on a pig."

Stacy Jo thought this over. "Forget it. I don't like that saying."

Now it was Hayley's turn to crack a smile.

There was a long pause. Hayley could see Stacy Jo thinking hard, eyes downcast.

Finally, she looked up at Hayley. "You were right. I lied. I did arrive in town on Saturday night and I did go to see Mickey."

Hayley nodded.

She didn't want to push Stacy Jo too much now that she was talking.

"I guess I didn't want anyone to know, because if

people found out I was with Mickey the night he was shot, the police would consider me a suspect. And I just couldn't risk people making assumptions about me, especially when I have a new album coming out in a few weeks. I didn't want to endanger my career."

"That's understandable," Hayley said. "So what did you two talk about when you saw him?"

"Oh, we had quite a row that night. You should've seen the scratches I left on his face," Stacy Jo said, laughing. And then she sobered up fast. "But I guess nobody saw them because he was burned to a crisp."

"Was the fight about him breaking up with you?"

Stacy Jo's eyes widened. "Where on earth do you get your information?"

"I read a lot of mystery novels," Hayley said.

"Well, you're right, we did quarrel about that. But not because he broke up with me. I couldn't have cared less about that. I was already over him. In case you didn't get a chance to meet him, he was a real grade A scuzzball."

"I did have the unfortunate experience of meeting Mickey, so at least the two of us have finally found one thing we have in common."

"Other than us both being jailbirds?"

"Okay, two things in common. So if you didn't have feelings for him anymore, what was the fight about?"

"It was the way he did it. He tweeted that I was a bad lay and he was bored with me because he had met someone else, a local here in Bar Harbor, who could really satisfy him in bed."

"He said that on Twitter?"

"Classy, huh?"

"So Mickey met someone here in town? Do you have any idea who it was?"

"He wasn't exactly forthcoming with a name. Just

said she was a real spitfire and much more fun than I ever was."

"What a bastard," Hayley spat out.

"Trust me, darling, the way he publicly humiliated me, all those horrible jokes about me on Twitter, I would've loved to have shot him between the eyes and then gone out for a bourbon, like my daddy does when he goes deer hunting, but I didn't. I left and crashed in Billy Ray's room. Billy Ray's a dear. He was going to back up my story about not arriving until Sunday night."

Hayley believed her.

Now the big question was, who in town was Mickey Pritchett sleeping with and could this mysterious local be the one who murdered him?

Island Food & Spirits
by
Hayley Powell

The other night as I was getting my new pressure cooker out from the cupboard under the kitchen counter to make a batch of country chili, my mind wandered back to last summer when I had purchased another pressure cooker for only $2 at a yard sale. I had been so excited to try it out with my new chili recipe that I immediately called a few friends, my brother, and his partner Sergio to come over for an impromptu southwestern chili party that evening.

I excitedly scurried around setting the table and whipping up a yummy batch of jalapeño and cheddar cheese corn muffins to go with our chili. I also made a colorful veggie tray along with a couple of dips, and I was even able to bake a nice apple crisp since we had just been apple picking the weekend before, and obviously got a little too carried away with the amount of apples we brought home!

Finally, it was on to the chili. I should mention here that this was my first time using a pressure cooker, and for my $2, I only got the pressure cooker. I did not get any instructions to go with it. But really. How hard could it be to toss a few ingredients inside the pot, raise the pressure, and come back in a little while to take a little taste to see if it's done? Martha Stewart assured me it was one of the easiest ways to cook. Well, she didn't tell me in person. I'm just a rabid fan of her show. And we all know Martha is *never* wrong!

Everyone arrived promptly at 6 P.M. And a good time was had by all. Mostly due to the mango margaritas I prepared to greet everyone as they walked through the door. Margaritas always go well with chili. Well, let's be honest, margaritas go well with just about *anything!*

My guests crowded into the kitchen because no matter how many times I tell anyone to go relax in the living room or outside on the deck or around my dining-room table, they will always, inevitably, stay hovering right in the kitchen, talking and laughing and watching me cook. Everyone was in great spirits, and someone—I think it was my brother, Randy—even tied a tiny green sombrero, that he got at a birthday party ages ago, onto Leroy's head. True to form, Leroy pranced around the kitchen like he was modeling on the catwalk during Fashion Week in New York City.

Well, it was finally time to eat.

Everyone was feeling rather festive thanks to the margaritas, so I thought it was best to get some food into my guests' stomachs. I needed to release the pressure on the cooker, but for some inexplicable reason, the lever wouldn't work. I tugged and tugged but it still wouldn't budge. Then, as I gave it one last yank, all of a sudden it snapped right off in my hand!

Before I could say anything, the top exploded right off the cooker and shot straight up in the air and smashed against the ceiling with the loudest crash! Not realizing what was happening, everyone was startled into silence for a moment.

But, then, without missing a beat, Sergio, our esteemed police chief, jumped into cop mode and was yelling for everyone to get down on the ground, with such authority that we all dropped to our knees and watched horrified as he automatically reached for his gun. Thankfully, he was in civilian clothes and not wearing his holster or carrying his gun. Otherwise, I might not be around to write about this unfortunate episode.

That's just about when it began raining chili on all of us while we were bunched together on the floor. Leroy was blissfully unaware of the splattering chili since his little green sombrero provided a perfect cover. He was just running and jumping all over us, completely thrilled to have so many people down at his level to play with him.

I learned a very valuable lesson that day, about buying used appliances. Know how to use them or otherwise just buy a new one that comes with very clear instructions! Luckily, I had enough people to help me clean up the mess. We even got to slather some of it onto our corn muffins, thanks to the small amount salvaged from the rim of Leroy's sombrero. I'm not sure that Martha would agree, but as far as I'm concerned, my southwestern chili party wound up being a smashing success, and one that none of us would soon forget!

Take my word for it, you will never go wrong serving frozen mango margaritas at your next southwestern chili party! They were an absolute hit at mine!

Frozen Mango Margaritas

Serves 2 to 3 (or 1 if you've had a really stressful day)

1 tablespoon kosher salt
1 lime, cut into four wedges
¼ cup gold tequila, or to taste
½ cup fresh lime juice
1 small mango, diced
Crushed ice

Sprinkle kosher salt on to a plate. Rub the rim of each margarita glass with one of the lime wedges and dip the rim into the salt.

Mix all the ingredients (except the salt and limes) in a blender until smooth.

Pour the mixture into a margarita glass. Bottoms up!

Pressure Cooker Country Chili

Note: if possible, buy a new pressure cooker or check yours for damage.

3 pounds stew meat
2 tablespoons olive oil, divided
1 yellow onion, chopped
1 small green bell pepper, finely
   chopped
1 jalapeño pepper, seeded and finely
   chopped
2 cloves garlic, minced
2 14.5-ounce cans dark red kidney
   beans, drained and rinsed
2 14.5-ounce cans diced tomatoes,
   undrained
3 tablespoons tomato paste
1 tablespoon dark brown sugar
¼ teaspoon crushed red pepper flakes
2 tablespoons chili powder
2 teaspoons cumin
Kosher salt to taste
2 cups water

Place the meat in a mixing bowl and toss with 1 tablespoon of the olive oil.

Following your pressure cooker instruction book, heat your 6-quart pressure cooker to high heat according to its directions (a lesson I learned the hard way!). Then heat the stew meat in batches to brown all sides. Then remove to a bowl.

Add remaining tablespoon of olive oil to the pressure cooker and adjust temperature to medium high heat and add onion, green pepper, and jalepeño pepper. Cook and stir until onion is translucent. Add garlic and cook about 30 more seconds. Return the meat to the pressure cooker; mix in kidney beans, diced tomatoes, tomato paste, brown sugar, red pepper flakes, chili powder, cumin, salt, and water.

Lock on the lid, bring the cooker up to pressure, reduce heat to maintain pressure, and cook 8 minutes. Remove cooker from heat and let pressure reduce on its own for 5 to 10 minutes.

When the pressure is fully released, remove lid, stir up your chili, and serve!

Delicioso!

Chapter 19

One big advantage of having your brother's significant other as the town's chief of police? There's not a big incentive to build a case against a family member. And since no real physical harm was done to anyone, and since neither Hayley nor Stacy Jo was interested in pressing any charges, Sergio was inclined to drop the whole matter.

On one condition.

That the two women refrain from any further public outbursts.

Both agreed, and were finally released from jail.

Stacy Jo immediately called Billy Ray using the police station's phone since her cell phone was dead after being dunked in the chilly Atlantic Ocean. He raced over to retrieve her. On her way out, Stacy Jo gave Hayley a cursory nod, making the point that despite their bonding behind bars, there was no way the two would ever be friends.

Hayley understood, and couldn't have agreed more. She just wanted to get back to the office before Sal fired her for taking a four-hour lunch.

Hayley popped her head into Sergio's office before leaving the station. Sergio sat behind his desk, sorting through paperwork. He looked dashing in his blue uniform. Tall, handsome, that perpetual South American tan. She knew exactly what her brother saw in him. "So I just wanted to thank you once again for forgetting about this little incident, Sergio."

Sergio shook his head and smiled. "If you don't stop getting arrested, someday they're going to have to put a gold plaque in the jail that says, 'Welcome to the Hayley Powell Memorial Cell.'"

"Last time. I promise," Hayley said, knowing full well it was probably a lie.

"Before you go, I thought you would want to know, I just came from a meeting with your friend Sabrina. . . ."

"Not my friend. But that's irrelevant. Go on," Hayley said.

"Well, Curtis King's gun was not the one used to kill Mickey Pritchett. King owns a Smith and Wesson thirty-eight, but Sabrina said the murder weapon couldn't have been a thirty-eight because of the circumcision of the entry wound."

Hayley had to think for a moment.

Circumcision.

Sergio sometimes mixed up his words in English because his first language was Portuguese.

"Circumference!" Hayley shouted, excited to figure it out like she was a contestant on *Jeopardy*. "The *circumference* of the entry wound. The size of the bullet hole!"

"Yes, that's what I said. Circumcision." Sergio sighed, slightly annoyed. "And she was proven correct when she removed the bullet. It was from a forty-five."

At that moment, Randy rushed in, panic on his face. "I just heard you were arrested again!"

Hayley hugged him and said, "Everything's fine. It

was just a little misunderstanding between me and Wade Springer's ex-wife. It's all over now."

"Stacy Jo Stanton is in town? I love her! Did you know she has her own clothing line? Or she did, anyway, until they busted some sweatshops her company was operating in Malaysia or somewhere like that. Do you think I could meet her?"

"We'll see. We're not exactly besties. She just tried drowning me in the harbor," Hayley said. "But the good news is you don't have to go on another date with Curtis King because he's in the clear."

Hayley bit her tongue.

Literally.

She tasted blood.

The second the words tumbled out of her mouth, she knew she had royally screwed up.

"Date?" Sergio asked in a deep intimidating tone.

"Not a date! Just dinner," Randy tried to explain, whipping his head around to stare daggers at his sister.

"Dinner?" Sergio asked in a deeper and even more intimidating tone.

"It was just a favor for Hayley. To buy her time to search Curtis's belongings for clues!"

Sergio swiveled his chair around to face Hayley, raising an eyebrow.

"So if you're going to be mad at anyone, be mad at her," Randy said weakly, turning to Hayley. "Sorry, it's just that I feel strongly that saving my relationship is more important right at this moment."

"So you're throwing me under the bus?" Hayley said.

"Someone tried to throw you under a bus?" Sergio said, jumping to his feet.

"It's just an expression, Sergio. I'm going to leave you two to work things out. Just remember. Randy loves you. I love you. We're a family. And families forgive and forget." Hayley checked her watch. "Sal's going to kill me! I have to get back to the office."

Hayley dashed out the door, feeling incredibly guilty for leaving her brother to explain everything to Sergio. But she didn't have time to hear another lecture from Sergio on why she should keep her nose out of his investigations. She already got enough grief from Bruce, who believed she was encroaching on his crime beat at the paper.

And maybe she was.

Maybe she should just stop this madness and focus on her work and family. Gemma was dating a boy that gave Hayley a knot in her stomach. She was sure it was because of his age. It was only a two-and-a-half-year difference, but he seemed so much older than Gemma and that made her nervous. She was afraid Reid might pressure Gemma into doing something she wasn't emotionally ready to do, and she wanted to be there for her.

Hayley decided she would sit Gemma down for a talk when she got home tonight to see where her head was at and if she was in need of some motherly support.

Of course, Gemma would say no.

But, as a mother, she had to at least try.

Hayley stopped. She wasn't walking back to the office. She was absentmindedly heading straight toward the Harborside Hotel.

She knew why.

A little voice inside was screaming at her to go to Mickey Pritchett's hotel room and see if she could find something the police missed.

This was crazy.

Sergio had discovered she hadn't really heard a rumor about Curtis King owning a gun, but that she had ransacked the tour bus where he was staying and found the gun herself.

And given her recent arrest, she knew she was walking on eggshells around Sergio.

Or, as he would put it, walking on egg beaters.

Hayley knew Sergio's officers had already done a thorough search of the room. But, let's face it, who did the search?

Donnie and Earl?

Sergio was a great cop, but his support staff left a lot to be desired.

Hayley knew she was convincing herself, and before she realized it, she was standing outside the Harborside.

How would she even get inside the room?

The reception desk would never just hand over a key.

Lisa O'Donnell.

Lisa and Hayley had grown up on the same street together. They had sat next to each other in homeroom through all of middle school because their last names were close in the alphabet. Lisa had gotten pregnant by her boyfriend during junior year in high school and had the baby by senior homecoming. To her credit, she had stayed in school and graduated and then married her boyfriend, and, beating the odds, they were still married to this day with four more kids.

Only Mona beat her in the "Most Likely to Have Tons of Kids" competition.

Now that all her kids were in school, Lisa was bored during the day and the family needed extra cash, so she got a job cleaning houses. That led to her being hired at the Harborside to run housekeeping, and as far as Hayley knew, she was still working there.

Whipping out her cell, Hayley called Lisa. Her

number was stored in Hayley's contacts because they often worked on the same parents' committees at their kids' schools.

Lisa picked up on the second ring. "Hi, this is Lisa."

"Lisa, it's me, Hayley!"

"Omigod, how are you? I haven't seen you in ages."

"I've been great. I've been thinking about you a lot. We really need to catch up. Are you still working at the Harborside?"

"Yes, I'm there now. We should grab a drink sometime."

"Great! Let's do it now! I'm standing outside the hotel."

"You are . . . ?"

Hayley spotted Lisa looking out a window, confused.

Hayley smiled and waved at her.

"I'm actually working until five, but I have a break coming up," Lisa said.

Hayley knew Lisa would help her. She was just that kind of girl. She also knew Lisa was a huge Wade Springer fan, too, and would probably be willing to do just about anything for a ticket to his concert. Since Hayley was now officially an employee of Wade's and didn't need the tickets Liddy had secured for her, she could offer one to Lisa.

Lisa met her in the lobby and was ecstatic. She jumped up and down like one of those Willie Wonka kids who won the golden ticket. And she was extremely grateful. Not only did she give Hayley the key to Mickey Pritchett's room but she also outfitted Hayley with a maid's uniform and a pushcart stocked with towels, soaps, and shampoo so as not to arouse suspicion.

Hayley stopped at the second-floor room, adjusted

her white apron over her drab gray fitted dress, and knocked on the door.

No answer.

Lisa had told her the next guests had not arrived to check in yet. Hayley just wanted to make sure she wasn't going to walk in and surprise anyone. There was no police tape because Mickey's body had been found in the tour bus.

Hayley looked up and down the hall before inserting the key and entering the room.

It was spotless. Lisa was definitely good at her job.

At first glance, there didn't seem to be anything out of the ordinary. Mickey's belongings had obviously been removed.

She poked her head in the bathroom.

Nothing.

She opened the cabinets.

Drawers.

Still nothing.

She then sat on the bed, frustrated. The police, the cleaning staff, even other guests had all been in this room since Mickey's murder. What was she hoping to find?

Hayley stood up, looked around once more, decided there was nothing else to find, and started for the door. Suddenly her cell phone chirped, startling her, and she dropped the set of keys Lisa had given her.

She answered the phone. "Hello?"

"Hayley, it's me, Lisa. Some guests have just checked in and are on their way up in the elevator with the bellboy. You have to get out of there!"

"I'm leaving right now!"

Hayley stuffed her phone in the pocket of the apron and bent down to retrieve the keys. That's when she noticed something under the bed.

A glint.

Like a small flash.

She got down on her belly and reached under the bed, patting the carpet with her hand.

What was that?

She was about to pull her hand out when she touched something small and hard. She picked it up with her fingers and looked at it.

A diamond. It was an earring.

Hayley's heart nearly stopped.

A diamond earring.

And she recognized it.

The earring belonged to Liddy. Liddy had been in Mickey Pritchett's hotel room.

Chapter 20

Hayley's head was spinning as she raced out of the hotel room and back to the office. Everyone had already left for the day. She scooped up the phone and tried calling Liddy several times on her cell but she wasn't picking up. She knew if Liddy was showing a lot of properties today, she would undoubtedly stop by Randy's bar to decompress when she was finished.

Hayley finished up her work at the paper, checked on the kids to make sure they would be home for dinner, and then drove over to Drinks Like A Fish, where, as expected, Liddy sat on a stool at the bar, nursing a gin and tonic and chatting with Randy, who was refilling a snack bowl with trail mix.

Liddy lit up and smiled when she spotted Hayley walking toward her. "Hey there, how was your day? Mine was a nightmare. Do you know how challenging it is selling a foreclosed property in desperate need of some tender loving care? I just don't have the energy to make it presentable to buyers. I've slashed the price four times already."

"We need to talk," Hayley said.

"Sure, sweetie, what's on your mind?"

"Somewhere private."

"Hayley, the only one here is Randy and I have no secrets from him."

"Okay. We need to talk about Mickey Pritchett."

Randy's ears perked up behind the bar.

Liddy's face went ashen and she grabbed her purse, which was sitting on top of the bar. "Randy, we'll be outside."

Randy shot Hayley a look: What the hell was going on?

Hayley gave him a thin smile and followed Liddy, who was now shaking as she scurried across the wooden floor, her heels clicking, and out the back door into the alley. Hayley was right behind her.

Outside, Liddy spun around to face Hayley, and put on the most innocent face she could muster. "Now, who do you want to talk about again? Mickey who?"

"Mickey Pritchett. The recent murder victim. You do know who I am talking about, don't you?"

"Yes, Hayley, I have a computer with Internet access and I occasionally read the paper. I know who he is."

"How *well* do you know him?"

"Well, just what I heard from you. That he was a drunk and a mess and Wade fired him the night he was shot and killed."

"Don't lie to me, Liddy. You're my best friend. I expect better."

"What are you talking about?"

Hayley reached into her pocket and pulled out the earring. She dangled it in front of Liddy's face. Liddy's eyes popped open in surprise.

"You found it!"

She grabbed the earring from Hayley, and caressed it lovingly.

"Yes, I found it," Hayley said evenly. "In Mickey Pritchett's hotel room."

"Oh," Liddy said, staring at the sparkling diamond as if in a trance.

"What was it doing there, Liddy? What were *you* doing there?"

"Maybe he stole it. He could've been stalking me around town. I drive a Mercedes, after all, and maybe I left the door unlocked when I went into the Big Apple to get some coffee or something, and he grabbed it."

"He stole one earring. From your car. And hid it underneath his bed."

"Well, it doesn't sound so plausible when you say it like that."

"You know what I think? You come here for a drink almost every night after work. Mickey had been coming here, too, until Randy kicked him out. I think the two of you met and hooked up and while you were having sex, your earring fell off and into his bed and when the housekeeper came the next morning to change the sheets, it somehow slipped through the space between the mattress and the headboard and onto the rug underneath the bed. Am I getting warm here?"

"What do you think I am, some kind of slut, Hayley? I would never do something that sordid. Mickey Pritchett? He's a drunken redneck!"

"That's why you were so anxious for me to find out about Stacy Jo. You were terrified I was going to discover your secret and so you were desperate to send me off into another direction."

"I'm not that calculating!"

"Then look me in the eye and tell me I'm wrong."

"I don't have to prove anything to you."

"Tell me, Liddy. And I'll forget the whole thing. Because we've been friends too long and I trust you."

Liddy stared at Hayley, her eyes brimming with tears. And then she started crying. "I can't lie to you. I just can't. You're my best friend."

"So I'm right."

"Yes. I was having a rough day. I was feeling bloated and miserable and I had two houses fall out of escrow and I had too many cocktails and Mickey turned on the charm and I just fell for it. I didn't realize what an ass he was until it was all over and he asked me to leave because he was tired and I had to endure a walk of shame through the hotel lobby to my car. If I could do it all over again, I *never* would have gone back to the room with him."

Hayley hugged Liddy, who was sobbing. "Please don't judge me, Hayley."

"No one's judging you."

"But the town will if anyone finds out. I can't get a reputation for being the town skank. If people find out I slept with Mickey, it could affect my business."

"You should be more concerned about being a murder suspect."

"What are you talking about?"

"Liddy, you had a relationship with the victim."

"Oh, please, it was a one-night stand, not a relationship."

"But you were intimate with him, and you were in his hotel room, and at the very least, I'm sure Sergio will want to question you."

"No! No one can know I was ever there. Please, Hayley, you have to support me on this. It will ruin me if this gets out."

Hayley was torn. On the one hand, she didn't want to be the reason Liddy became the talk of the town. But, on the other hand, she didn't want Sergio getting mad at her for withholding vital information pertinent to the case.

Suddenly she sniffed the air. "Do you smell something?"

Liddy wiped away her tears. "No."

"It smells like smoke," Hayley said, and turned around. There was a green Dumpster a few feet away from them. Hayley spotted a waft of smoke floating up from behind it.

"Is there a fire?" Liddy asked, clutching Hayley's shirt.

"No. It's cigarette smoke. Who's there? Come out here right now."

There was a long pause.

And then Bruce Linney walked out from behind the Dumpster, a lit cigarette between his fingers.

"Omigod, Hayley, Bruce was having a drink at the bar before you arrived. I thought he left, but . . . ."

"Just came outside for a quick smoke," Bruce said, his eyes darting back and forth between Hayley and Liddy.

"How much did you hear?" Hayley asked.

"Pretty much all of it."

Liddy threw her hands to her mouth and gasped. "Oh, Hayley, talk to him. He can't print anything I said."

"Bruce, please . . . ," Hayley pleaded. But she knew it was hopeless. There was no way Bruce would ever ignore a bombshell like this.

"Sorry, Liddy. But I have to do my job," Bruce said, flicking the cigarette to the pavement and crushing it with the heel of his shoe.

He walked back inside with a smile on his face and Liddy fell into Hayley's arms, weeping.

Chapter 21

Hayley spent the next hour comforting Liddy, and assuring her that this would all eventually blow over, and people would quickly forget about her sordid association with the now-famous, boorish, and dead country fried redneck. And it wasn't as if everyone who read Bruce's articles didn't have their own embarrassing secrets and scandals. No one in town had the right to judge.

Liddy was already on the phone calling her lawyer to sue Bruce for libel, but Hayley gently dissuaded her, and convinced her to at least wait until the story actually came out in the paper.

After making Liddy promise to call Sergio in the morning and come clean about her connection to Mickey Pritchett, she waited until Liddy climbed behind the wheel of her Mercedes and roared off down the street before Hayley got in her Subaru wagon and drove home.

When she pulled into the driveway, Hayley instantly sensed something was wrong.

It was already dark outside and all the lights in the house were off. The kids hadn't come home yet, but the back door was wide open.

Hayley got out of her car and looked around. She had this strange, eerie feeling someone was watching her. She hurried inside and snapped on some lights in the kitchen.

Then it struck her what was wrong.

No Leroy.

Her spoiled little boy always greeted her at the door, running around in circles, begging for a treat. But tonight he was nowhere to be seen.

"Leroy, here boy!" Hayley called.

Nothing.

Maybe she accidentally shut him in her bedroom when she left for work this morning. She could only imagine the destruction he would cause to the bottom underwear drawer she'd left open.

She clomped up the stairs and switched on the upstairs light in the hallway, but her bedroom door was open. As were the doors to the kids' rooms.

So much for that theory.

Hayley ran back down the stairs and felt her phone buzzing in her back pocket. She pulled it out and checked the screen.

A text from Gemma.

She was uptown having ice cream with Reid and Carrie. Where was Dustin? She checked her watch.

His curfew wasn't for another twenty minutes. And he always breezed in at the last possible second.

Hayley went back outside.

"Leroy!"

Still nothing.

Hayley noticed a few lights on in some neighbors' houses but otherwise it was completely dark up and down the street. A wind kicked up and some orange and yellow fall leaves rustled past her feet. Just beyond her house was a thicket of trees swaying in the night breeze.

Where the hell did Leroy go?

He never strayed far from the house even when he spotted a wayward squirrel and chased after it. He always came back panting, his little pink tongue hanging out of his mouth.

Hayley suddenly heard something.

A whimpering.

Was it a dog?

Was it Leroy?

She listened intently.

Yes, it sounded like a dog in trouble.

Maybe bitten by something or in distress.

Hayley ran toward the woods, straining to pinpoint where the whimpering was coming from and frantically calling for Leroy.

She was now several hundred yards from the house, pushing her way through thick tree branches, still calling for Leroy.

She stopped and stood very still, trying to listen. Then she heard a sharp muzzled yelp, like a dog trying to call out but unable to, as if someone was forcibly keeping his mouth closed.

Hayley called out again. "Leroy! Where are you?"

She spun around, scanning the whole area, but the woods were pitch-black and she could hardly see anything.

Suddenly she heard more leaves rustling.

Something was running at her fast.

Maybe a deer?

No, it wasn't big enough to be a deer.

And, then, as it got closer, she saw a white flash.

And teeth.

A pronounced underbite.

It was Leroy!

Panting. His pink tongue flapping up and down.

He leaped off the ground and into Hayley's waiting

arms. She squeezed him to her chest as he excitedly licked her face.

"How on earth did you get way out here?" Hayley asked, half expecting her smart little pup to answer her.

A voice from behind startled her. "You really should talk to your kids about keeping the back door to your house locked."

Hayley spun around.

It was dark, but she recognized him right away.

It was Jesse DeSoto.

"What are you doing out here, Jesse?"

"Just taking a walk. Found your dog wandering around lost. You really should be more careful. He's a small little thing. A pack of coyotes could have snatched him up for their dinner."

"How did you know my back door was unlocked? Did you go into my house and take him?"

"I would never do that because entering someone's house without permission is against the law, and I'm out on bail, and doing something like that would send me right back behind bars."

"So you didn't steal my dog in order to lure me out here into the woods?"

"That sounds so creepy. You must watch a lot of TV crime shows about serial killers and shit like that."

Jesse DeSoto took a step toward Hayley.

She slowly backed away.

"Am I really that scary?"

Hayley wasn't about to answer him and give the kid that kind of power.

But Jesse saw she was shaking.

So was Leroy.

"Good. I'm glad I scare you. Because maybe you'll take what I say seriously."

"And what is that, Jesse?"

"Don't testify against me in court."

"Is that what this is all about? You stole a car and drove it into a tree. The case against you doesn't exactly hinge on my testimony, or my daughter's testimony."

"Yeah, but my lawyer says if you don't testify, we can maybe cut a deal and I can get off with a fine and some lame-shit community service. But if you do, it's just going to make me look bad and I could be sent to prison and I am not gonna let that happen."

"I'm sorry, Jesse. I can't help you. I saw you steal that car."

"And so did your daughter. Maybe I should go talk to her."

Leroy growled.

Hayley gently petted his curly white fur and shushed him before raising her eyes to meet Jesse's.

"Come anywhere near my daughter, and I will kill you myself, and save the state the cost of your trial."

Jesse opened his mouth and laughed, disgusting Hayley with his stained, crooked teeth.

Didn't his mother believe in dentists?

Then he caught the look on Hayley's face—the determination, the anger—and suddenly her threat didn't seem so far-fetched.

His smile faded.

But Jesse kept up his bravado.

"I'd like to see you try," he said, a crack in his voice.

And he ran off into the night.

Hayley watched him disappear into the trees. She clutched Leroy, who was snuggling into her chest, exhausted from his ordeal. Hayley knew deep down that Jesse was just full of empty threats. He was a messed-up kid who was in a lot of trouble and probably panicking over the fact that he was facing serious jail time.

Still, he had entered her house and taken her dog.

She should call Sergio and report him and maybe get him thrown back in jail until the trial.

But she had no proof.

And going after Jesse would just exascerbate the situation.

But warning Gemma to stick close to her friends was her utmost priority. There was no way she wanted her daughter in close proximity to any danger.

Just the thought of it made her shudder.

Chapter 22

Three nights later was Wade Springer's first charity concert. When Hayley showed up at the Criterion Theatre, Billy Ray escorted her to a trailer parked out back, which served as Wade's makeshift dressing room. It was bigger than the whole first floor of Hayley's house. Framed gold records of Wade's singles adorned the wall. A Country Music Association award that Hayley at first assumed was a lamp sat on a side table. The furniture was plush and cushiony, the bar was fully stocked, and there was an entire buffet of assorted cheeses and finger foods set up off to the side.

Wade sat on the couch in a pair of crisp, dark blue jeans and a black shirt open enough to show off hints of his curly chest hair. His cowboy hat rested next to him and he was strumming his guitar.

After Billy Ray had ushered her inside, he then stepped back out, closing the door behind him.

Wade looked up and smiled.

"Hey there, stranger," he said. "Haven't seen you around much lately."

"It's been a crazy couple of days," Hayley said. "I hope you've been getting your meals on time."

"Oh, yeah, and they're so mouth-wateringly delicious, I just may have to kidnap you when I'm done here and whisk you away with me."

Hayley's heart fluttered.

He looked so handsome, and the scent of his cologne wafted over to her and made her nose tingle.

"So what's been keeping you so busy?" Wade asked.

"My work at the office, my column, my kids," she said, shrugging. "The usual stuff."

Hayley didn't want to admit to her own haphazard investigation into the Mickey Pritchett murder, or her recent run-in with town thug Jesse DeSoto, which had rocked her world off its orbit, and how she was terrified the creep might come within spitting distance of her daughter, Gemma.

She had spent the whole day lecturing Gemma on the phone to keep an eye out, to definitely not separate from her friends, and to come home right after school and keep the doors of the house locked.

Gemma wasn't nearly as concerned. She knew Jesse DeSoto and said she had no doubts she could take him in a fight. And if for some reason she couldn't, her boyfriend Reid would protect her. He was twice Jesse's size.

That was some comfort, but Hayley was still haunted by the delinquent's threats.

"Why don't you have some food?" Wade said. "There's enough there to feed the entire Grand Ole Opry. I don't know why they stock this place with so much. Seems like such a waste."

Hayley wandered over to the table and speared a fresh shrimp with a toothpick, slathered on some cocktail sauce, and popped it in her mouth.

Wade patted the couch. "Now, why don't you sashay on over here and take a load off, Hayley. There's something I want to share with you."

Hayley did as she was told.

She sashayed. And sat down on the couch.

Hayley made sure she was as far away from Wade as possible. She didn't know why she did that. But she was nervous and jumpy and didn't want to give Wade the wrong impression.

Wade gave her a funny look and then shuffled over closer to her. He strummed his guitar some more and started to sing.

A quiet ballad.

About a woman in love with a man.

And how she gets the man to fall in love with her by cooking for him.

And how the way to a man's heart is through his stomach.

Exactly what everyone assumed she was doing with Wade.

Did Wade actually believe this?

Hayley shifted uncomfortably, her eyes downcast, her face burning with embarrassment.

Wade continued singing the chorus.

"The way to a man's heart."

That had to be the title of the song.

And then he segued into another refrain.

How the man couldn't stop thinking about the woman's food.

And how she put so much tender loving care into each and every dish, it was as if they were her own children.

And how a man like him couldn't help but fall in love with a woman like that.

And how, when you've found someone you love that much, there's always room for dessert.

Wade sang the chorus again. *The way to a man's heart* . . .

Hayley reached out and grabbed the hand that was strumming the guitar strings. "Wade, please, stop."

"What's wrong? You don't like the song?"

"It's beautiful. But I'm just humiliated that you think by cooking for you, I'm trying to get you to fall in love with me. I admit, I tried to meet you through my cooking, but it was more as a fan meeting her idol. I had no pretensions that you and I would ever . . ."

"You think this song is about you?"

"Well, you wrote it. You tell me."

"Hayley, I didn't write this song."

"Then who did?"

"Mickey Pritchett."

It was like a kick in the solar plexus.

Hayley reared back, her mouth agape. "Mickey? Are you serious? How?"

"Mickey's been an aspiring songwriter for years. He's tried to sell me so many songs, I lost count. But none of them have ever really spoken to me. I kept putting him off, telling him to keep at it, work harder. I was beginning to think he just didn't have what it takes, until he showed up with this one."

"Oh. Hearing the lyrics, it just sounded a lot like it was based on me and you," Hayley said, deeply embarrassed.

"Maybe it was. I read your column about me. You wanting to impress me with your country fried chicken recipe. Mickey could've seen it, too, and been inspired to write this song."

It sounded plausible.

But no less embarrassing.

"I was going to try it out tonight," Wade said.

"Tonight?" Hayley gasped, realizing the whole town was now seated in the theater and would immediately know who Wade was probably singing about.

"I won't if you don't want me to," Wade said. "But I was hoping to record it on my next album and donate all the proceeds to Mickey's brother Clarence. He's a sweet and kind young man. Nothing like Mickey. He's just trying to make something of himself and could really use a little money to give him a boost."

Now Hayley felt like a heel.

She couldn't stand in the way of Clarence getting a little financial relief from his brother doing doing one thing right: writing a hit song recorded by Wade Springer.

"Of course, you have to sing it," Hayley said. "I want you to."

Wade smiled. "I'm just joshin' ya, Hayley. I'm not going to sing it tonight. I still have some work I want to do on it first. I just wanted to see your face when you thought the whole town was about to hear it."

Hayley gave him a playful slap on his arm.

She could feel the muscles.

Now her whole body tingled.

Wade gave her a hug.

He squeezed so tight, Hayley couldn't breathe.

Or maybe it was his cologne.

Either way, she wasn't complaining.

Wade slowly pulled away and stared at Hayley, a grave look on his face. "Hayley, I just want to say, I'm so, so sorry for all this trouble I've brought to your town."

"You . . . ?"

"Well, it's my tour and Mickey's murder has caused all kinds of chaos and I can't help but feel responsible . . ."

"This isn't your fault, Wade. It's becoming clear Mickey had a lot of enemies. That has nothing to do with you. So don't worry. Sergio is going to solve this case and clear up this whole awful mess."

There was a rap on the door and from outside they heard Billy Ray shouting, "Five minutes, Wade!"

"Now forget about all that, because you know what they say . . . ," Hayley said, smiling.

Wade nodded and they both said in unison, "The show must go on."

Wade slung his guitar over his shoulder and grabbed his cowboy hat off the couch and opened the door for Hayley.

The two of them stepped outside. Wade took her by the hand and led her through the door to the backstage of the theater. He escorted her to the side, hidden out of view from the audience by the curtain, and put his hands on her shoulders.

"Best view in the house," he said, reaching around and giving her a quick peck on the cheek. Hayley resisted the urge to spin around and grab him by the neck and plant a big kiss on his lips.

Especially after hearing that song.

Wade stepped around her and sauntered out on the stage, and the crowd erupted in thunderous applause. Even Hayley found herself clapping and whistling and hooting and hollering.

On Wade's cue, the band started playing and Wade launched into one of his biggest hits—and Hayley's favorite—"I'm Not a Wife Beater, I Just Wear One." Hayley started bopping up and down to the music.

She had dreamt of this moment.

Seeing Wade Springer live.

She never imagined she would be his personal guest backstage.

Sometimes life really was full of surprises.

And, then, suddenly, without warning, Hayley felt something thrown around her neck like a rope or a cord, and it instantly tightened like a noose. She clawed at it with her fingers she was yanked back, out of the lights, into a dark corner backstage. She struggled.

There was someone pressed up against her from behind, pulling on the cord. She couldn't breathe.

Omigod.

Someone was strangling her.

She saw Billy Ray on the other side of the stage and reached out to him, trying to scream for help.

But he couldn't see her.

And the cord around her neck prevented her from screaming.

Her attacker wasn't letting up, choking her until she was gasping for air.

And he was strong.

Whenever she tried to break free, he anticipated her move and squeezed harder, until she was about to pass out and her eyes rolled back in her head.

Chapter 23

Hayley knew she was moments away from slipping into unconsciousness. She had to act fast. She worked her hands up to the cord and tried to pull it away from her neck but her assailant was holding tight.

She managed to focus her eyes again for a split second, and she could see Wade standing out on the stage in the spotlight, strumming his guitar, at one with the audience, singing his heart out, blissfully unaware that Hayley was being strangled to death only a couple hundred feet away.

The music, so deafening just a few moments before, was now fading into nothingness as the vision of Wade became cloudy and blurry and she knew she was seconds away from blacking out.

Hayley went limp and fell back against her attacker's chest, and for a second he thought she had passed out. He relaxed his grip just a bit, allowing Hayley the moment she needed.

She thrust her head back with her last ounce of strength, cracking the man's nose with a sickening crunch. She heard a wail in her ear as her attacker let go completely. She saw blood spurt past her as she lifted her right leg and nailed it down on the guy's foot.

He stumbled back, allowing her to rip the cord off her neck and hurl it to the ground. Then she felt a hand shoving her forward. Her whole body smacked against a giant speaker set off just out of view of the audience.

The impact knocked the wind out of her and she fell to the ground, her forehead cracking against the hardwood floor.

She was going to have a nasty bruise.

But she was alive.

At least for now.

Hayley scrambled to her feet and spun around to get a look at her attacker. He was dressed all in black and had his hands in front of his face to conceal his identity. And then he whirled around and bolted out the backstage door into the parking lot where Wade's mobile dressing room was parked.

Still woozy from her head hitting the floor, Hayley stumbled after him, determined not to allow him to get away. She went to open the door he'd run out, but it didn't budge. She stepped back, and threw a flying kick at the door.

She heard a sharp crack but it still wasn't opening.

She tried again, insistent that those karate classes she'd spent a fortune on for Dustin—and spent hours watching—would somehow pay off.

And, finally, they did.

Another kick and the door flew open.

A piece of wood her attacker had jammed up against the doorknob snapped in half and went flying in two different directions.

Hayley raced outside.

She spotted the attacker, sitting atop a Harley-Davidson, strapping on a black helmet, and frantically trying to kick-start his motorcycle.

Hayley started yelling and running at him.

Which, upon reflection, was a really dumb thing to do since she was chasing after an attempted murderer with no backup.

But she was pumped full of adrenaline and not thinking clearly, and she definitely didn't want this creep getting away.

The attacker kept glancing up at Hayley and back down at his kick-starter.

It was a race against time and she was only a few feet away when the Harley finally roared to life, and the attacker cranked the handlebar accelerator and took off with a cloud of smoke trailing out from the exhaust pipe.

Hayley stopped in her tracks and bent over, trying to catch her breath.

Suddenly a pickup truck veered around the corner into the parking lot, cutting off the motorcyclist, who had to swerve to avoid a head-on collision.

The Harley spun out and the attacker lost control and crashed into a Dumpster. He was momentarily stunned.

The bike was tipped over but the engine was still running.

Hayley saw Mona getting out of the truck in her bulky sweatshirt and faded jeans. Obviously dressed for the concert.

"Mona, don't let him get away!" Hayley screamed.

That's all Mona needed to hear.

She advanced on the motorcyclist, arms stretched out like a New England Patriots linebacker trying to stop a touchdown.

The attacker hustled to his feet and lifted his Harley off the ground and swung a leg over just as Mona reached him. She grabbed the back of his jacket and tried pulling him off again, but she was a hair too late as he revved the bike and roared off.

Mona was able to hold on for a few seconds, being dragged along behind him, but she eventually lost her grip and went hurtling to the ground.

Hayley's attacker fled off on the Harley into the night.

Hayley raced to Mona, who was rolling over on her back and clutching her hands to her side.

"Shit, that hurts!" Mona spat out.

"Come on, I'll get you to the hospital."

"I don't need no doctor. I got six rambunctious kids, last count. This is nothing compared to the physical abuse I take from them every day."

Hayley helped Mona to her feet.

"Who the hell was that?" Mona asked.

"I don't know. But he tried to strangle me backstage during Wade's first song."

"What?" a voice screamed from behind Hayley.

It was Liddy, who was jumping out the passenger-side door of Mona's pickup. "Somebody tried to kill you?"

"I have the welt on my neck and a bunch of bruises to prove it," Hayley said, checking Mona for injuries.

Mona swatted Hayley's hand away. "I told you, I'm fine. No point fussing over me. Let's just call the cops and report this."

"Can't we wait until after the concert? I've already missed the first few songs," Liddy said.

Mona looked at Hayley. "Tell me she didn't just say that out loud."

"Well, I'm sorry," Liddy cried. "But it's not my fault. We wouldn't have been so late if your wild-child Ethan hadn't tried to microwave Judy's pet hamster."

Hayley gasped. "One of your kids tried to microwave Mr. Wiggles?"

"He's fine. He couldn't quite reach the start button before I caught him," Mona said before turning her attention to Liddy. "But you catching the concert isn't the hot topic right now. Finding this Jack the Ripper guy who tried to take out Hayley is what we should be concerned about."

"You're right, I'm sorry," Liddy said, chastised. "We should call Sergio so he can put out an ATM or ABC or whatever it is they put out to catch criminals."

"APB," Mona said, annoyed.

"Yeah, whatever," Liddy moaned.

"Really, I'm fine, Liddy, if you want to go inside, Mona and I can handle it from here," Hayley said.

Liddy looked at Hayley expectantly, a smile forming on her face, but then she shifted focus to Mona, who was scowling and shaking her head.

"No, forget it," Liddy said. "I'm not going to let Mona hold this over me for years to come. But this proves I'm just as good a friend to you as she is, Hayley. And don't let her try to tell you otherwise."

"Can we discuss who is a better friend to Hayley *after* we call the cops?" Mona said, ready to lose it.

Liddy threw her hands up in surrender and nodded.

Then she pulled off her leopard-print scarf and handed it to Hayley.

"Here, honey, wear this," Liddy said. "It's Hermes."

"It's beautiful, but, why?"

"You don't want Wade seeing that disgusting splotchy red mark on your neck."

Mona growled and nearly lunged at Liddy, whose eyes popped open in surprise.

"What? What did I say?" Liddy shrieked.

Hayley held Mona back with one hand as she flipped open her cell phone and dialed 911 with the other.

Chapter 24

Wade Springer rushed to Hayley's side at the Bar Harbor police station once he walked off stage following his final encore and heard the disturbing news of the attack.

Hayley was just finishing up giving a statement to Sergio when Wade arrived. She spent the next half hour trying to convince Wade not to cancel his second concert, for the sake of the college.

Wade was resistant at first. The whole situation was getting too dangerous, and someone trying to strangle Hayley backstage while he was singing really shook him. It was the last straw.

But Hayley insisted he not disappoint the students and faculty at the College of the Atlantic who were counting on those ocean research funds. They went back and forth for a few rounds before Wade finally saw the grim determination in Hayley's eyes. She was not going to let this one incident jeopardize all the good the concerts would do.

No way. No how.

Wade put his arms around Hayley and squeezed her tightly. "I'm just so glad you're safe, darling."

"I'm fine," Hayley said. "I've been through worse, believe me."

"Do you need a ride back to the hotel, Wade?" Liddy asked, appearing out of nowhere and sidling up next to him. "My car's right outside."

"No, ma'am. Billy Ray will take me back. But thank you just the same," Wade said, then turned to Hayley. "I've rented the adjoining suite for you and your kids at the hotel. Curtis will make sure nobody bothers you."

"That's not necessary, Wade. My kids and I will be fine."

"I don't want you staying at your house tonight. If this attacker knows where you live, he just might try again."

"Mona's already picked up the kids and taken them over to my brother's house. He lives with the police chief. I don't think anybody's dumb enough to go after me there."

Wade nodded, satisfied. "All right, then. I'll see you tomorrow. But don't be bringing me breakfast or anything. I'll be fine. You just get some rest and spend time with your kids."

Hayley was going to protest, but realized that after what she had just been through, Wade was right. She just wanted to be with her kids. "Okay."

Wade reached down and gave her a peck on the cheek and then sauntered out of the station.

Hayley turned to Liddy, who had a crushed look on her face.

"What is it, Liddy? What's wrong?"

"Ma'am? How old does he think I am to be calling me ma'am?"

"It's a southern thing."

"Well, it's rude," Liddy said, spinning around and sweeping out of the station. "Come on. I'll drop you off at Randy's."

Hayley dutifully followed.

Gemma and Dustin had only been told sketchy details about the attack backstage, because Mona didn't want to scare them, but Hayley knew they would find out all the gory details at school on Monday, true or not, so she thought it was best to sit them down in Randy's living room and tell them everything she knew. They were both just relieved that their mother wasn't seriously harmed.

The comforting smell of freshly baked chocolate chip cookies wafted in from the kitchen and Randy brought out a tray of hot cocoa with marshmallows for Hayley and the kids. They were going to have a family slumber party without the scary movies, because they had all had enough frights for one night.

Instead, Randy downloaded a Kristen Wiig comedy from Netflix and it played in the background as Hayley, Randy, Gemma, and Dustin munched on cookies and sipped cocoa.

Hayley felt relaxed for the first time in days. She just wanted to sit with her brother and kids and forget all about the trauma of nearly dying tonight.

"So who do you think tried taking you out?" Dustin asked.

So much for that.

"I have no idea, Dustin," Hayley said. "I'd rather not talk about it."

"But if you were to guess," Gemma jumped in. "Do you think it's the same person who shot Mickey Pritchett?"

"Maybe. Who knows?" Hayley said, grabbing another cookie off the plate.

"That's enough, you guys," Randy said sternly. "Your mother needs to stay calm and rest and she doesn't need you two shooting questions at her and bringing up unpleasant memories. Now watch the movie."

Gemma and Dustin sighed and settled in on the cushiony couch and stared at the TV.

Randy poured some more miniature marshmallows from the bag into his cocoa and glanced at Hayley. Proceeding gingerly, he said, "Personally, I don't think it was anyone related to the Pritchett killing. My money's on that delinquent Jesse DeSoto."

"Randy!"

"You're right. I'm sorry," Randy said, popping a marshmallow in his mouth. "Let's not talk about it."

Hayley tried concentrating on the movie, but her mind was racing.

She cocked her head in Randy's direction. "So what has Sergio told you about the murder so far? Any leads we don't know about?"

"You know I can't talk about that," Randy said.

"You're right. I'm sorry."

She knew she just had to wait a few seconds for him to break. Randy was a die-hard gossip. Her kids knew it, too, because Dustin picked up the remote and hit the mute button on the TV so they could hear what he'd say.

"Uncle Randy, we all know you're going to talk. You'll make us promise not to say anything and after we do you'll spill everything."

"Oh, is that right? You think you know me so well, but you don't. I'm not going to make you promise because I'm not going to tell you anything."

Gemma picked up the plate and held it in front of Randy.

He took another cookie. "Thank you."

They waited.

It was only a matter of time.

The silence in the room was deafening.

"If I *did* tell you something, do you promise not to say anything?"

Hayley, Gemma, and Dustin all scooted closer to Randy.

"Now wait a minute. I said *if* I tell you . . ."

"We promise, we promise," Gemma said. "What?"

Randy looked at Hayley, who crossed her heart with her index finger.

Randy took a deep breath and exhaled. "Okay, here's the weird thing. Sergio and his team first suspected Mickey stole the tour bus to leave town, and that the killer either flagged him down or was with him when he left. But when they combed the bus, there was no evidence he was leaving. All of his belongings were back in his hotel room."

"So where was he going?" Gemma asked.

"No one but Mickey and the killer knows that."

"Do you think the killer shot Mickey in his hotel room, and then put the body in the bus, drove to Albert Meadow, and set it on fire?" Hayley asked.

"No. Someone would have heard the gunshot or at least seen someone dragging his body out of the hotel," Randy said. "My guess is the killer forced Mickey into the bus at gunpoint and then drove it to Albert Meadow where it's quiet and more remote and that's where the killer shot him before setting the bus on fire."

"Is that what Sergio thinks?"

"Yes. Mickey's suitcase was open on the bed and half his clothes were packed. Somebody must have shown up at the door when he was getting ready to leave," Randy said. "And there was a grocery bag on the table with some toiletries and snacks and booze. There was no receipt, but the bag was from the Shop 'n Save."

"So Mickey went shopping before he was killed. Does anyone at the store remember seeing him?"

"No, that's what's so strange. The Shop 'n Save is dead that time of night so it doesn't make sense that no one saw him enter or leave. Not even the cashier who was on duty. She would've had to check him out. And Sergio went through all the receipts and there was nothing in their records that showed anyone buying those items. And there was nothing on the surveillance cameras that showed Mickey was ever inside the store."

"So it would've been impossible for him to shoplift all of that stuff," Gemma said.

"Mickey's cell phone records show he called the store at eight thirty-five and talked with someone for five minutes, but Sergio interviewed everyone on duty—the cashier, the manager, the bag boy—and they all deny ever talking to Mickey."

"So who did he talk to?" Hayley asked, more to herself.

Dustin gasped. "Spanky!"

"Spanky McFarland?" Gemma asked incredulously.

"Yes! He's a stock boy at the Shop 'n Save. Uncle Randy, was Spanky working that night?"

"Yes, I saw his name on the interview list. But he told Sergio he never spoke to Mickey on the phone or in person. Ever."

"He's lying," Dustin said, slapping his palm on the coffee table.

"How do you know?" Hayley asked.

"Because Spanky was hanging out at Rosalie's Pizza after school a few days ago and he was throwing money around, buying all the kids pizza, trying to be Mr. Popular. He said he got a big tip making a delivery."

"So why would he lie about that?" Randy asked.

"The booze!" Gemma screamed. "Spanky's underage. He's not allowed to deliver alcohol. But if there was the promise of a big tip, I bet Spanky just bagged everything Mickey wanted and snuck it out of the store."

"Which would explain why there was no receipt," Randy said.

"And Spanky works there, so he knows where all the surveillance cameras are located! He probably smuggled the bag out the back, knowing he wouldn't wind up on tape," Dustin said.

"So Spanky McFarland may have been the last one to see Mickey Pritchett alive," Randy said.

"And quite possibly he may have seen the killer," Hayley said.

"Or *is* the killer!" Dustin shouted, arms in the air.

Hayley grimaced.

Her kids were getting way too excited about this case.

Island Food & Spirits
by
Hayley Powell

With winter fast approaching, I realized we just didn't have too many weekends or evenings left to enjoy the things we like to do outside, because we all get so busy. So I decided to take a break, wrangle up my kids, and call my friend Mona to invite her and her own kids to go on a picnic with us. I knew she would appreciate the break. Her brood loves hanging out with mine, mostly because they look up to my kids as an older brother and sister.

I didn't feel like a picnic at the beach. So Mona and I piled everyone in her van and headed into Acadia National Park since it's practically in our own back yard, and I knew we'd quickly find a nice private area for the kids to run around so Mona and I could relax and catch up on some long-overdue gossip.

After finding a scenic spot, we pulled over and parked. All the kids tumbled out of the van and went wildly running off as if we'd just been on a ten-hour excursion instead of a ten-minute ride to our picnic area.

While my two older kids kept an eye on Mona's hellions, she and I spread out a couple of blankets and began to unpack our joint picnic baskets of thick sliced ham-and-cheese sandwiches on homemade country oatmeal bread, Mona's specialty! I brought a country potato salad, coleslaw, and thermoses of sweet tea, as I am still exploring good ole home-style country cooking as a part-time employee of Wade Springer's. (I might have previously mentioned that.)

Anyway, the kids were having a grand time exploring, climbing rocks and trees, which thankfully allowed Mona and me to finally have some good old girl time to catch up on everything going on in our lives.

Which took about five minutes.

It wasn't long before the kids got tired of running around and wandered back over to us, stomachs growling. So we all gathered around for a delicious cold lunch.

But, as usual, all good things must come to an end. Little Timmy started scratching himself to the point where Mona finally had to shout, "For God's sake, Timmy, what is with all that scratching?"

That was just about the time Judy started scratching her arms. And I'm sure you know what's coming. One by one, *all* the kids began digging and scratching at their arms and legs, jumping up and down, yelling and complaining louder and louder.

Mona and I just stared at each other. It was like watching a horror movie! Then we sprang into action, grabbing the kids one by one to inspect them. At first I suspected we were sitting atop a giant red ants' nest because I started feeling itchy myself. But, Mona, waving her arms, screamed, "Don't touch them, Hayley, it's poison ivy!"

That did it. My daughter went into full panic mode, wailing, "Oh, no! My face! My face! Tell me it's not on my face!" Then she pushed and shoved her way past the furiously scratching kids, actually knocking some of them down to the ground, which made them cry even louder as she ran to the van to inspect every inch of her face in the side mirror. That's my daughter! Always thinking of others!

My daughter spied a small red bump on her face and let out such a bloodcurdling howl, it startled the little ones into silence for a split second. I swear to you, I heard an answering howl from a coyote in the distance.

Luckily, Mona once again took control and began barking orders for everyone to get in the van, sit as still as they could, and don't touch anything or anyone (especially me and her!). I threw what was left of our picnic lunches into the baskets and tossed them in the back of the van, then jumped in the front beside Mona. She looked at me and let out a big sigh as we peeled away for home. I knew what she was thinking.

Why didn't we just follow through with our plan, after high school, to travel to California, find our fame and fortune, and lead wonderfully exciting lives? Well, that obviously didn't pan out so we both just smiled and shrugged our shoulders.

When we arrived at Mona's house, she raided the pantry for boxes of oatmeal she had stocked up on for her country bread and prepared an oatmeal bath in her tub for the kids, to relieve their itching.

Suffice it to say, the next time we go on a picnic, I'm going to suggest we go to the beach for some swimming. What possibly could go wrong there? Sharks don't make it up to the Maine coast all that often, do they?

Well, after that exhausting adventure, I found myself with an extra thermos of sweet tea, so I decided to make myself a very strong sweet tea cocktail.

Today, I'm going to share with you Mona's country oatmeal bread recipe. But, first, I recommend you start with a nice refreshing whiskey sweet tea!

Whiskey Sweet Tea

½ ounce whiskey
½ ounce Southern Comfort
Sweet tea
Lemon slice for garnish (optional)
Ice

In a rocks glass, fill with ice and add whiskey and Southern Comfort. Top with sweet tea. Stir and add lemon slice for garnish and enjoy!

Mona's Country Oatmeal Bread

1 cup boiling water
1 cup old-fashioned oats
1 package active dry yeast
⅓ cup warm water
¼ cup honey
1 tablespoon butter
1 teaspoon salt
3 to 3½ cups all purpose flour
Additional oats and melted butter

In a large bowl, add oats and boiling water to combine; let stand until warm. In a small bowl, dissolve yeast in the ⅓ cup warm water, then add to oat mixture. Add honey, butter, salt, and 2 cups of the flour; beat until smooth. Add enough of the remaining flour to form a soft dough. Turn onto a floured surface and knead until smooth and elastic, about 5 to 7 minutes.

Place in a greased bowl and let rise in a warm place for about an hour until doubled. Punch the dough down and shape into a loaf. Place in a greased 8-inch by 4-inch loaf pan, brush with the melted butter, and sprinkle with oats. Place in a warm spot for about 30 minutes until doubled again. Bake at 350 degrees for 50 to 55 minutes or until golden brown. Yummy!

Chapter 25

Hayley waited until early the next morning before stepping out onto Randy's front porch—so as not to wake anybody inside the house—and calling Spanky McFarland's mother, with whom she was friendly because they had once shared a table at the library bake sale.

Carla McFarland's apple turnovers were to die for.

And Carla enjoyed Hayley's sense of humor and love of sweets.

But today Carla seemed tense and out of sorts when she picked up the phone. Hayley chalked it up to her calling so early. It was just a few minutes past eight in the morning.

"Yes. Who is this?" Carla barked.

"Hi, Carla, it's Hayley Powell."

"Oh, Hayley. I thought you were a telemarketer or someone trying to sell me something."

"I'm sorry I'm calling so early, but I was hoping to speak to Spanky."

"Spanky? I'm afraid he's not here. He's gone kayaking with Nate."

Nate was Spanky's older brother, a senior in high school.

"Do you know when he'll be back?"

"Not until later this afternoon. Why? What's he done now?"

"Nothing. I'm just planning a surprise birthday party for Dustin, and I was hoping Spanky might help me come up with names for the guest list."

"Oh, good. I thought he was in some kind of trouble again."

"Oh, no, of course not."

Hayley decided not to mention the whole stealing groceries and alcohol and selling them for a profit scheme.

Why add to Carla's stress so early in the day?

"Well, I'll give Spanky the message and have him call you. And I'll be sure to make some of my apple turnovers for the party."

"You are too good to me, Carla. Thank you. By the way, I used to love kayaking. Where did the boys go?"

Actually, Hayley had never been kayaking in her life.

"They set off from the beach in front of the Bar Harbor Inn and were going to go around Frenchman's Bay."

"Oh, that sounds lovely. Well, you have a great Saturday, Carla."

"You, too, Hayley."

Hayley quickly ended the call and speed-dialed Mona at her house.

When Mona picked up, Hayley could hear screaming kids in the background.

"What?" Mona yelled, even more tense than Carla had sounded.

Why was Hayley the only morning person?

"Mona, it's me. I need to borrow one of your

motorboats. I need to track down a couple of kayaks somewhere in Frenchman's Bay.

"Of course you do. Meet me at the pier in five. If I don't get out of this house, I think I'm going to have a stroke! Hold on."

Hayley heard rustling on the other end of the line.

Then Mona was screaming, "Do not, I repeat, do not throw eggs at your sister! I'm warning you! Don't you do it! Aw, hell, Hayley, make it ten. I have to chase down one of my kids."

Click.

She was gone.

Hayley considered waking Dustin and taking him with her. Spanky might be more inclined to talk if a friend was there. But, then again, if she had to strong-arm the kid, she didn't want to embarrass Dustin or damage his friendship with Spanky in any way.

She hopped in her Subaru and drove down to the town pier solo, parking in an empty spot.

Waiting by the dock were a couple of Mona's boats tied to wooden posts sticking above the water.

Fifteen minutes passed.

Then thirty.

Finally, Mona's pickup truck came roaring down the hill from the center of town and pulled into the spot next to Hayley's.

When Mona jumped out of the truck, there were bits of yellow scrambled egg in her hair and juice stains on her sweatshirt.

"It's friggin' World War Three at my house. Thank God you called. I was going stir crazy. It started when two of my rugrats wanted to watch *SpongeBob* and the oldest insisted on *iCarly* and it all went south from there."

Hayley hugged Mona and their cheeks touched.

"Your face is sticky," Hayley said.

"Maple syrup. I got caught in the cross fire."

"Is your husband watching the kids?"

"If you call zoning out in front of the TV glued to a ball game while the walls of the house collapse around him watching the kids, then yes, he's watching the kids."

Mona barreled down the walkway to the dock, wiping her face with her sleeve, and then cracked her knuckles and set about untying a small army green boat with an outboard motor from the dock.

"So who are we looking for?"

"Spanky McFarland."

"The stock boy from the Shop 'n Save?"

"Yes. He may have information about the death of Mickey Pritchett and I don't want to wait until the end of the day to talk to him because as you know, time is of the essence when it comes to murder investigations and—"

Mona held up a hand. "You don't need to explain. I'm just happy to be out of the house. Let's go."

Mona steadied the boat and waved Hayley aboard and then she jumped in after her, tossed Hayley an orange life jacket, and yanked the cord until the motor sputtered to life.

Within seconds, they were chugging out into the harbor and around the small islands that dotted Frenchman's Bay.

The bright morning sun beat down on them.

And she forgot her sunscreen.

Great.

It took about twenty minutes before Hayley and Mona spotted two kayaks off in the distance gliding across the water at an impressive speed. Mona steered the motor in their direction and they soon caught up with them.

Hayley stood up, keeping her balance, and waved her arms at the boys. "Spanky! Nate! It's me, Hayley Powell! Dustin's mother!"

The two boys stopped paddling and exchanged confused looks.

Nate spoke first. "Hi, Mrs. Powell. What are you doing out here?"

"I need to talk to Spanky."

Spanky shifted nervously in his kayak. "About what?"

"Mickey Pritchett."

That was all he needed to hear.

Spanky suddenly started frantically paddling in the opposite direction.

"Is this kid serious?" Mona asked, shaking her head.

She gunned the motor and the boat shot off ahead of Spanky.

Mona veered in front of him, cutting him off.

"Give it up, Frankie. This is a Yamaha outboard with twenty-five horsepower. You're not going to out-paddle it."

"It's Spanky," the kid mumbled.

"What?"

"His name is Spanky, not Frankie," Hayley offered.

"What the hell does it matter? I can't even keep the names of my own kids straight."

Hayley patted Mona's back, giving her the signal that she would take over now, so Mona plopped down on the wooden seat in the boat and started combing her hair for egg bits.

Hayley smiled at Spanky. "Now, Spanky, I don't want to get you into any kind of trouble . . ."

"I didn't do anything!" Spanky protested.

His brother Nate was watching the scene curiously.

"I know you took some groceries over to Mickey

Pritchett at the Harborside Hotel the night he was
killed."

Spanky was shaking now. "You can't prove it!
Nobody saw me take anything!"

Nate rolled his eyes. "You did *what?*"

"Nothing," Hayley said. "I don't care how you got
the groceries or what they were or how much Mickey
paid you for them."

"You don't?" Spanky asked, his eyes as big as saucers.

"No. It's none of my business and, like I said, I'm
not here to get you into trouble. I just need to ask you
a couple of questions about Mickey, about when you
brought him the bag of groceries. What did he say
to you?"

"Not much. He was kind of a jerk. He seemed . . . I
don't know . . . like something was on his mind."

"He was preoccupied?"

"Yes. And nervous or agi . . . agi . . ."

"Agitated?"

"Yeah, that's the word. Agitated. And he was eating
a greasy piece of chicken and it was all over his face
and he kept wiping his hands on his shirt. It was kind
of gross."

Hayley resisted the urge to defend her chicken. It
was not greasy!

"What else do you remember?"

"Nothing. He gave me my money and then shut the
door in my face and I went home because my shift at
the store was over."

"So you didn't see anyone else around when you
got there?"

"No. Nobody."

Hayley sighed.

She was going to get sunburned for nothing.

She turned to Mona. "Let's head back to shore, Mona."

"Only when I was leaving."

"Wait. What did you say?"

"I didn't see anyone when I showed up. Only when I was leaving."

"Who was it?"

"I don't know. It was a girl. She walked right past me and knocked on the guy's door and he let her in."

"Girl? You mean a woman? Stacy Jo Stanton? Did she have blond hair and big boobs?"

Nate chuckled.

All teenage boys chuckle at the mention of boobs.

Spanky shook his head. "No. Not really. I don't remember much about her. She wasn't exactly a hottie."

"How old would you say she was?"

Spanky shrugged. "Way older than me, like a sophomore or junior."

So, about a year or two older.

"What did she look like?" Hayley said.

"I don't know. Brown hair. Fat. Well, not fat, but not skinny, that's for sure."

"What else?"

"Oh, she had this big ugly mole on her face."

Hayley's heart nearly stopped.

A mole.

That the girl probably hated.

Spanky was talking about Carrie Weston.

Gemma's best friend.

Carrie had been in Mickey Pritchett's hotel room the night he was murdered.

Chapter 26

As the boat cut through the waves back toward the town pier, Hayley was on her cell phone calling Randy's house and asking for Gemma.

Randy's voice was scratchy and his mood was grumpy when he picked up the phone. He obviously hadn't had his morning coffee yet. "She's not here."

"Where did she go?"

"The Lobster Festival down at the ball field."

"Right. I forgot that was today. Who did she go with?"

"One of her friends."

Carrie Weston.

Hayley remembered overhearing Gemma talking with Carrie on the phone last night and making plans to meet there today.

"Thanks, Randy," Hayley said.

"Who can eat lobster this early in the morning?" Randy said.

Hayley checked her watch.

It was after ten now.

The life of a bar owner rarely began before noon.

Hayley clicked off her phone just as Mona's boat

bumped into the side of the dock, nearly causing Hayley to topple over.

She hopped out and hurried up the walkway to her car. "I'll call you later, Mona! I have to get to the Lobster Festival."

Mona waved and then grabbed some rope and started tying it around a post to secure her little motorboat. "Crap. I knew there was something else I had to do today. I'm sponsoring the whole damn thing. Okay! I'll see you there!"

Hayley jumped in her car and roared up the hill along Main Street, straight through town, all the way to the other end where the town ball field was located. Normally a couple of Little League teams would be in the middle of a Saturday morning game. Maybe a few locals would be tossing a ball for their dogs to chase after. But, today, booths with steaming pots of lobster and other seafoods grilling and frying and rows and rows of picnic tables had been set up. Even though the crowd wouldn't swell until closer to lunchtime, already there were lots of people milling around, checking out the food and playing a few of the carnival games with their kids.

Because the festival wasn't yet in full swing, Hayley had no trouble finding a parking space. She tried tracking down Gemma on her cell phone but the call went straight to voice mail.

The sun was so blinding Hayley had to fish through her bag for some sunglasses. She slid them on so she could scan the festival-goers for any sign of her daughter.

It took about ten minutes to locate her, but finally she spotted Gemma and Carrie chowing down on blueberry muffins they must have purchased at the

Jordan's restaurant booth on the north side of the ball field.

Hayley made her way through the crowd and over to them just in time to hear Gemma say, "I've never felt this way about a guy before, and I'm not sure what I'm going to do about it."

Hayley froze in her tracks.

This is not what she needed to hear at this moment.

But she couldn't very well address it now.

That was a whole other discussion.

Instead, she just smiled and said, "Hi, girls."

Gemma spun around, a look of concern on her face.

Hayley lowered her sunglasses and her blazing eyes told Gemma that she had overheard her talking about Reid. It was a signal that said they would definitely be discussing it later.

"Hi, Mrs. Powell," Carrie said flatly, before taking a bite of her muffin.

"Want half my muffin?" Gemma said in a sweet voice, trying to deflect attention from her earlier words. "It's really, really good and I know how much you like blueberries."

"No, I'm fine."

"Uh-oh. What's wrong?" Gemma asked before turning to Carrie, who looked at Hayley curiously. "My mom never turns down food. Something is seriously wrong."

"I need to talk to you," Hayley said grimly.

"Look, we're just dating. I know you think we're doing the nasty behind your back but the truth is we're not. We're just . . ."

"I wasn't talking to you, Gemma. But that doesn't mean we're not going to get into all that at length later. Right now, I'm talking to Carrie."

"*Me*?" Carrie said, her eyes wide with surprise.

"I just spoke with someone who saw you enter Mickey Pritchett's room at the Harborside Hotel on the night he was murdered."

There was a long awkward moment.

"I . . . I don't know what you're talking about," Carrie stammered.

"Mom! Please!" Gemma wailed.

"I need to know what you were doing there," Hayley pressed.

"Mom!"

Hayley held up her hand. "Gemma, stay out of it."

Carrie folded her arms and looked down. She was embarrassed and more than a little scared. It was clear panic was slowly rising up inside her.

Hayley hated interrogating the poor girl like this, but she had to know. "Carrie, it's all going to come out eventually. If you don't talk to me now, you'll eventually have to talk to the police."

Carrie's eyes nearly popped out of her head. "The police? No! Please! I don't want to go to jail!"

Hayley softened. "Talk to me, Carrie. I want to help you."

Carrie looked at Gemma, who nodded. "Go ahead. Tell her."

"Yes, I was there that night," Carrie said softly, still not making eye contact with Hayley.

Suddenly a deep voice coming from behind them startled all three of them. "Carrie, we're going home. Go wait in the car."

Hayley turned to see Ned Weston, Carrie's father, hovering over them, a stern look on his face, his fists clenched.

Carrie didn't make a move.

"I said, go wait in the car," Ned barked.

They all jumped again.

And Carrie immediately scooted across the grass toward a row of parked cars.

"Ned, I really need to talk to Carrie because it seems she might know something about . . ."

"I really don't care, Hayley," Ned growled. "Stop badgering my daughter."

"I'm not badgering her. I'm just trying to . . ."

"I'm warning you," Ned said, pointing a finger in Hayley's face. "Leave us alone."

He stalked off, leaving Hayley and Gemma standing in the middle of the ball field, engulfed in white steam from all the boiling lobster pots.

"I'm supposed to meet Reid over by the information booth," Gemma said, attempting a fast getaway.

Hayley reached out and grabbed her by the arm. "You're not going anywhere until you tell me what you know."

"I promised Carrie I wouldn't say anything."

"Gemma, you can't hide something like this from me. We're talking about a murder investigation. This is serious."

Gemma wrinkled her nose and sighed, wavering. "If Carrie finds out I said anything, she'll never talk to me again."

"Why? Gemma, please."

Gemma looked around and then back at her mother before speaking in a hushed tone. "Carrie was dying to meet Wade Springer, just like you were. I mean, he's like her idol and she has all his music on her iPod just like . . ."

"I know. Just like me. Go on."

"Well, there was no way she was ever going to get close to him on her own. She knew that the night you two tried to crash the hotel bar to meet him. But if she got to know someone close to Wade, maybe he could make an introduction."

"Mickey Pritchett."

"We ran into him when he was coming out of Uncle Randy's bar one night. And Carrie just went for it and asked him, and he said he'd be glad to help us."

"So did he introduce her?"

Gemma shook her head. "No. It never got that far. Because Mickey told her nothing comes free in life and if she really wanted to meet Wade then she was going to have to . . ."

"Oh, no."

Sexual favors.

A chill went up Hayley's spine.

"Gemma, please tell me she didn't . . ."

"No! I mean, she considered it. You know what a huge fan she is of Wade's. Carrie was willing to do almost anything to get in the same room with him. But, come on. That guy was so gross!"

"If Carrie turned Mickey down, why did she go to his hotel room that night?"

Gemma shrugged. "I don't know. You'll have to ask her."

"Gemma, what makes you so sure she didn't agree to Mickey's demands?"

"Because she told me so. And she's my best friend and I believe her."

Hayley silently prayed Gemma was right. But if Carrie was willing to do something so desperate to meet her idol, there was a strong chance she might hide it from her best friend out of sheer embarrassment and humiliation.

One thing was certain.

Hayley had to somehow circumvent Ned Weston and get to his daughter to find out the truth.

Chapter 27

"Mona, it's me," Hayley said.

"What now? You want another boat ride?"

"No. I need to know if Ned Weston ever orders seafood from your shop."

"Everybody in town does. Ned's no different."

"Good. Where are you now?"

"At the Lobster Festival trying to corral my kids, who are running around raising hell right now. I got nobody working my booth."

"I can call Gemma. She'd love to help you out. The kids adore her so they'll listen to her and she can work the register while you're gone."

"Where am I going?"

"Ned Weston's house."

"And why am I going there?"

"To deliver fifteen lobsters he ordered."

"But he didn't order any lobsters."

"Yes."

"You want me to keep him busy by making him think I'm an idiot who got an order screwed up so you can play Nancy Drudge?"

"Nancy Drew."

"I didn't read much as a kid. Don't read much now,

come to think of it. Guess I haven't changed much. But who the hell has time with those hellions I'm trying to raise . . ."

"Mona, I really need you to do this."

"How long do I have to stall him?"

"Just five minutes. Until I get a chance to talk to Carrie."

"Fine. Call Gemma and I'll be there in ten."

"Thank you, Mona!"

"But this is the last time I go undercover while you're snooping."

"Technically, you're not going undercover. You're just being yourself."

"But I'm pretending that I got an order wrong, which, by the way, I never do. So I would say that's operating undercover."

"Not really, because going undercover is assuming a false identity . . ."

"You really want to argue with me over this right before I do you this huge favor, Hayley?"

"You're right. Thanks for going undercover. I'm calling Gemma."

Hayley called Gemma, who was giggling over something Reid said when she picked up. She wasn't too happy about having to drop everything to go work at Aunt Mona's booth, but when Reid suggested it might be fun, Gemma quickly reversed her opinion and told Hayley they were heading over there immediately.

Hayley jumped in her Subaru and raced over to the Weston house, parking a block away so Ned would not spot her car. Then she walked the rest of the way, darting behind a tree as she rounded the corner and saw Mona pulling a silver cooler out of the back of her truck and carrying it up the walk to the Weston's doorstep and ringing the bell.

Ned answered with a puzzled look on his face and Mona broke into a big, warm smile.

"Looks like you're putting on quite a feast tonight, Ned. Where's my invitation?" Mona chuckled.

"What the hell are you talking about?"

Mona put down the cooler and pulled a receipt out of her jeans pocket. "Here you go. Fifteen lobsters. Billed to your account. I threw in some mussels, on the house."

Ned snatched the receipt out of her hand and studied it. "I didn't order any lobsters."

That was Hayley's cue.

Ned's face was buried in the piece of paper, allowing Hayley a precious few moments to run out from behind the tree and up the driveway toward the back of the house.

The yard was immaculately landscaped. Ned Weston was not one to allow even one blade of grass to grow too high.

He was controlling that way.

Hayley was careful not to step in his beautiful flower bed as she reached down and picked up a few pebbles and started throwing them up at a second-story window. She knew this was Carrie's room from the many times she had picked up or dropped off Gemma.

One time when Ned wasn't home and the girls were blasting music in Carrie's room and didn't hear Hayley honking the horn outside or ringing the bell, she had to walk around and call up to them from the back yard.

Hayley tapped the window with three tiny pebbles.

None got Carrie's attention.

She didn't want to call her name for fear of alerting Ned so she picked up the garden hose, turned it on, and started spraying the window with water.

That did it.

Behind the waterfall of water cascading down the glass, Hayley could see Carrie looking outside.

She dropped the hose and waved at her.

Carrie opened the window. "Mrs. Powell, what are you doing here?"

"We didn't get a chance to finish our conversation at the Lobster Festival."

Carrie looked around fearfully. "Please. My dad is home."

"He's busy right now. We have a few minutes to chat."

"What do you want?"

Hayley didn't want to betray Gemma's confidence. She couldn't very well say she was aware of Mickey Pritchett's offer of an introduction to Wade in exchange for sex. But she also didn't have an infinite amount of time to sugarcoat it.

"You already told me you went to see Mickey Pritchett on the night he was murdered. Why?"

Carrie spoke softly, her eyes still darting back and forth for any sign of her father. "He said he'd introduce me to Wade and I was so excited, but then he said it was going to cost me and . . . and, well, I just couldn't do something like that. Especially with him."

"So you didn't know he was going to proposition you until you got there that night? You just thought you were going to meet Wade?"

"No. All that happened before. I talked to Gemma about it and she told me not to do it."

"So why did you go to his room that night, Carrie?"

"I . . . I . . . just went to tell him to forget it. I wasn't going to go through with it."

"That seems like a risky move. You could've just called the hotel and told him over the phone. Why would you put yourself in that kind of position? Mickey was a predator and he could've forced you to stay."

"I don't know. I wasn't thinking. I guess a part of me hoped he might change his mind and introduce me to Wade without making me do anything for it. But it was clear when I got there that was never going to happen."

"Did he try anything?"

"Yes. He tried to kiss me. It was so gross. He had chicken grease all over his face. I pushed him away and threatened to scream and then I ran out."

"Did he chase you?"

"No. He was laughing. He was such an asshole."

Hayley heard Mona's booming voice coming from the front of the house. "Sorry for the mix-up, Ned. You and your daughter enjoy these lobsters on me. Invite some friends over."

Ned grumbled a reply, but Hayley couldn't make out what he said.

Time had run out.

She had to get out of there.

"So you didn't get angry with him and do something to him? Because, let's face it, Carrie, right now it looks like you were the last one to see him alive."

"Me? I can't even kill a spider! Mickey Pritchett was shot, wasn't he? Where would I get a gun?"

She was right. It was a tough sell that Carrie Weston would show up brandishing a revolver, shoot a hole through Mickey Pritchett, and then somehow manage to drag his body out of the hotel and drive it in a huge tour bus to Albert Meadow and set it on fire.

Hayley heard the front door slam.

Ned was back in the house and probably on his way upstairs to check on Carrie.

"Okay. Thank you, Carrie."

"Please, Mrs. Powell. My father can't find out about any of this."

Hayley gave her the thumbs-up and then dashed

back around the house to the street and the cover of the tree.

She poked her head around to make sure Ned hadn't spotted her and then slowly made her way back to her car.

When she reached the Subaru, there was a piece of paper underneath the windshield wiper, flapping in the breeze.

Oh, no.

Not another parking ticket.

Hayley couldn't afford another ticket.

But then she realized she was on a residential street. There were no parking restrictions.

She scooped up the piece of paper and unfolded it.

Was it a flyer?

No. Definitely not a flyer.

Scrawled in black magic marker were the words SILENCE OR DEATH! YOUR CHOICE!

Hayley looked around. A stray cat sped across the street after a squirrel, which scrambled up a tree. Otherwise, the whole street was empty. Not a soul out.

Hayley trembled.

Someone was following her and threatening her, and she had a pretty good idea who that person was.

Chapter 28

Hayley knew exactly where Jesse DeSoto's mother lived because the police had been called out a number of times to the apartment house answering disturbance calls. Hayley heard about every one on her trusty police scanner, which sat atop her refrigerator.

Jesse's mother, Freda, who was a few grades ahead of Hayley in school, was a hard drinker and a nasty drunk who had been ejected from Randy's bar once for picking a fight with the part-time bartender/cocktail waitress, Michelle, a sweet girl whose greatest threat to Freda was her young and pretty face.

Needless to say, Freda's taste in men was at best questionable, and most of the neighbors' complaints came on nights when she was blotto and beating up on her various boyfriends. A couple of them hit back, causing Freda to unleash a torrent of swear words and insults at the top of her lungs and waking up half the residents on the street.

Hayley and Freda had run into each other on occasion, shopping at the grocery store or in line at the bank, and had exchanged nods and good mornings, but other than that they kept their distance, since Freda had a grudge against Randy for kicking her out of the bar and Hayley was guilty by association.

Freda DeSoto and Mickey Pritchett would have probably been the best of friends if they had ever had the chance to meet before he burned up in that bus.

Hayley parked her car on Cottage Street and ambled down a side street toward the shore front. The apartment house where Freda lived with Jesse was in desperate need of a paint job and the roof looked like it was about to cave in. But the rent was cheap.

Still, Hayley had no idea how Freda kept herself and her son from being evicted since she never saw Freda work a day in her life. There were rumors running rampant that Jesse was supporting them with his take from the rash of robberies, but Hayley couldn't bring herself to engage in the gossip, because she didn't believe Freda was that atrocious a mother. Whenever she saw them together, Freda had a smile on her face, like she was proud of her son. Maybe she hadn't known what he was up to in his spare time before, but she certainly did now that he had been arrested. She probably got one of her boyfriends to post the kid's bail.

Hayley walked up the creaky uneven steps to the second floor of the building and knocked on a cracked and chipped door. She heard sounds from a television inside the apartment. It sounded like *Locked Up Abroad* or one of those inside prison shows they aired every weekend on MSNBC.

After a minute went by, Hayley knocked again, this time louder.

The door swung open fast, startling her, and

Hayley stared into a hardened face with a grayish hue from too many packs of cigarettes and bottles of bourbon.

"Hayley Powell. What brings you to this neighborhood? You giving cooking lessons door to door now?"

"I need to talk to Jesse," Hayley said.

"He ain't here," Freda growled before coughing and then snorting the phlegm in her throat up toward her nose.

Charming.

"When do you expect him back, Freda?"

"What'd he do now?"

"I think he may have left a note on my car."

"A note, huh? Like a love note? Aren't you a little up there to be chasing after my boy?"

"Trust me. It was no love note."

"Anyway I hear you go more for the older type, you know what I'm talking about? A stud with a fancy cowboy hat on his head and a sweet love ballad on his lips. I'm sure his bank account helps a hell of a lot, too, huh, Hayley?"

She stepped closer and cackled.

The smell of bourbon on her breath was overpowering.

"I see you read more than just my column."

"I like to keep up on all the news in town."

The two women stared each other down for a moment.

Hayley finally spoke. "When Jesse gets home, tell him I'm looking for him and if he knows what's best for him, he'll get in touch with me so we can sort this out."

Freda shrugged. "I'll tell him. If he comes home. I don't know where he goes half the time. You know kids. And I don't have time to grill him about where he's been and what he's been up to."

Freda was obviously the poster child for bad parenting.

Hayley peered past the door into the living area where the TV was blasting and a half-empty bottle of bourbon sat on a TV tray. "Yes. I can see you're very busy."

Freda's sneer morphed into a scowl.

She didn't like to be insulted.

She stepped back and slammed the door in Hayley's face.

Well, that was a waste of time.

Hayley walked carefully back down the wobbly steps and was walking up toward Cottage Street when her eye caught a glint of something.

In the alley between the apartment building and the house next door.

It was a motorcycle!

She ran over into the alley for a closer look.

It was a Harley Davidson.

Just like the one her attacker had sped off on last night.

Her suspicions were confirmed.

Jesse DeSoto was the one who tried strangling her backstage at the Criterion Theatre.

"What do you want?" a voice said behind her.

Hayley spun around.

Jesse was standing there in jeans and a ratty ripped t-shirt that said "I'm Sleeping With Your Girlfriend."

Charming.

Just like his mother.

He also had a scuffed black motorcycle helmet that he held by the strap in one hand.

"Why did you come here?" he said in a low threatening voice.

"Because I know it was you who came after me at the Wade Springer concert and tried to kill me," Hayley said, standing her ground.

But scared out of her mind.

"You don't know nothing," Jesse said menacingly.

He advanced toward her, backing her up against a Dumpster at the end of the alley.

"Stay away from me," Hayley warned.

"What are you going to do about it?" Jesse said, eyes narrowing.

He was just about on top of her when Hayley reached into her coat pocket and yanked out a small bottle of pepper spray. She pointed it right between Jesse's eyes.

He quickly jumped back and hoisted the helmet in front of his face as a shield.

"Don't spray me with that shit!"

Hayley sprang away from the Dumpster and knocked the helmet out of Jesse's hand. It went clattering to the pavement and now she was the aggressor, wielding the pepper spray, pointing it at his face.

"How stupid are you, Jesse? You know I'm probably going to be the main witness against you in court! If anything happens to me, you are the first person everyone will suspect."

"I know."

"Then why did you take such a risk?"

"I needed cash to pay back my mother's boyfriend for posting my bail . . ."

Hayley stopped cold. "Cash? Someone paid you?"

Jesse was squinting, holding his hands up to protect himself just in case Hayley let loose with the pepper spray.

"Never mind. Forget it."

"Jesse, talk to me. Who paid you?"

"I wasn't going to kill you or anything. I was just supposed to scare you."

Hayley felt her cheeks flushing and her heart thumping wildly. The revelation that someone in town had hired Jesse to attack her made her head woozy.

It was almost too shocking for her to take.

But she kept the spray aimed squarely at Jesse's face.

"I'm warning you for the last time, Jesse. Tell me or it's one squirt and you'll be as blind as Stevie Wonder."

"I don't even know who that is," Jesse wailed, covering his eyes.

Suddenly, Hayley sensed someone rushing up behind her.

"Get away from my son, you bitch!"

Freda DeSoto.

Mother of the Year.

She grabbed Hayley around the neck and hauled her away from Jesse, who looked like he was going to make a run for it.

But he didn't.

He just stood there watching his mother grapple with Hayley like some Vince McMahon women's wrestling match gone horribly wrong.

Freda tried prying the pepper spray out of Hayley's hand. "I'm sick of you oversexed cougars eyeing my son. He's got enough problems."

"I told you, I have no interest in your son."

"That's what the other one said. The blonde."

"Mom!" Jesse shouted, panic in his voice.

"What blonde?"

"The one with the big rack. I saw Jesse and her

hanging out together and when I told her to find someone her own age, she told me the same thing you did."

"Stacy Jo Stanton? The country singer?"

"How the hell should I know?" Freda spat out. "I hate country music!"

It was suddenly crystal clear.

Stacy Jo Stanton hired Jesse to attack her.

Chapter 29

"I have absolutely no idea what you are talking about!" Stacy Jo scoffed as she attempted to push past Hayley, who had confronted her at the entrance to the Harborside Hotel.

Anticipating her move, Hayley backed up a few steps and blocked Stacy Jo's escape. "So you deny paying Jesse DeSoto to come after me?"

"Darling, as much as you would like to think you are on everyone's mind all day and all night, I am a Grammy-winning country artist. I don't have time to spend plotting against you."

"Jesse says otherwise."

"Well, the boy's a liar. And so is his white trash mother."

Stacy Jo gave Hayley a shove, and sent her stumbling back. "Now get out of my way. I thought our days of street brawling were over after we went diving off the town pier and wound up in the slammer."

Stacy Jo was halfway inside the hotel lobby and almost to the elevator before Hayley called after her, "I *never* said anything about his mother!"

Stacy Jo froze in her tracks.

Her back was to Hayley, so she couldn't see her face.

Just a massive amount of blond hair piled high on top of Stacy Jo's head.

"Funny. Freda DeSoto told me all about her warning you to stay away from her son. And, yet, I never mentioned her to you. If you don't know what I'm talking about, then how did you know about her?"

Stacy Jo still wasn't moving.

"I'd like to know what all this is about, too," a man's voice said.

Hayley turned to see Wade returning to the hotel with a six-pack of beer in one hand and car keys in the other.

"Mind explaining what's going on here, Stacy Jo?"

Stacy Jo finally spun around, a tight smile on her face. "She's delusional, Wade. She just showed up here accusing me of all kinds of crazy things. I really think you should consider getting a new chef. This one likes to stir the pot too much, and not in the way she's been hired to do."

Wade looked at Hayley.

"You want to tell him, Stacy Jo, or should I?" Hayley said.

Stacy Jo just stood there, mouth agape, eyes bulging.

"Fine," Hayley said. "I'll tell him. It was a thug named Jesse DeSoto who tried to strangle me at your concert. And it was Stacy Jo who hired him to do it."

"She needs help, Wade. She's had some kind of psychotic break," Stacy Jo wailed, knowing she was losing the fight.

"Jesse's mother saw them together and thought Stacy Jo was hitting on her son so she warned her to stay away from him."

"He was a fan who just wanted an autograph. You of all people must understand that, Wade."

"And Jesse admitted Stacy Jo paid him a nice sum to scare me away."

Wade's disbelieving eyes went to Stacy Jo, who suddenly went pale. "It's not true, Wade. I swear."

"Jesse happily agreed to do the job because I was already on his radar as the main witness to testify against him in court on a car theft charge," Hayley said. "So it was essentially killing two birds with one stone."

"There wasn't supposed to be any killing," Stacy Jo screamed, before catching herself and covering her mouth with her hand, which was now shaking.

"So Hayley is right. You gave that boy money?" Wade asked, staring at her grimly.

"Yes," Stacy Jo sighed. "But he wasn't supposed to harm her in any way. He was just supposed to scare her. Warn her to stay away from you. It was killing me to listen to you go on and on about how delicious Hayley's cooking is. The crew telling me all about your romantic walks with your dogs in the early morning dew. I just couldn't take it, Wade."

"But, Stacy Jo, have you forgotten we're divorced?"

"Yes. But you divorced me. That doesn't mean I ever stopped loving you. Seeing you doting on another woman, it's like a knife through the heart," Stacy Jo said, eyes welling up with tears.

"Stacy Jo, don't you get it? You could be charged with conspiracy to commit murder!" Wade said, stepping protectively in front of Hayley.

"Maybe here up north. In the south, they'd just call it a squabble between girlfriends. He wasn't supposed to touch so much as a hair on her head. Just show up and verbally threaten her. But the boy got carried away."

"That makes me feel so much better," Hayley said.

"How on earth did you come across this kid?" Wade asked.

"When I got to town and saw Hayley in your room, I just got crazy jealous and I asked around to find someone who might be open to doing some extra work that might not be one hundred percent legal. All fingers pointed to Jesse, who apparently has quite the reputation in town. So I tracked him down and offered him a nice sum to just give Hayley a little push, and show her that dating you might not be in her best interest. I promise he was just supposed to talk to you. Not physically attack you! I guess he had a different agenda on his mind because of his upcoming court case."

"Stacy Jo, you are unbelievable," Wade said quietly.

"I tried to call it off. After Hayley and I got arrested and spent that time in jail together, I actually grew to like her. And when we got out, I called the number Jesse had given me, to cancel, but his cell had been turned off. I guess he didn't pay his bill. I couldn't reach him and I didn't know where to find him. His mother certainly wasn't going to help me. And then it was too late and I heard what happened backstage at your concert last night."

Wade shook his head as he took it all in.

Stacy Jo folded her arms across her chest to hug herself—as much as she could, given her cleavage—and sobbed. "I'm so sorry, Hayley. Truly, I am."

"And what about Mickey?" Hayley asked, flashing Stacy Jo an accusing glance. "Did you hire Jesse to scare him, too?"

"No!" Stacy Jo wailed. "I had nothing to do with that! I swear!"

"You just swore you had nothing to do with what happened to Hayley. How are we supposed to believe you?"

Stacy Jo sank to her knees, her shoulders shaking, her choked sobs drawing attention from the hotel staff working in the lobby.

Wade casually walked over and knelt down beside her. "You've made a fool of me and a bigger fool of yourself and I think it'd be best for everyone if you went upstairs, packed up your bags, and got the hell out of Dodge. Am I making myself clear, Stacy Jo?"

Stacy Jo nodded.

But she didn't move.

Wade cleared his throat.

She looked up at him, black mascara running down her face.

Wade, his eyes flaring, took her by the elbow and hauled her to her feet. "Now, Stacy Jo."

He gave her a slight nudge that sent her scampering toward the elevator.

And then he turned to Hayley and mouthed the words, "I'm sorry."

Hayley smiled.

She felt bad for Stacy Jo.

Instinctively, she knew Stacy Jo wasn't involved in the Mickey Pritchett murder. But she sure wasn't going to miss her.

And deep down she felt a thrill over the fact that Wade Springer had once again come so gallantly to her defense.

What a man.

Island Food & Spirits
by
Hayley Powell

Y'all won't believe what happened to me the other night! Oh, listen to me. I'm even starting to sound a little southern, after all the visitors we've had in town lately.

Anyway, I had just picked up my daughter at the high school after a late basketball tryout, and we were heading home. Of course, my daughter had the radio blasting through the car speakers, and was screaming over the sound of the music, telling me all about how the tryouts went. She was very confident she would get a spot on the team.

As usual, Eagle Lake Road was pitch-black, and since it was a foggy night, I couldn't see five feet in front of me. Anyone who knows me is well aware that I hate driving in fog or in snow!

We were descending McFarland Hill when suddenly the thick fog parted as if on cue and standing right in the middle of the road not more than fifty feet away was the biggest, meanest-looking buck I've ever seen! His cold black eyes stared right at me through my car windshield. That's when I realized I'd seen this giant buck before! It was Bucky, the now six-point buck, who had chased Leroy and me through the woods not too long ago.

This might sound crazy, but I swear he gave me a look like he was out for revenge! If you recall, he had an unfortunate accident the last time he chased us.

My daughter took a much needed breath from talking and noticed I wasn't paying attention to her. She glanced in front of us and let out a bloodcurdling, terrified scream, because we were heading straight toward that massive buck! My daughter's screaming shook me out of my thoughts and I slammed on the brakes as hard as I could. (I knew the old brakes weren't as good as they used to be, so I prayed for the best.) Trying not to lose control of my trusty old Subaru wagon, I veered the wheel to the left and then swung back to the right. None of my defensive driving seemed to work. We were still careening straight toward poor Bucky! He just stood there, not moving a muscle, just glaring at me with his dark beady eyes as if he was daring me to hit him!

There wasn't much we could do except brace ourselves for the impact. I gave one final stomp on the brakes and closed my eyes, waiting for the sickening crunch of the impact. My last thought was, how was I ever going to pay for the damage to my car? Sorry, Bucky.

As we sat there in silence, I quickly realized the car was stopped and there was no crash. I slowly opened my eyes and, there illuminated by the headlights of my Subaru, was Bucky, still looking right at me. The staring contest went on for another few seconds, and then Bucky dropped out of view. Gone in an instant. He just fell over and hit the ground with a loud thud.

I don't know what it is about a deer being hit by a car on the island. You can be driving along and not see another car for miles. But once you hit a deer, the next thing you know, suddenly there is a line of cars and trucks on the scene, and a bunch of men ready to take the animal off your hands! And that's exactly what happened! Four men pulled over and offered to take home that giant buck if I didn't want him.

I told them that whomever was on the scene first could have him, and after some arguing and grumbling, the men decided Old Joe McKinley, one of our retired fishermen in town, was there first. So Old Joe happily carted Bucky off toward his army green pickup truck. The other onlookers were visibly disappointed, but they knew it wouldn't be a long wait for another car versus deer incident on the island.

Oh, and, just so you know, the men looked over poor Bucky, and came to the conclusion that I never even hit him! It looked to them like he just died of fright! The shock of my car speeding toward him was probably what killed him. As Old Joe said when he hauled his prize away, "When it's your time, it's your time!"

With all that excitement over Bucky the six point buck, I found myself craving a mincemeat pie, so for today's recipe, mincemeat it is! But, after a very stressful evening, I decided to take the edge off before I got to cooking. And we all know there is nothing that cures stress better than some warm relaxing cocktails on a cool evening. So I think a hot buttered rum is exactly what the doctor ordered. Although, at this point, I'm afraid it's not going to help poor Bucky.

Hot Buttered Rum

Serves 10 or more. (You might want to invite a friend over, depending on how thirsty you are.)

1 stick unsalted butter, room temperature
2 cups brown sugar
1 teaspoon ground cinnamon
½ teaspoon grated fresh nutmeg
Pinch of ground cloves
Pinch of salt
1 bottle dark rum
Boiling water

In a bowl, cream together butter, sugar, cinnamon, nutmeg, cloves, and salt. Place into the refrigerator until almost firm. Spoon 2 tablespoons of the butter mixture into a mug. Pour 3 ounces of rum into the mug and top with boiling water. Stir well and serve. If serving guests, just add more mugs and repeat.

Mincemeat Pie

2 pie crusts, for bottom and top (use your favorite recipe; I like to use the refrigerated Pillsbury pie crusts from the grocery store, which come two in a pack)
¼ pound ground mincemeat
2 cups apple juice
1 cup dark seedless raisins
½ cup dried cherries (sweet or sour)
1½ cups peeled and chopped apples
¼ pound ground venison
1 teaspoon cinnamon
1 teaspoon ground cloves
1 teaspoon ground ginger
½ teaspoon salt
½ teaspoon ground nutmeg
¼ teaspoon allspice

In a 2-quart saucepan, combine apple juice, raisins, and cherries. Cover and bring to a boil over high heat. Reduce heat to low and simmer for 30 minutes, stirring occasionally.

Add apples, venison, mincemeat, cinnamon, cloves, ginger, salt, nutmeg, and allspice. Simmer for 2 hours. Check occasionally; add water to keep mincemeat from sticking to bottom of pan. Remove from heat and cool to room temperature.

Place bottom crust in 1 inch pie pan. Add mincemeat mixture and place second crust on top. Crimp the edges and remove excess crust. Make 5 or 6 slits with a knife on the top crust for steam to escape. Place in preheated 350 degree oven and bake 50 to 55 minutes, until crust is lightly browned and filling is bubbling.

Chapter 30

Hayley finished her column around 7:30 P.M. and e-mailed it to the office. She poured herself a glass of red wine and relaxed on the sofa with Leroy, who snuggled in her lap. She closed her eyes, trying to forget all the drama of the last week. Sunday night would be Wade's last concert and then the crew would pack up and move on Monday morning.

Whether Mickey Pritchett's murder was solved or not.

She sipped some wine.

She felt a crick in her neck.

Undoubtedly from Jesse DeSoto trying to squeeze the air out of it.

She rubbed the sore spot.

Let out a deep breath.

She had read that breathing exercises and meditation were healthy for you, but who had the time with a full-time job and looking after two demanding teenagers?

Not to mention chasing after clues in a murder investigation.

It was unusually quiet in the house.

Especially for a Saturday night.

A text from Gemma explained her absence.

Out with Reid.

No surprise there.

Dustin was home and in his room, but there was no blaring noise from the television nor the annoying sounds of sonic rings, or creepy piano music, or fireball explosions from his wide array of video games.

There was no noise at all.

And that was a bit worrisome.

Hayley gently moved Leroy's head off her lap and lowered it onto a throw pillow. She stood up, set her glass of wine down, and headed up the stairs.

She saw a light coming from under Dustin's bedroom door.

She knew there was zero chance he was doing homework on a Saturday night. Hayley cautiously approached the door and pushed it open, the hinges squeaking. Dustin was on his bed texting on a cell phone. His eyes bulged open at the sight of his mother and he instinctively stuffed the phone underneath his pillow.

"If you ever want to raise a red flag, that's definitely the way to do it," Hayley said, arching an eyebrow. "What are you doing?"

"Nothing," Dustin said, shrugging.

"Who are you texting?"

"Nobody. Just a friend."

"Which is it? Nobody, or a friend?"

Dustin was sweating.

And it was forty degrees outside.

Gemma was much more adept at covering her tracks when she was up to no good.

Hayley entered the room and thrust out her hand. "Give me the phone."

"Mom! Come on. I'm just chatting with Spanky."

"Spanky McFarland?"

"Yeah, it's no big deal."

"Then why did you hide the phone underneath your pillow when I came into your room?"

"Spanky was just telling me some private stuff and I promised not to tell anyone."

"What kind of stuff?" Hayley wanted to know.

"Nothing!"

Hayley marched over to the bed and rummaged underneath the pillow.

Dustin sat up in his bed. "Mom! No! Spanky's going to think I ratted him out."

"You didn't tell me anything. It's not your fault I just happened to find your phone and read your conversation while cleaning this pigsty of a room."

Hayley scrolled up the long series of word bubbles on Dustin's screen until she saw a mention of a gun.

"A gun?" Hayley asked, eyeing Dustin curiously. "A real one?"

"It's not his!" Dustin said, huffing and puffing to show his annoyance.

"Where did he get it?"

"He and his brother found it while kayaking over to Bar Island. It was just lying there on the beach covered in seaweed."

Hayley shoved the phone at Dustin. "Ask him if it's a forty-five handgun."

Dustin sighed. "Okay. Okay."

He used his thumbs to text Spanky.

Hayley marveled at how fast kids could type on their phones.

It took her two minutes just to text the word hello.

Dustin waited.

Then there was a ping indicating Spanky's response.

"Yeah, it's a forty-five."

It had to be the murder weapon that killed Mickey Pritchett.

The killer probably tossed it in the ocean after shooting Mickey and setting fire to the tour bus. The gun could have conceivably washed up with the tide on Bar Island, a small privately owned island located directly across the bay from the town pier. One could actually walk over to it during low tide.

She had to call Sergio.

This could break the case wide open.

Hayley did an about-face to the door and was scurrying out when Dustin pleaded, "Mom, you can't say anything! I gave Spanky my word!"

She stopped and turned back around. "I have to tell Uncle Sergio. This could be a crucial piece of evidence in his murder case."

"Spanky said not to tell *you* especially, since you have a habit of sticking your nose in everybody's business," Dustin said.

Okay.

Spanky was right.

The little brat.

But Hayley knew she couldn't keep a lid on something like this. Sergio had to know.

"Maybe there's a way I can let Uncle Sergio know without him realizing it's coming from me," Hayley said.

"You mean an anonymous tip?" Dustin asked.

"Yes."

Dustin rolled his eyes. "He's going to know it's you."

"Not if I'm playing a character. I did a couple of plays in high school. I know how to act."

"You played a Shark in *West Side Story*. With no lines. Remember? You made us watch the video."

"He won't know it's me."

Hayley marched out of Dustin's room and back down the stairs.

She picked up the phone in the kitchen, took a long, deep breath, and called Sergio at home.

She expected Randy to pick up and was surprised when she heard Sergio's thick Brazilian accent instead.

"Yes. This is Sergio."

Hayley had not taken much time to perfect her character, but she attempted a Swedish accent only because she had given some college-age Swedish tourists on mountain bikes directions to Cadillac Mountain recently and they were fresh in her mind.

"I have some information regarding the Mickey Pritchett murder," Hayley said, her Swedish accent coming across more like Russian.

Where was that glass of wine?

"I am sorry. I do not understand you," Sergio said, puzzled.

"I know where you can find the gun that killed Mickey Pritchett," Hayley said, now doing a dead-on Count Chocula impression.

"Hayley, is that you?" Sergio asked.

Dustin was right.

Smart kid.

Damn.

"Why do you sound so funny?" Sergio asked.

"Look who's talking," was all Hayley could think of to say.

"Did you say somebody killed Ricky Martin?"

"Mickey Pritchett! I know where you can find the gun!"

There was a long pause.

Sergio was probably grabbing a piece of paper and a pen. "Okay, talk."

Hayley told him everything. And she asked Sergio

not to reveal the source of his information when he showed up at Spanky McFarland's front door. But she knew the kid would probably put two and two together and blame Dustin. It was a risk she had to take. There was a killer on the loose and she was determined to keep her own family safe.

Sergio promised to call her back once he picked up the gun from Spanky and ran a search on the registration.

After apologizing to Dustin for forcing him to breach his friend's trust, Hayley waited by the phone in her bedroom for Sergio to call back.

Time ticked by.

She watched a mindless action movie starring Jason Statham on cable. She had a crush on the rugged English bloke with the shaved head and the sexy bad attitude.

She checked the clock.

8:30 P.M.

Still no call.

Leroy found her and jumped up on the bed with her and she pulled her white down comforter up to her chest and hugged a pillow and closed her eyes. She had drifted off to sleep when the ringing of the phone suddenly snapped her awake.

The clock read 9:38 P.M.

She scooped up the receiver. "Sergio?"

"Yes," he said in a monotone voice.

"So who is the gun registered to?"

"Ned Weston."

The name barely registered at first, it was so unexpected.

Ned Weston.

The father of Carrie Weston.

Gemma's best friend.

Hayley immediately updated Sergio on Carrie's

run-in with Mickey Pritchett. Ned had probably found out about it and decided to take action on behalf of his daughter, to protect her from Mickey's slimy advances.

"I'm heading over there in a few minutes," Sergio said. "I'll call you in the morning with an update."

Hayley was in a daze.

She crawled out of bed and went into the hallway.

Dustin was still up and watching the end of the same Jason Statham movie on his TV. Gemma's room was dark.

"Did your sister tell you when she would be home?"

Dustin propped his head up with his hand, elbow on his pillow. "Reid dropped her off hours ago, before you even got home."

"Well, where is she?"

"She went over to spend the night at Carrie's house."

Hayley's heart stopped.

"She left you a note," Dustin said, yawning.

"The only note I got was a text message telling me she was going out with Reid."

"That was from this afternoon. You didn't see a newer note?"

"No!"

"Oh, wait. She asked me to tell you. I forgot. Sorry."

Hayley started shaking.

"What's the matter, Mom?"

Hayley threw on some tennis shoes, grabbed her car keys, dashed down the stairs, and ran out the door.

The only thought in her mind was that at this moment her daughter was inside the house of a possible killer.

Chapter 31

Hayley banged on the door of the Weston house, desperately trying to stay calm.

The porch light flicked on, and the door swung open.

Ned Weston stood in the doorway in a red-and-black plaid shirt, blue jeans, and an annoyed look on his face. He lowered his reading glasses and gripped the newspaper in his fist.

"What are you doing here? It's almost ten o'clock at night!"

"I need to speak with my daughter. It's important."

"Couldn't you have just called?"

"Now, Ned," Hayley barked.

Ned rolled his eyes and stepped back inside, calling upstairs, "Gemma! Your mother's here! She wants to talk to you!"

Hayley could hear music playing upstairs.

She recognized the tune.

Some British songstress barely old enough to vote. Adele.

Ned yelled again. "Gemma!"

"She obviously can't hear you because the music's

too loud. Let me go get her," Hayley said, pushing her way into the house.

Ned blocked her path. "You can't just come into my house uninvited."

Hayley exhaled a breath and stepped back outside. "Fine, Ned. Just get my daughter for me and I'll leave."

Ned gave her a curious look. "Why are you acting so strange?"

Hayley was tapping her foot nervously.

She ignored the question.

"I'll go get her," Ned said, eyeing Hayley suspiciously and then pounding up the stairs.

Hayley glanced around.

Everything appeared normal as far as she could see.

After a few moments, Gemma hurried down the stairs, Carrie and Ned on her heels, and stared at her mother, perplexed.

"What's going on? Why are you here?"

"I need you to come home with me," Hayley said evenly.

"Why?"

"I don't want the third degree. I just want you to come with me right now."

"Is something wrong, Mrs. Powell?" Carrie asked in a soft voice.

"No, Carrie. Everything's fine."

"Then I don't understand why I have to leave," Gemma said, anger rising in her voice.

Hayley took Gemma by the arm and squeezed tight. It was her usual signal that she was in no mood to argue and there would be painful consequences if Gemma did not start cooperating immediately.

Gemma shrugged and turned to Carrie. "I'll call you when I get home."

"Carrie, why don't you walk us out?" Hayley asked as casually as she could.

"No, Carrie, I want you to stay here," Ned said, shifting uncomfortably, trying to figure out what was going on here.

"Dad, I'm just going to walk them to the car. You can see me the whole time from here, okay?"

Ned didn't want to appear too controlling so he nodded, his eyes fixed on Hayley like a laser, his mind racing.

"Let me just go get my stuff," Gemma said, turning to go back upstairs, but Hayley squeezed her arm tighter.

"We can pick it up tomorrow," Hayley said, forcefully pulling her daughter outside and toward the car.

Carrie followed them.

They were halfway across the street when, out the corner of her eye, Hayley spotted Sergio's police cruiser rounding the corner and heading down the street toward the Weston house, the blue lights flashing.

She picked up the pace, dragging Gemma alongside her. Carrie was still a few feet behind them, oblivious to the approaching cop car.

Hayley fished in her coat pocket for her car keys and remotely unlocked the doors of the Subaru.

She glanced back. Ned Weston's tall frame was still filling the doorway. Even in the dark from across the street, she could see his angry eyes glaring at her.

The blue lights from the cruiser washed over Ned's face and he suddenly snapped to attention and jerked his head around to see the approaching police car.

Hayley was distracted by Carrie, who was tugging on her coat sleeve. "Mrs. Powell, what's happening?"

Carrie had noticed the cruiser.

Now, so did Gemma.

Hayley didn't know what to say.

"Mom . . . ?" Gemma asked, her voice trailing off.

The police cruiser stopped in front of the house and Sergio, accompanied by Officer Donnie, stepped out of the vehicle.

Hayley glanced back to the front door of the Weston house.

Ned was gone.

"What are the police doing here?" Carrie wanted to know.

"They want to speak to your father," Hayley said quietly.

"My father? About what?"

Hayley couldn't bring herself to answer.

Sergio and Donnie were now on the front stoop, looking around, wondering why the front door was left wide open. Sergio turned around to see Hayley and the two girls standing by Hayley's white Subaru wagon. He raised an eyebrow, surprised to see her here.

"Hayley?" Sergio asked.

"I just came by to pick up Gemma and take her home."

Sergio nodded, understanding instantly. "Carrie, is your father home?"

"Yes. He must have gone back inside," Carrie said.

"Mind if we go inside and have a talk with him?"

Carrie nodded, and Hayley put an arm around her, sensing how frightened she was, not knowing why the cops wanted to question her father.

Sergio and Donnie walked inside the house and began calling for Ned.

But Hayley knew they wouldn't find him.

She knew Ned Weston would have run off into the night when he saw the cops in front of his house.

And it just made him look guiltier.

Hayley still had her arm around Carrie.

"Why are the police looking for Mr. Weston, Mom?" Gemma asked.

"I'll explain when we get home. Carrie, why don't you come stay at our house tonight?"

"No! I'm not going anywhere until Chief Alvares tells me what he thinks my father has done!"

Carrie broke away from Hayley and dashed back inside the house.

"Mom, we can't just leave her," Gemma pleaded.

Hayley felt vulnerable in the pitch-black night.

Ned Weston was on the loose.

He could be anywhere.

And her single thought was getting her daughter home safe.

"Gemma, in the car," Hayley said.

Gemma got her mother's tone immediately.

Without another word, she opened the passenger-side door and slid onto the seat.

Hayley got behind the wheel, and they pulled away in time to see Sergio talking to Carrie, who looked scared and alone.

Chapter 32

After Hayley explained to Gemma about the re-covered gun being registered to Carrie's father and how they suspected it might have been used in the murder of Mickey Pritchett, Gemma frantically began texting Carrie to see if she was all right.

After what seemed like an eternity, Carrie texted back that she was fine and at her house with Sergio waiting on word from her father. There was still no sign of him.

It was now after eleven, and Hayley could barely manage to keep her eyes open. Gemma retreated to her room, while Dustin was already asleep when they'd arrived home.

Leroy followed Hayley up the stairs to her bed-room, jumped up on a footstool, and looked outside, tail wagging, as Hayley undressed, slipped on some sweats and a ratty old t-shirt, and climbed into bed. She made a whistling sound and patted the comforter for Leroy to join her, but he was staring at something on the street. She noticed his tiny tail stop wagging and a low growl building.

The growl erupted into a bark and Hayley sighed, throwing off the comforter and putting her feet down on the cold hardwood floor to snatch her pup away from the window. Leroy barked at anything that moved outside so she assumed it was just a squirrel or a night owl or a deer that had wandered into the yard to munch on her flower bed again.

It was none of those things.

It was the figure of a man.

Standing in the shadows just outside the glow of a street lamp.

Watching her house.

It was Ned Weston.

Hayley wasn't going to waste a moment speculating on why he was stalking her. Her nervous behavior had certainly tipped him off that something was about to go down. He knew her relationship with Sergio. It was no coincidence that the police had showed up only minutes after she had pounded on his door demanding to take her daughter home. He knew Hayley was responsible and maybe he was here for revenge.

But it didn't matter.

What mattered was protecting her kids.

So, like any threatened mama bear, she slipped on some shoes, snuck into Dustin's room and grabbed a baseball bat from his closet, and marched down the stairs.

She didn't stop to think about what she was doing, because she didn't want time for fear to take over.

She kicked open the front door and saw the man in the shadows jump back. She raised the bat over her head and broke into a run, heading straight for him.

"Whoa! Wait! Stop!" the man yelled, throwing his hands up in surrender.

It wasn't Ned Weston.

She saw the silhouette of a cowboy hat.

It was Wade Springer.

"Wade! What are you doing lurking around here at this time of night?" Hayley asked, relieved, still holding the baseball bat above her head.

Wade cautiously reached over and lowered the tip of the bat with his index finger. "I was debating on whether I should bother you so late. But, hell, honey, I can see now that you were still up!"

"You scared me half to death," Hayley said, clutching her chest.

"That makes two of us, darling," Wade said, wiping his brow.

"Why are you here? What's happened now?"

"Nothing. I heard they caught the killer and I wanted to come by and see if were okay. But when I got here I realized how late it was and you were probably already sleeping. Hell, maybe I was just looking for an excuse to see you. I still feel responsible for all this."

"I already told you, none of this is your fault!"

"Like hell it isn't. I've turned this town upside down just by being here. Nice, quiet little place and then after I show up, there's murder and scandal and Lord knows what else. Seems like a tornado of troubles always seems to follow me around. And I threw you right in front of it with Mickey putting the moves on you and Stacy Jo's insanity, hiring that kid to scare you. Let's face it, if I never came here in the first place, you wouldn't have had to deal with any of this craziness."

"Well, I got to meet my idol, so in a weird way, it was worth it."

Wade smiled.

Tipped his hat.

"So now that the murder's been solved, what do you say we start all over again. Let me take you out after the show tomorrow night."

"Who told you the murder was solved?"

"That reporter who works with you, Bruce something . . ."

"Bruce Linney."

"Yeah, he dropped by the hotel bar for a drink about twenty minutes ago and said he heard some local man shot Mickey because he made unwanted advances toward his daughter."

Bruce no doubt heard about the search for Ned Weston on the police scanner.

It must have driven Bruce crazy to find out Hayley was so far ahead of him.

"So what do you say? Dinner? On me? Tomorrow night after the show? I know it'll be late, but I'm betting I can convince at least one restaurant to stay open. I'm Wade Springer, after all!" Wade said, flashing his killer smile.

"I'm sorry, Wade, but I can't."

Wade looked crestfallen. "Why not?"

"Ned Weston is still on the loose and I'm not going to be able to concentrate on anything, especially enjoying dinner with you, until the police have him in custody."

There was no arguing her point.

Wade nodded. "I understand."

There was a chill in the air.

Hayley hugged herself to keep warm.

"You still coming to the concert?"

"I hope to. We'll see."

Wade tipped his hat again and started to go, but then he stopped. He took Hayley by the chin and gave her a soft, lingering kiss on the lips.

"Good night, darling."

And he was gone.

Hayley looked around to make sure there weren't any more men skulking in the shadows outside her house and then hurried back inside.

Chapter 33

The following morning, the day of Wade's second and final concert in Bar Harbor, Hayley was up early only to discover, much to her horror, that she was out of coffee. Not ten minutes ago, she had reluctantly agreed to let Gemma drive over to Reid's to pick him up and take him out for Sunday brunch. She still wasn't comfortable with the idea of Gemma driving, let alone dating so seriously, but she did feel better that Gemma was not alone and had a good, strong, hearty boy around her, given recent events.

Hayley desperately needed coffee. She hooked the worn red nylon leash onto Leroy's collar and headed out to the nearest corner store. It was only a half mile from the house, on lower Main Street, and she could use the exercise.

She cut through an alley to shorten the distance, as her head was already pounding from a severe lack of caffeine. This led her onto a tree-lined side street. It was chilly and there was a heavy mist and the cars parked along the street had morning dew on their windshields.

Leroy scampered along, tongue hanging out, just excited to be out walking.

But then, suddenly, he stopped.

His ears perked up.

And there was that low growl again.

Just like last night when he saw Wade lurking outside the house.

Leroy began barking.

Hayley looked around, but there was no sign of anyone out.

She tugged on the leash.

"Quiet, Leroy. You'll wake the whole neighborhood."

Her firm yank on the leash caught Leroy's bark in his throat and he settled back into his familiar low growl.

Hayley decided it was just a squirrel or a cat and hustled past Leroy, pulling him along.

He put up a fight.

He wasn't going anywhere.

His little butt dragged across the pavement as she forced him.

"What is the matter with you?"

Leroy stopped barking and stared past her.

Suddenly, Hayley felt someone behind her.

She spun around.

Ned Weston.

Hayley shuddered.

"Don't scream, or so help me . . ."

"What, Ned? You're going to shoot me? Like you shot Mickey Pritchett?"

"You don't know anything," Ned spat out.

Hayley surmised Ned had to have been hiding behind one of the trees waiting for her to approach so he could confront her, and Leroy had spotted him peeking around the trunk and started to bark as a warning.

God, she loved her dog.

But since she hadn't paid attention to him, the poor little guy was no longer in any position to help her.

Ned's face was drawn, with dark circles under his eyes. He probably hadn't slept all night, trying to avoid Sergio and his officers. He also smelled. But not of sweat and dirt.

No, it was a sharp, distinct, familiar fishy smell.

"I'm warning you, Hayley, leave this thing alone. I don't want to hurt you. But if you keep poking around playing detective, I'm afraid I'm going to do something we'll both regret."

"Innocent men don't make such blatant threats, Ned."

First Jesse DeSoto.

Now Ned Weston.

How many more men would threaten her with bodily harm before all this was over?

Ned pointed a finger in her face. "I'm not going to tell you again!"

He got right up close and the smell was overpowering.

It nearly brought tears to her eyes.

Ned kept his finger pointed at her and Hayley noticed it was shaking slightly. Like he was scared.

Meanwhile, Leroy's yapping was getting louder, and Hayley noticed a couple of people looking out their windows out of curiosity. The barking startled Ned enough that he stuffed his hands in his coat pocket, brushed past Hayley, and ran off down the street.

Hayley didn't follow him.

She knew where he was probably going.

Coffee would have to wait.

She picked up Leroy and ran back home, since she had forgotten to bring her cell phone with her.

She slammed through the front door, grabbed the

phone off the kitchen counter where she'd left it, and
speed-dialed Sergio, who picked up on the first ring.

"This is Sergio."

"I know where you can find Ned Weston."

"I'm all earrings."

"Ears, Sergio. It's just ears."

"I'm listening!"

"I just ran into him."

"Where?"

"Doesn't matter. He took off. But I know exactly
where he is going. Lex Bansfield's fishing boat.
There's a nice little futon below deck. He's hiding out
there."

"How do you know?"

"Because I've been there. I'm an adult, Sergio. If I
want to spend some quality time with a man on his
boat, then that's nobody's business but . . ."

"I meant how do you know Ned is there?"

"Oh. Right. Because I recognized the smell. A fishy
odor. And Ned stunk to high heaven of it. It's the
same odor Lex had when I saw him the day before he
left town for a couple weeks. And I remember him
telling me he had been cleaning out his boat because he was going to lend it to Ned Weston while he
was gone."

"Good work, Hayley. I'll call you when we catch
him."

Hayley put the phone down in its cradle and felt a
wave of relief.

The sooner Ned was behind bars, the safer she
would feel.

And she wouldn't be so worried about her kids
leaving the house once Mickey Pritchett's killer was
safely behind bars.

She fed Leroy a doggie treat and cleaned up the kitchen.

Less than an hour later, the phone rang.

It was Sergio.

"Did you find him?"

"Yes. We brought him in for questioning. He admitted it was his gun."

"And did he confess to killing Mickey Pritchett?"

"Yes. Just as you suspected. Weston found out Pritchett was pressuring his daughter, demanding sexual favors in exchange for an introduction to Wade Springer, and he just lost it. Grabbed his gun and went hunting for him. He went to the hotel and found Pritchett in one of the tour buses in the parking lot and shot him dead. Then, in a panic, he drove the tour bus with Pritchett's body to Albert Meadow and torched it, hoping to destroy any evidence. Then he tried to get rid of the murder weapon by tossing it into the Atlantic."

"You mean, all of this is finally over?"

"Thanks to you. You told us where to find him."

Hayley's first thought was of Carrie.

How was she ever going to handle this? She was already struggling with the normal teen issues. This was going to be a huge burden to take on.

Hayley was determined to help her.

And she knew Gemma would be there for her as well.

She could hardly believe it.

Ned Weston.

A brutal killer.

She had never liked him.

It made perfect sense.

An overly protective father defending his only daughter's honor.

Going to unimaginable extremes.
But, now, he was finally caught and behind bars.
So why didn't she feel better?
She had a queasy feeling in the pit of her stomach.
Like this entire ordeal was far from over.

Chapter 34

"He didn't do it. He couldn't have," Liddy said as she picked the top off one of Hayley's homemade blueberry muffins and popped it in her mouth.

Hayley put on a checkered oven mitt and pulled a tray out of the oven with eight bubbling piping-hot orange cranberry muffins. She upended them into a wicker basket lined with a paper towel to cool. "How do you know that?"

"Because I know he has an alibi on the night of the murder."

"God, Liddy, please, don't tell me that in addition to Mickey Pritchett, you were also seeing Ned Weston on the side!"

"Of course not! Just the thought of Ned Weston makes my skin crawl."

"And Mickey Pritchett was such a winner?"

"I didn't say I'm not capable of misjudgment. Mickey was new to town. He was fresh meat. A charmer. He swept me off my feet before I realized what a complete loser he was. Ned, on the other hand, well, he's been around forever. Long enough for me to know better!"

After receiving the call from Sergio about Ned's

confession, Hayley went into baking mode, something she often did to calm her nerves.

Hayley knew she should be feeling an enormous sense of relief now that Mickey Pritchett's killer was finally behind bars.

But she didn't.

Far from it.

She was antsy, and worried about Carrie, and still trying to put all the pieces together in her mind.

Something just didn't add up.

Liddy had dropped by unexpectedly—as she always did, since she didn't really believe in calling first—in time to be the taster for all the different kinds of muffins Hayley was baking. Hayley figured she could drive the muffins over to the Criterion and hand them out to Wade's band and crew before the concert.

Liddy picked the top off one of the orange cranberry muffins and took a bite. "Oh, these are even better than the blueberry ones."

"Liddy, why do you think Ned Weston is innocent?"

"Ask Michelle."

"Michelle Butterworth? Who works part time at my brother's bar?"

"Yes. Rumor has it she's been secretly seeing Ned."

"Are you serious? Michelle is so pretty and nice and Ned is so . . ."

"There's no accounting for taste."

"You should know," Hayley said, grinning.

"Do you constantly have to remind me of my brief foray into utter insanity? It's never going to happen again. Trust me."

"Yes. Now that Mickey Pritchett is dead."

"Look, this isn't about me. This is about Ned and Michelle. And I know for a fact that the two of them have been canoodling on Lex's boat the last couple of weeks. He's been after her for some time and she finally relented."

"Okay, so let's assume this is true, what you're saying. How does this give Ned an alibi on the night of Mickey's murder?"

Liddy dropped the bottom uneaten half of her orange cranberry muffin dramatically and stared at Hayley. "Because Mona told me she saw them sharing a bottle of wine on Lex Bansfield's boat around ten-thirty on the night of the murder when she went to drop some new lobster traps off at her own boat, which is tied up near Lex's. She was in her outboarder and when they heard her approaching, they made a big production of grabbing the bottle and hurrying below deck so she wouldn't see them together. Mona spent the next two hours stacking the traps and they never left.

"Given the time frame of the murder, there was no way Ned could've slipped away and shot Mickey, let alone drive the tour bus to Albert Meadow and set it on fire."

"Why didn't Mona say anything to me?"

"You know how annoying Mona can be about not getting involved in other people's business. It really drives me nuts. And, besides, Ned Weston wasn't a suspect at the time, so she probably didn't even think to say anything. The only reason she told me is because she was making fun of me for sleeping with that skeevy Pritchett character. She said I had worse taste than Michelle when it came to men. That peaked my interest and I got her to tell me what she saw."

"Why were Ned and Michelle keeping their relationship a secret?"

"Michelle used to babysit Ned's daughter, Carrie. They were very close when Carrie was a little girl.

They probably didn't want her to be weirded out by her dad dating the babysitter."

Hayley methodically stirred some batter in a large bowl with a wooden spoon, her mind working overtime. "Well, she's going to have to fess up. Once she finds out Ned is being accused of murder, she's going to have to come forth and provide him with an alibi."

"What I don't understand is, why didn't Ned immediately admit to being with Michelle when he was arrested," Liddy said. "Sergio could have just brought Michelle in and she could've cleared the whole thing up. I mean, I understand protecting your daughter's feelings, but it's a little extreme to be willing to take the rap for murder just so she doesn't find out you're banging the babysitter!"

"Of course!" Hayley screamed, dropping the bowl to the floor, shattering it.

The batter seeped out in a thick gooey mess.

Leroy was on the spilled batter in seconds, excitedly lapping it up.

"What?" Liddy asked.

"Mona is a pretty reliable witness, so we can assume Ned Weston was on that boat the whole time. So *why* would Ned confess?"

"He has to be covering for someone else," Liddy offered, suddenly intrigued, and grabbed another muffin from the basket.

"And there's only one person in the whole world Ned loves enough to lie for and to risk a life sentence for murder."

"I don't like muffins," Ned growled, turning away from Hayley.

Hayley held up her wicker basket and took a whiff.

"Come on, Ned. They smell delicious and they taste even better."

Ned faced the cement wall in the jail cell. He refused to even look at Hayley. "What do you want? I told Sergio I didn't want to see anyone."

"Not even Carrie?"

Hayley saw Ned flinch.

There was a long moment of silence before he spoke again.

"Especially Carrie. How could any father want his daughter to see him like this?"

"I know we're not the best of friends, Ned . . ."

"That's putting it mildly . . ."

"But we're both parents and I know how much we both love our kids. And I know the lengths we'd go to, to protect them . . ."

"Forget it, Hayley. I'm in no mood for a bonding session with you."

"Where is Carrie now?"

"With her grandmother in Bangor. I made sure Sergio delivered her there safely while I deal with all this. So don't even think about bothering her. The last thing she needs is to worry."

"But she's going to find out, Ned. And then what do you think she's going to do? Let you rot in prison? When she knows you didn't do it."

"What are you talking about? I confessed. It's over. Done. Case closed."

"I'm sorry, Ned. We both know it's not. I have a very reliable eyewitness who can place you on Lex Bansfield's boat with Michelle Butterworth on the night of the murder. I'm sure Michelle will be scared enough of a perjury charge to back the witness up."

Ned slowly turned around to face Hayley, eyes blazing. "What are you trying to say?"

"I'm saying you are covering for someone. And we both know who that is."

Ned glared at her and his lips tightened.

"Carrie already told me she went to the Harborside Hotel the night Mickey Pritchett was murdered. Mickey was pressuring her to have sex with him, but she decided meeting Wade Springer wasn't worth all that. So she went to the hotel to tell him it was a no-go."

"So what? That doesn't mean she killed him."

"Who else would know where you stash your gun in the house? Carrie probably figured she might need protection when she went to tell Mickey she wasn't going to give him what he wanted. He could've lured her onto the tour bus. Maybe he got a little rough. Tried to force himself on her. I know from personal experience, Mickey was that kind of creep. So Carrie would have had no choice but to shoot him."

Ned shook his head, eyes pleading with Hayley to stop.

But she couldn't.

"And then Carrie probably panicked and somehow drove the tour bus to Albert Meadow and set it on fire to cover her tracks."

Even as she was saying it, Hayley didn't quite believe it.

When Hayley had gone to talk to Carrie at her house while Mona distracted Ned with that bogus lobster order, Carrie had seemed so convincing.

Hayley had no reason to doubt what Carrie had told her. That when she left Mickey, he was still alive.

But there was the possibility that Carrie was just so scared of going to jail, she put on the performance of a lifetime to deflect suspicion.

Carrie Weston had to be lying.

Hayley stepped closer to the bars and spoke softly. "When those kids found your gun washed up on the rocks on Bar Island, you knew right then and there, in your gut, what really happened. And you made a vow to protect Carrie at all costs, no matter what."

Ned sprang off the cot and rushed toward the steel bars separating them. He shot his arm through to make a grab for Hayley's throat.

Muffins flew in every direction as the basket fell from Hayley's arms and hit the floor.

She managed to avoid Ned's grasp by jumping back.

Ned was hollering at the top of his lungs. "You leave her out of this! Do you hear me, Hayley? I will kill you if you drag her into this!"

Hayley just stood there, her back pressed to the wall opposite the cell, near tears, trying to catch her breath as Sergio pounded down the hall.

"What happened here? Hayley, are you all right?"

Hayley nodded.

"She's out of her mind, Sergio," Ned wailed. "She's making things up!"

Hayley fixed her gaze on Ned, who now paced the cell like a caged tiger, ready to attack again given the slightest opportunity.

"Hayley . . . ?" Sergio said, a confused look on his face.

She didn't have to say anything.

She could let Ned take the fall and Carrie would be raised by her grandmother and nobody would ever have to know the truth.

It was an accident, after all.

Carrie wasn't some cold-blooded, calculating killer. Or was she?

It wasn't fair to anyone to conceal something like this.

If she stayed silent, Hayley would never be able to live with herself.

"Sergio, we need to talk," Hayley said, starting to choke up.

Ned sank to his knees, weeping.

The thought of his baby girl going to jail was just too much to bear.

Chapter 35

Sergio

Hayley

Hayley was exhausted by the time she left the police
station. Sergio dispatched Donnie and Earl to drive to
Bangor and pick up Carrie at her grandmother's
house. It was only a matter of time before word spread
around town that Carrie Weston was actually the one
responsible for the death of Wade Springer's roadie.

The sun was already going down, and Hayley had
to race home to get ready for Wade's concert.

But there was something important she had to do
first.

She had to talk to Gemma.

Hayley didn't want her hearing about Carrie on
Facebook or Twitter or any of the other social media
sites she and her friends used to chat and keep abreast
of all the latest gossip.

Hayley knew in her heart Carrie had to have killed
Mickey Pritchett in self-defense. She saw firsthand the
kind of guy Mickey Pritchett was. And there wasn't a
mean bone in Carrie's body as far as she could see.

But she also knew Gemma would take the news
about her close friend hard. And she wanted to break
it to her gently.

When Hayley walked through the back door of

the house, she could hear the TV blasting in the living room.

It was music from the movie *Hairspray*.

Gemma's favorite movie of all time.

It was the song "Mama, I'm a Big Girl Now." And Hayley had to stop and smile. How appropriate.

She spent half her time worrying about Gemma. The other half, she spent worrying about Dustin.

But with Gemma's blossoming romance with Reid, Hayley had been particularly concerned about her daughter growing up so fast. So maybe this was a sign from the universe to let go just a little bit and recognize her daughter as the young woman she was becoming, capable of making smart decisions.

Yeah, right.

Like that was going to happen.

Maybe when Gemma was thirty-five, Hayley would stop worrying.

What if this was just part of being a mother and she would worry no matter how old her kids were?

That was just too much to think about.

Hayley rounded the corner into the living room and was not surprised to see Gemma nestled on the couch, her head on Reid's broad shoulder, watching the movie.

"Hi, Mrs. Powell," Reid said in an upbeat, chipper tone.

"Hello, Reid," Hayley said, trying not to sigh with disappointment that Gemma had a boy in the house without her permission.

Gemma held up a half-full bowl of popcorn. "We have snacks. Want to watch with us? Your favorite part is coming up—John Travolta in drag dancing with Christopher Walken."

Hayley smiled. "That's your uncle Randy's favorite part. I'm all about Queen Latifah singing 'Big, Blonde and Beautiful' because, inside, I've always thought of myself as all those things even though I'm not blonde or beautiful, but I'm certainly big!"

Reid chuckled.

Hayley cleared her throat. "Reid, I was wondering if I could talk to Gemma alone."

"Sure, Mrs. Powell," Reid said, stretching and making a move to stand up.

Gemma grabbed his sweater and pulled him back down. "Mom, please, anything you say to me you can say in front of Reid."

"It's about Carrie," Hayley said.

Gemma gasped and jumped off the couch. "What? Has something happened to her?"

"Reid, would you mind taking Leroy out for a walk around the block? He's been cooped up inside all day and I'm sure he needs to do his business. There are plastic bags—"

"Mom!" Gemma interrupted. "Reid is Carrie's friend, too. I'm sure he'll want to know what's going on."

"Okay," Hayley said, putting an arm around her daughter. "She wasn't totally truthful with me when I went to talk to her about the night of Mickey Pritchett's murder. She said when she left Mickey, he was still alive. But it turns out she stole her father's gun and shot him. Now, I'm sure he must have tried to attack her, and so obviously if it was self-defense there's a chance . . ."

"Mom, there's no way Carrie shot that guy."

"It turns out her father's gun is the same one that was used to kill Mickey. But Ned Weston was nowhere near the scene of the murder and Carrie was the only one who had access to it, and we already know she was being propositioned by Mickey. All the pieces fit."

"But I know for a fact that when she left Mickey he was still alive."

"How?"

Gemma glanced at Reid and swallowed before locking eyes with her mother. "Because I was with her."

"Gemma, why didn't you tell me this before?"

"I didn't want you to freak out and ground me or punish me by saying I couldn't spend time with Reid."

Reid's eyes were downcast and he was probably wishing he had accepted Hayley's request to take Leroy for a walk and clean up after him right about now.

Gemma sat back down next to Reid and put a hand on his knee. "Carrie called me that night to say she was going over to the hotel to tell Mickey to go to hell. She was never going to sleep with him. Under any circumstances. I begged her not to go. I knew Mickey might not take no for an answer. So I borrowed your car and raced over there to make sure she was all right. I know, I didn't ask or leave a note. I'm sorry. I was just so worried about Carrie."

"That's okay. Go on," Hayley said.

"I got there just in time to see Carrie running out of the hotel. That greaseball Mickey was right behind her still trying to paw her and talk to her. I waved her into the car and we took off leaving him in the dust. Then we dropped the car off here at our house and walked back to her place where I spent the night. Her father wasn't home."

"Yes. I know where Ned was that night."

"Carrie never said anything to you about me being there because she didn't want to get me into trouble," Gemma said. "She didn't have a gun, Mom. Carrie gets freaked out by guns. And she never left my side again the whole night so there was no way she could've doubled back and shot Mickey and driven him to Albert Meadow."

Reid took Gemma's hand, which was resting on his knee, and squeezed it. "Gemma, are you just saying this to cover for Carrie? I know you'd do anything for her. She's your best friend."

Hayley was surprised Reid was saying what she was thinking.

Gemma arched her back, indignant. "Of course not. I wouldn't do something like that. Carrie is innocent. And she shouldn't go to jail for something she didn't do."

Hayley believed her. She nodded. "You two get back to your movie. I'm going upstairs to get ready for Wade's concert."

Hayley's head was swimming.

She was frustrated to be back at square one.

What was she missing?

Who was left?

Wade.

Stacy Jo.

Curtis.

Ned.

Carrie.

Even Liddy.

All cleared.

There had to be someone who was slipping under the radar.

Someone she hadn't even considered.

But who?

Chapter 36

After calling Sergio to inform him that Gemma was offering herself as Carrie's alibi and that according to her trust-worthy daughter there was no way Carrie was directly involved in the death of Mickey Pritchett, Hayley showered, applied a little mascara, and brushed out her hair. Then she rummaged through her closet for a dressy sweater to wear to the concert. Her mind wasn't on her appearance at all because she was too consumed by Gemma's admission. The facts of the case kept swirling about in her head, making her more and more confused as to who could've done it.

She did a quick once-over in the mirror, grabbed her bag, and walked out of the bedroom.

Dustin was in his room doing his homework, which was due in the morning. Hayley stopped.

Where was she? In an alternate universe? Dustin doing his homework?

She decided not to question it. She just kissed him lightly on the forehead.

He squirmed, irritated, like most teenage boys do, and she gently patted his back before heading out.

She was at the top of the staircase and stopped suddenly.

She heard a song.

But it wasn't from *Hairspray*.

Gemma and Reid had stopped watching the movie and turned off the TV.

No, this was a live performance.

Someone in her living room strumming a guitar.

Obviously Reid.

He was singing Gemma a song.

It was a quiet ballad.

Strangely familiar.

About a woman in love with a man.

And how she gets the man to fall in love with her by cooking for him.

And how the way to a man's heart is through his stomach.

Wait.

She had heard this song before.

Wade sang it to her in his dressing room.

Reid continued singing the chorus.

The way to a man's heart.

And then he segued into another refrain.

How the man couldn't stop thinking about the woman's food.

And how she put so much tender loving care into each and every dish, it was as if they were her own children.

And how a man like him couldn't help but fall in love with a woman like that.

And how, when you've found someone you love that much, there's always room for dessert.

Reid sang the chorus again. "The way to a man's heart . . ."

This was Mickey Pritchett's song.

The one he wrote and submitted to Wade.

But Wade had yet to record it or even perform it because he said he had more work to do on it.

Then how on earth did Reid know the song?

Where could he have possibly heard it?

Hayley's blood ran cold as she listened to Reid singing the song to her daughter.

She instinctively pulled her cell phone out of her pants pocket and began recording Reid singing.

The pieces of the puzzle were finally starting to come together.

Chapter 37

Hayley continued recording Reid singing, holding her cell phone in the palm of her right hand as she slowly descended the stairs, trying to stay calm. When she reached the bottom, she saw Gemma beaming as Reid sang to her. He finished just as Hayley walked into the room.

"Isn't it beautiful, Mom? Reid wrote it," Gemma cooed.

"I smell a hit," Hayley said, forcing a smile. "Gemma, I'm in the mood to do some baking. Could you run to the store for me and pick up a few things? I'm a little low on the essentials. Milk, eggs, flour."

"Now? You just baked enough muffins this morning to feed my entire class," Gemma said.

Hayley pulled a twenty from her wallet and handed it to Gemma. "I'd really appreciate it."

Gemma knew her mother was not going to budge. "Fine. Let's go, Reid."

Reid set his guitar down on the couch and started to get up.

"No, why don't you go and Reid can stay here. It'll give us a chance to get to know one another," Hayley said, eyeing Reid, who smiled.

"No way! I am not going to leave him here so you can give him the third degree!" Gemma said, stuffing the twenty dollar bill in the pocket of her pink sweat jacket.

"I don't mind, Gemma," Reid said. "Your Mom's pretty cool. I'd love to hang out and chat with her if she wants."

Gemma eyed Hayley suspiciously.

She definitely did not want to leave her boyfriend at the mercy of her mother.

But she was outnumbered.

"Whatever," Gemma sighed. "But I'll be back in ten minutes!"

Gemma then pointed a finger at Reid. "You call me if she gets to be too much!"

Reid laughed. "I promise."

And Gemma trudged out of the house.

"Can I get you something to drink, Reid?" Hayley asked pleasantly.

"No, I'm fine. Thank you, Mrs. Powell."

"You have a beautiful voice. I was bowled over by your talent that first night Gemma and I came to see you at the coffeehouse."

"That's very nice of you to say. I really want to make it as a singer-songwriter someday."

"Well, you have the talent. That's for sure. But it's a tough business. A lot of stiff competition."

"Oh, I know what I'm in for, believe me."

"A lot of lowlifes and bottom-feeders who will try to take advantage of you and use you and take you for everything."

Reid nodded, not quite sure where Hayley was going with this.

"Like Mickey Pritchett, for instance."

Reid tried not to change his expression.

He was still smiling.

But Hayley detected a slight flinch.

A flash of surprise in his eyes at hearing Mickey's name.

"You knew Mickey, right?"

"I knew of him. I knew he tried to get in Carrie's pants. And I certainly don't blame her father for taking matters into his own hands."

"But Ned Weston didn't kill Mickey. He was nowhere near the murder scene that night. He was on a boat in the harbor with his girlfriend. And you just heard Gemma say she was with Carrie the whole night. So Mickey Pritchett had to have been killed for an entirely different reason."

Reid nodded.

There was a trickle of sweat on his forehead.

"And everyone else who had a motive to kill Mickey has been cleared by the police. That just leaves one person unaccounted for."

"Who?"

"You, Reid."

"Me? Why would I kill a guy I didn't even know?" Reid said, picking up his guitar again.

"But you did know him, Reid. You had to."

Reid began nervously strumming the guitar, keeping his eyes on his strings and not looking at Hayley. "Why do you say that?"

"That song you were just singing to Gemma. The song *you* wrote."

"Yeah, what about it?"

"Wade sang me that same song in his dressing room the night of his first concert at the Criterion. He told me Mickey wrote it."

Reid stopped strumming his guitar but did not lift his eyes to meet Hayley's.

"But you were really the one who wrote that song, and I'm guessing you were obviously inspired by my obsession with Wade Springer. You saw me trying to win him over with my cooking and what you didn't see, I'm sure Gemma told you. And so you wrote a song about it."

Reid shrugged, not yet willing to admit anything.

"You knew Carrie had met Mickey and you saw an opportunity. Why not ask Mickey if he could help you get your song to Wade? So you had Carrie make an introduction, and Mickey really liked the song, and he told you he'd pass it along to Wade. I'm sure you were flying high. Until you found out Mickey sang the song for Wade and claimed he was the one who wrote it. You were enraged. That song was your ticket to stardom."

"You're just making all this up as you go along."

"Wade said he had never played the song for anyone. He wanted to do some work on it first, before he performed it in public or recorded it. There was no way you could have heard it before. Unless the song really was Mickey's and he sang it to you."

Reid couldn't help himself. "Are you kidding? That loud mouthed idiot drunk couldn't write his own name!"

"Which means he stole it from you and that gives you a motive for murder."

"Even if all that's true, it doesn't mean I killed him. He was shot with Ned Weston's gun. How would I ever get my hands on it?"

"Very easily. You and Gemma hung out at Carrie's house all the time. You saw where Ned kept it."

Reid's foot began tapping nervously.

Hayley was getting to him.

She kept going. "Then there was the night you asked me to drop you off at Carrie's house because you left your guitar there and wanted to pick it up. You said Carrie told you where they hid the key to the house. You were free to come and go as you pleased. You just waited until no one was home and snuck in and made off with the gun sometime before the murder."

Reid stood up, a hardened look on his face.

"You were out for revenge," Hayley said, taking a step back. "You wanted to get back at Mickey and then somehow prove to Wade that it was you who wrote the song. And by shooting Mickey with Ned Weston's gun, you could insure Ned would take the fall. You hated him for being so strict with Carrie. Why not steal his gun and make it look like Ned was furious about Mickey putting the moves on his teenage daughter? You knew Carrie and Gemma would back you up. But the thing is, Ned may be a jerk but he's no killer."

"If I did it, why aren't my prints on the gun?"

"You're a smart kid. I'm sure you watch all the *CSI* shows. You probably wore gloves. You showed up at the Harborside Hotel and ran into Mickey, who was leaving town. You pulled the gun on him."

"I read the papers. Nobody inside the hotel heard any shots."

"Because you forced Mickey into the tour bus and had him drive you to Albert Meadow, which is just off the shore path. The loud crashing of waves against the rocks would cover the sound of a gun firing. It was there you shot him dead. Then you set the tour bus on fire, hoping it would destroy any evidence of you ever being there."

Reid clenched his fists.

His face ashen.

His foot tapping incessantly.

"And you tossed the gun into the Atlantic knowing if it was ever found and linked to Mickey's murder, Ned would be the one arrested because his motive would be clear, once it became public knowledge that

Mickey was sexually propositioning his daughter, Carrie."

Reid finally raised his eyes to meet Hayley's.

They were full of hate.

Unrecognizable from the sweet boy who had worked so hard to make a good impression on her earlier.

No, this was a totally different person in her living room now.

Mean.

Menacing.

Dangerous.

Chapter 38

Reid took a small step forward.

He was much taller than Hayley.

Broad shouldered.

A strong kid.

Hayley took another step back.

"Did I miss anything, Reid?"

Reid shook his head. "No. You got it right. But who are you going to tell about it?"

Hayley had one thought swirling in her head. Thank God she got Gemma out of the house.

But Dustin was still upstairs in his room. Probably done with his homework and watching TV, completely oblivious to the danger downstairs.

And she intended to keep it that way.

There was no way she was going to involve her son in any of this.

Hayley held up the cell phone cupped in her hand and showed it to Reid.

He grimaced upon seeing the image of a microphone on the screen.

Hayley took a deep breath. "I got it all. The song. Your admission. Everything."

"Give it to me, Mrs. Powell." Reid stuck out his large hand. "I'm not going to ask you twice."

Hayley kept eye contact with Reid but her thumb was working the screen.

Reid noticed her finger moving. "What are you doing?"

Hayley didn't answer.

She quickly glanced down at the screen and tapped the SEND button.

Reid suddenly realized what she was doing. "No!"

He lunged forward and grabbed her around the neck with his hands.

Hayley fell back against the wall. "It's over, Reid. I just e-mailed the recording to Chief Alvares. He'll be here any minute."

But Reid didn't let go.

He squeezed Hayley's neck harder. "You ruined everything!"

"Reid, please . . . ," Hayley choked out, gasping for breath.

He was out of his mind.

All his hopes and dreams.

Suddenly shattered.

Hayley reached for a lamp.

The tips of her fingers touched it, but there was no way to get a good grip on it and use it as a weapon.

Leroy, alerted to the scuffle, came bounding down the stairs, barking wildly and nipping at Reid's heels.

The ultimate protector.

Too bad he was the size of a ladies' small handbag.

Reid just kicked him away.

Hayley was a mere seconds from passing out.

Reid was about to finish the job Jesse DeSoto had started.

She still couldn't reach the lamp.

Then, from the top of the stairs, Dustin called down, "Mom, is everything all right down there?"

Leroy's barking must have finally alerted him to the commotion.

Dustin's voice distracted Reid long enough for Hayley to inch her way toward the lamp where she was able to finally grab it and smash it into the side of Reid's head.

He let go of her neck.

Hayley ran for the kitchen.

Reid felt for blood on his scalp, then, filled with fury, chased after Hayley.

She grabbed a coffeepot off the stove and swung it at him.

He ducked.

She hurled it at him and he raised his arm up, the pot bouncing off his elbow.

He wailed again.

Madder than hell.

And kept charging her.

Hayley threw open the screen door leading outside to the deck and flew down the steps and into the driveway.

Better to draw him away from the house for Dustin's protection.

Reid hurled himself off the deck in an attempt to tackle Hayley, but she was far enough out of his reach that he failed to get a hold of her.

He landed in the middle of the driveway just as Gemma, behind the wheel of Hayley's Subaru, pulled in.

Reid made a grab for Hayley, but she shoved him back, right into the path of the car.

Hayley could see the look of shock on her daughter's face as she slammed on the brakes, but not fast enough. The car rammed into Reid and he went sprawling to the pavement.

Gemma just sat behind the wheel, screaming.

Hayley took a step forward to examine Reid.

He was moaning, clutching his elbow. "I think I broke my arm."

Reid was no longer a threat.

Gemma stopped screaming and jumped out of the car. "Omigod! Omigod! Reid, are you all right?"

She ran toward him, but Hayley intercepted her.

There was no way she was going to allow her daughter to get any closer.

"No, Gemma. Stay away from him."

"I saw you push him! I know you don't like him, but do you have to *kill* him?" Gemma yelled.

Flashing blue lights flooded the driveway as Sergio pulled in behind the Subaru and got out of the car.

"He's hurt, Sergio, but he'll live," Hayley said.

Sergio nodded, and then pulled his handcuffs off his belt and walked over to talk to Reid, who was sitting up now, rocking back and forth, still moaning.

Hayley took Gemma by the arm and walked her inside.

She sat her down on the couch and explained everything.

Gemma tried arguing at first.

That it was impossible.

Reid wasn't that kind of boy.

Hayley was overreacting.

But then Hayley pulled out her phone and played the entire recording for her daughter.

The truth finally sunk in, and Gemma cried.

Hayley hugged her.

"How could I have fallen for someone like that?" Gemma asked, wiping away her tears and sniffling.

"You're sixteen. You're supposed to make mistakes."

"But, Mom, he's a killer!"

"Okay, some mistakes are bigger than others. That's why I'm here."

Gemma rested her head on Hayley's shoulders. "I am so going to break up with him!"

Hayley smiled and kissed her daughter on top of her head.

Then Gemma sprang to her feet. "I have to call Carrie."

She ran up the stairs, punching numbers into her cell phone.

Hayley checked the time on her own phone.

She had missed most of Wade's concert.

It was almost over.

And thankfully so was this entire country fried nightmare.

Chapter 39

Just before you cross the bridge to Mount Desert Island, where the town of Bar Harbor is located, there is a beautiful oceanfront picnic grounds called Thompson Island, a picturesque spot for tourists with a visitors' center. A lot of travelers buy steamed lobsters from the nearby pound and gather with friends and family to enjoy the ocean view. But, today, Wade Springer's tour crew had taken it over for their own farewell lobster feed to celebrate the money they'd succeeded in raising for the college. Mona provided all the seafood and Hayley spent the morning preparing a feast of side dishes with a decidedly southern flavor for the picnic. It was a tasty fushion of East Coast seafood and southern-style home cooking. The menu proved to be a monstrous hit. In addition to the crew, Hayley invited Liddy and Mona, who arrived with her army of kids, and Ned Weston and his daughter, Carrie, who sat at a wooden picnic table with Gemma and Dustin.

Hayley was happy to see Ned smiling. Maybe it took the fear of his daughter going to prison to make him appreciate the smaller moments in life, and to just enjoy his time with her and not try to be so controlling.

It seemed to be working.

Hayley had mixed feelings about Wade leaving.

A part of her was happy the town would finally be able to get back to normal. Another part of her was going to miss his intoxicating charm and killer smile.

Another tour bus had been driven up from Nashville to transport the crew to their next concert in New York City and both buses were now packed and ready to hit the road once the picnic festivities wound down.

"I really hate to say good-bye," Wade said in a deep southern drawl as he put a hand on Hayley's shoulder.

She turned around and smiled. "I'm going to miss having you around here."

"You don't have to. You could come with me."

Hayley felt butterflies in her stomach.

Gemma's ears perked up. She was sitting at a picnic table only a few feet away.

"I want you to come on tour with me," Wade said, suddenly serious.

"As your personal chef?" Hayley asked.

"You can cook if you want to, but that's not a requirement," he said, giving her a wink.

"Can she bring her adorable, loving children?" Gemma asked, now up from the picnic table and at her mother's side.

Wade chuckled. "Of course. The more, the merrier."

Hayley turned to Gemma. "What about school?"

"We can hire a tutor. Like all the child stars!" Gemma offered.

Hayley took Gemma by the shoulders, turned her around, and sent her back to her table.

She then took Wade by the hand. "As enticing an offer as that sounds, I'm afraid I'm going to have to say no."

Wade couldn't hide his disappointment.

"My life is here, Wade," Hayley said. "My kids are in

school here. My friends are here. And even though it's a dream come true to have a superstar like Wade Springer asking me to go on tour . . ."

"I suspect I have some competition," Wade said, nodding.

"The man I told you about. He's a good man. And I need to give him a chance."

Wade leaned in to give Hayley a kiss. She turned away slightly and he got her on the cheek. She knew if he kissed her on the lips, she just might change her mind.

"Well, I got to say, Hayley, my heart's a little broken. But at least I won't have to suffer alone."

"What do you mean?"

"I'm not the only one who got dumped today."

He pointed to his dog Delilah, who was chasing after Leroy, sniffing his butt. But Leroy, no longer interested, just kept scampering away from his oversized admirer. As far away as possible. Delilah finally gave up, and slogged slowly and sadly back over to Wade, who rubbed her head lovingly.

"He's very fickle," Hayley said, watching as Dustin picked up Leroy and fed him a piece of white lobster meat.

Wade gave Hayley one last look and then led Delilah to the tour bus, where they climbed aboard.

Within minutes, the two buses were on the road and Wade Springer was gone from Bar Harbor.

Hayley sighed.

Chapter 40

After filing her last southern-cooking column and finally putting to rest the rumors that she was Wade Springer's new girlfriend, Hayley left work at five o'clock, and headed over to Randy's bar to meet Liddy and Mona for an after-work cocktail.

She arrived early.

The bar was empty.

Except for Michelle, who was working the bar.

Hayley ordered her favorite, a Lemon Drop Martini, and after Michelle poured it from the shaker into a glass and slid it over to her, Hayley asked, "So what's new, Michelle?"

Michelle grinned. "Oh, I think you know, Hayley."

Ned Weston and Michelle were now dating out in the open, thanks to his new lease on life.

And from what Gemma had told her, Carrie was very accepting of it and happy for her dad.

Michelle went to take an order from another customer and Hayley took a sip of her martini.

Delicious.

With a nice kick.

The perfect cocktail to drown her sorrows.

She was already missing Wade.

"Miss me?"

Hayley spun around on her bar stool.

It was him.

Lex was back.

"Of course I missed you."

Lex leaned in and took Hayley by the chin and kissed her.

Suddenly, all thoughts of Wade Springer were gone in an instant.

"When did you get back?"

"Just flew in about forty-five minutes ago. Called you at home and the kids said you were here."

Michelle walked over to them. "Can I get you anything, Lex?"

"Amstel Light. Thanks, Michelle."

She nodded and went to the cooler at the other end of the bar.

"So," Lex said, sitting on the stool next to Hayley and putting an arm around her. "Anything interesting happen while I was gone?"

"Nope. The usual boring small-town stuff. Nothing interesting at all."

Hayley rested her head on the warm checkered flannel shirt he was wearing, feeling safe against his broad chest.

Lex was finally home.

And the best part was, she couldn't remember being so happy to see him.

Island Food & Spirits
by
Hayley Powell

Whew! Can I just say these past few weeks have been one wild ride, as I imagine they must say in the south? Never in a million years would I have thought that I, Hayley Powell, of Bar Harbor, Maine, would in my lifetime meet my favorite country singing idol, Wade Springer, so up close and personal—and, to top it off, become his personal chef! But I can honestly say that with all the excitement and changes that came with his visit, it just made me appreciate living a quieter life on this beautiful island.

Of course, I was sad to see everyone go. But, as you all know, this town is usually filled to the brim all summer long with lots of interesting people visiting our treasured Acadia National Park, restaurants, and stores, and, since we are also a cruise ship port, you never know who you might meet!

Speaking of never knowing who you might meet, the other night after all the brouhaha had finally seemed to settle down, it was time for me to wind down, too, so I mixed up a nice Lemon Drop Martini and planted myself in a chair out on the deck next to Leroy, who was already fast asleep and exhausted from his own little romance and adventure.

I must have dozed off for a bit, because I was suddenly startled awake by Leroy's frantic barking, coming from behind the garage. I struggled up off the deck chair and headed in the direction of his now high-pitched barking, which could only mean one thing . . . a cat. Whenever Leroy spots a cat, he just starts shaking and whining and barking as if he's having some kind of seizure. It's one of his annoying habits, which all of my neighbors are acutely aware of, but luckily seem to take in stride.

As I raced off in the direction of his barking, I tripped over a skateboard lying in the driveway. I cursed myself for not replacing the outside motion detector spotlight bulb, because it only seemed to pop on when it wanted to, and right now it was pitch-black outside and I could barely see Leroy jumping up and down in the grass behind the garage. I called to him, but, true to form, he didn't listen.

"Leave that poor cat alone!" I screamed.

I could barely make out the poor animal's black outline in the tall grass just about ten feet from Leroy. I figured it must be our neighbor's large black cat, Midnight, who always takes a perverse pleasure in tormenting Leroy.

Leroy had now worked himself up into a frenzy and was darting and lunging and snapping at the poor cat. My only course of action was to rush him from behind and grab the little bugger before he sensed my presence and ducked away from me. I was almost in the perfect position to grab his collar when he suddenly lunged at the cat and out of my reach. I tripped over a branch and fell flat on my face.

Face down in the dirt with a free mud facial (I like to look at the bright side), I heard a strange hissing sound and then Leroy yelped. I pushed myself up on my knees, and at that exact moment, my motion detector spotlight finally decided to snap on. I just stared in horror as Leroy came racing at me, suddenly bathed in light. But it wasn't him I was looking at. It was the biggest skunk I had ever seen, staring right at me. I swear he winked at me, as if to say, "Joke's on you," before he turned around and lumbered away.

I now focused my attention on the dog running at me and it was in that moment that I realized the joke truly was on me.

Just as Leroy leapt into my arms, the foulest, most awful stench wafted up into my nostrils! It made my eyes water. The poor dog reeked to high heaven. Yes, I had to face the truth. He had just been sprayed by the big old skunk and was now wiggling in my arms and licking my face. Yup. Now I was going to be a skunk spray victim, too.

As I trudged back to the house with my horribly smelly dog in my arms, I actually found myself thankful for last summer's tomato bounty in the garden. I had made quarts and quarts of homemade tomato soup to freeze for the winter. I had plenty left, so I had the necessary ingredients to give myself and Leroy a tomato bath to get the smell off us.

And, after the last couple of busy weeks, I think I just might have a nice hot bowlful of homemade tomato soup, too!

Homemade Creamy Tomato Soup

2 tablespoons butter
2 tablespoons olive oil
1 large onion, diced
1 tablespoon minced garlic
2 tablespoons flour
3½ pounds ripe tomatoes, chopped
2 tablespoons tomato paste
2 tablespoons sugar
3 cups vegetable broth
⅛ teaspoon ground cloves
Salt and pepper to taste
½ cup Half & Half

Melt the butter with the oil over low heat in a pot.

Add onion and garlic and cook over low heat until translucent, stirring occasionally.

Sprinkle with the flour and cook 3 more minutes.

Add tomatoes, tomato paste, sugar, and broth.

Bring to a boil, reduce heat to simmer; cover and simmer for 30 minutes.

Season with cloves, and salt and pepper to taste.

Remove from heat.

Puree the soup in a food processor or blender, a little at a time.

Pour soup through a strainer into a pot.

Stir in the Half & Half.

Warm soup before serving.

A delicious treat after scrubbing off the stench from a skunk!

Please turn the page for an exciting
sneak peek of the next
Hayley Powell mystery

DEATH OF A COUPON CLIPPER

coming soon from Kensington Publishing!

Chapter 1

It would be a cold day in hell before Sal Moretti allowed his employees at the *Island Times* newspaper to go home early. The picturesque little hamlet of Bar Harbor, Maine, certainly wasn't hell. In fact, to hikers and mountain bikers and cruise ship passengers and lobster lovers and vacationing families from all over the world who flocked to Mount Desert Island for the breathtaking scenery of Acadia National Park, it was a nature lover's paradise.

But that was during the summer months. Today, on this midafternoon during a particularly brutal February, the temperature was hovering just below ten degrees and outside the picture window of the main office where Hayley Powell sat at her desk, all she could see was a white blanket of snow. She couldn't remember the last time she had seen it come down so hard.

Hayley stood up and poured herself a cup of hot coffee from the pot she had just brewed and took a big gulp to warm herself up. Sal had allowed her to turn the thermostat up a few degrees earlier that morning, but kept a watchful eye to make sure she didn't crank it too high and send his heating bill soaring.

She had dressed appropriately for the workday.

Long underwear. Flannel shirt. Bulky wool sweater. Jeans. Fleece snow pants over the jeans. Big clunky boots. But looking outside at the nasty weather still chilled her bones.

Bruce Linney, the paper's handsome crime reporter, with whom Hayley maintained a love-hate relationship, ambled out to the front office to get some coffee. He wore an expensive black cashmere sweater and khaki pants.

"Hayley, would you mind running out and picking up some of those delicious warm blueberry muffins from the Morning Glory Bakery?" he said. "I'm sure the reporters would appreciate it."

"Of course, Bruce. Let me just get my dogsled team ready and I'll be on my merry way," Hayley said, shaking her head.

She couldn't believe he was serious.

Maybe their relationship was more tolerate-hate.

"Is that you being sarcastic?" Bruce sighed.

"That's me saying no, Bruce!" Hayley said. "The Morning Glory is clear across town and the streets aren't plowed yet and even if they were, the roads are so icy I'd probably lose control of my car and skid right off the town pier!"

"Man, Hayley, sometimes you can be such a drama queen," Bruce said, shrugging. "I just asked for some muffins. Maybe if you thought ahead, you would have considered the weather reports, and whipped up some of your own muffins in your kitchen this morning so you wouldn't have to go out in this nasty storm to buy us some now."

"You're not getting muffins, Bruce!" Hayley said.

Sal Moretti charged out of his office and bellowed, "Would you two pipe down? This is a newspaper, not a marriage counselor's office!"

Hayley and Bruce exchanged a look and called a

silent truce. They both knew it was best not to tick off the boss right now, because Sal was already on edge. His wife had left him for a week to go visit her mother in North Carolina, so there was no one to take care of him at home.

And this was painfully obvious. His shirts were wrinkled. There were a half-dozen empty bottles of Tums on his desk from all the late-night gorging on pepperoni pizza. The poor guy was scattered and off his game. It was clear he missed his wife terribly and didn't like being home alone.

"They're saying on the Weather Channel that this storm's only going to get worse. So I think we should all just call it a day and go home," Sal said.

Stunned silence.

Sal was dismissing the staff for the day?

And it wasn't even three o'clock in the afternoon.

Bruce did his best Rod Serling voice. "You're about to enter another dimension. Next stop, the Twilight Zone!"

"Shut up, Bruce," Sal snapped. "I want everybody to be careful driving home. It's a mess out there."

Sal rubbed his eyes and ambled back to his office.

Hayley wasn't going to wait for him to change his mind. She quickly shut down her computer and grabbed her green L.L.Bean winter jacket from the office closet. She threw it on, laced up her black boots, and was out the door.

She carefully navigated the frozen walkway from the office to the street. But she still nearly lost her balance on the slippery ice and had to flap her arms like a crazy person to keep herself from falling flat on her back.

Once she managed to reach her white Subaru wagon, which was parked up the street, she pulled on a pair of mittens her mother had knitted her twenty years ago and began brushing all the fresh snow off the car. Then, she clicked the remote key to unlock the doors, and rummaged through all the kids' athletic equipment and empty fast-food cartons and discarded paper coffee cups in the back seat to find her red wooden-handled ice scraper.

Hayley began hacking at the clumps of ice that had formed on her windshield, clearing enough so she could at least see where she was going on the short drive home. Then she climbed behind the wheel, shut the door, started the engine, and cranked up the heat. She waited a few minutes for the car to warm up before slowly pulling away from the curb.

She could hear the wheels crunching through the snow and she hadn't even maneuvered the vehicle all the way into the street before the car hit a patch of ice and began slipping and sliding into the opposite lane. Luckily, no one was stupid enough to be out driving in this mess and there were no cars to collide with, so Hayley counted her blessings.

Hayley stayed focused, never taking her eyes off the road, gently pressing her foot down on the accelerator; not too much, just enough to keep the car going in a forward motion. She didn't want to chance losing control again and smashing into a tree or a fire hydrant or, God forbid, a storefront window.

What was normally a five-minute drive home took thirty minutes, but Hayley finally managed to get herself and her Subaru home safely. She turned into the driveway of her gray two-story house. Well, it was gray when she left for work this morning. Now it was completely white. At least the snow covered the fact that her house was in desperate need of a new coat of paint. Which she couldn't afford. Maybe she would get a nice tax refund this year, which she could use to paint the house in the spring.

Wishful thinking.

Lex Bansfield, the man Hayley had been dating off and on for the past year and a half, usually would clear her driveway with his snowplow truck during a storm, but he hadn't had a chance to swing by yet, so Hayley assumed he was busy clearing the roads on the expansive seaside estate where he worked as a caretaker.

It was slow going, the tires of her Subaru skidding through the mound of snow piled high in the driveway as she pulled in and opened the garage door with her remote. Hayley had to press her foot harder down on the accelerator to keep the car moving forward. Then, suddenly, without warning, the tires freed themselves from the packed snow and the car took off, speeding toward the open doorway of the garage. Hayley slammed on the brakes to stop the vehicle before it hurtled through the garage and crashed right through the back wall and into her neighbor's adjoining yard. Luckily the car squealed to an abrupt stop just inches from the wall.

And Hayley breathed a deep sigh of relief.

The last thing she needed right now was a costly repair. She got out of the car and was about to head into the house when she stopped.

She distinctly heard a creaking sound.

Hayley looked around.

Nothing appeared out of the ordinary.

She couldn't make out where the sound had come from.

She continued to walk out of the garage.

Another creak.

This time louder.

What was that?

It seemed to be coming from the roof.

She looked up.

One of the wooden beams supporting the roof

looked warped. As if it was bending and about to snap
in half. That couldn't be.

She knew she would need to reinforce the roof at
some point. Lex had warned her many times. But she just
didn't have the money to do it right now. Besides, Lex
told her she was probably fine unless there was a lot of
weight on it. Only then might it give way to the pressure.

But there wasn't a squirrel or a raccoon up there
climbing around and putting extra weight on it so it
looked like she was in the clear.

Wait.

It was true there wasn't a small animal on top of
her roof.

But there was about two-and-a-half feet of heavy
snowfall.

The wooden beam suddenly snapped and Hayley
heard a rumbling sound. She dashed out of the
garage just as she caught a glimpse of the entire roof
over her garage caving in, landing on top of her white
Subaru wagon and crushing it.

No. This was not happening.

Hayley just stood there in a state of shock. Flakes of
snow landed on her rosy red cheeks. She was about to
cry, but choked back the tears. She was afraid if she
did cry, the tears would freeze right on her face.

She heard her white shih tzu (with pronounced
underbite), Leroy, inside the house barking, undoubtedly spooked from the thunderous crash of
the roof collapsing. Hayley decided to deal with the
garage when the snow stopped. But with her car
buried underneath the rubble, she was probably
going to have to borrow some snowshoes to get to the
office the next morning.

Hayley entered the house through the back door
into the kitchen. Leroy was there, jumping up and
down to greet her. The sight of her devoted pup in-

stantly put Hayley at ease, and the little guy leapt into her arms when she knelt down to say hello. He began licking frantically at her face, attracted to the wet snow. Hayley noticed Leroy's nose was running and he was shivering. She set him down and took off her coat. That's when she realized the temperature inside the house felt like twenty degrees. Maybe even colder. She knew she had left the heat on when she went to work. What could have possibly happened?

Dear God, no.

Not the furnace.

Lex had also warned her that her furnace was barely hanging on and the odds of it making it through another winter weren't very good. She had brushed off his comments, not because she didn't believe him, but mostly because she just couldn't bear the thought of having to invest in a new one. She just didn't have the money. Hayley opened the door to the basement, snapped on the light, and descended the stairs, with Leroy scampering right behind her.

When she reached the bottom of the steps, she knew in her gut the situation was dire. She touched the furnace. Ice cold. She played with the buttons and readings. Nothing.

It was dead.

And she was screwed.

Unable to hold it in any longer, Hayley finally started to cry. Why was all this happening at once? How was she ever going to pay for all this? She sat down on the bottom step of the basement and let the waterworks flow.

She was going to allow herself a few minutes of self-pity, and then she would steel herself and work on solving the problems at hand.

Her cell phone rang.

Hayley reached into the back pocket of her snow

pants and pulled out her phone. It was Gemma. Calling from her dad's in Iowa.

Hayley's two kids, sixteen-year-old Gemma and fourteen-year-old Dustin, were spending the winter break with their dad, Hayley's ex-husband, in Des Moines, Iowa, where he worked as a manager at Walmart.

Hayley got a lump in her throat. She missed them. The three of them were a team, and now faced with all this sudden adversity, she wished they were home with her to calm her nerves. Just having them around made her feel better. But they were so far away and she felt so alone right now.

Hayley wiped away the tears, cleared her throat, composed herself, and then clicked on the phone.

"Gemma, honey, how are you?"

"It's freezing here, Mom. I wish we were back in Bar Harbor."

"It's pretty much the same here, so you're not missing anything. How's your brother?"

"The same. Still annoying. Dad's got a new girlfriend. Nice, but trying too hard to impress us. Just like the last three. What's going on with you?"

"Not much," Hayley said. "I just got home from work."

"It's only three o'clock there. Are you sick?"

"No, I'm fine."

"You don't sound fine. You sound stressed," Gemma said.

"No, Gemma, everything's just fine. Believe me."

But things were not fine.

Not fine at all.

And they were about to get a whole lot worse, because a collapsed roof, a crushed car, and a busted furnace would soon be the least of Hayley Powell's problems.